DIAL
577
R-A-P-E

Lillian O'Donnell

DIAL

577

R-A-P-E

G. P. Putnam's Sons
New York

Within the New York Police Department there are many squads and within these again many officers with the rank of sergeant, lieutenant, and captain, so that a character bearing such a title is readily acceptable as fictional. There is, however, only one Rape Analysis and Investigation Squad and one Lieutenant heading it. The character in this book is not intended to portray the real commander of the RAI, though we hope that in purpose and dedication she will accept kinship with her counterpart.

L. O.

Sex Crimes Analysis Unit

The Sex Crimes Analysis Unit is a subdivision of the Chief of Detectives' Office of the New York City Police Department.

Our Unit has as its primary function the gathering of information and intelligence leading to the identity and ultimate apprehension, arrest and conviction of perpetrators of the crimes of Rape and Sodomy and their attempts.

This Unit is staffed by ten (10) female investigators who have had previous investigative experience and are sensitive to the needs of females. It is commanded by a female Lieutenant with one (1) male Sergeant assigned as a Supervisor. One (1) Management Intern, one (1) Stenographer, three (3) female and one (1) male Police Administrative Aides are also assigned.

In 1972, there were 3,271 cases of forcible rapes reported in New York City—this is approximately 250 cases per month.

—NEW YORK CITY POLICE DEPARTMENT

1

It was a fine night for strolling, but Gabriella Constante hurried. Before turning the corner to Riverside Drive, she cast a quick, nervous look over her shoulder. Nobody in sight. The handful of people who had come out of the subway two and one-half blocks back had dispersed, and the entire stretch behind her was now deserted. *Gracias a Dios!* She slowed down to ease the stitch in her side.

The September night was a summer leftover, hot and close. Though she was wearing a sleeveless cotton dress, bare but modest, Gabriella Constante was covered with perspiration—she could feel a heavy band of it across her brow and rivulets of it trickling down between her breasts. Even here, close to the river, there was no relief. Not a leaf on the trees along the embankment stirred. A harvest moon encrusted each one in golden immobility. The moon was so bright it washed out both the streetlamps and their shadows, outshone the high-voltage signs on the Jersey Palisades, overlaid their multicolored reflections on the sludge waters of the Hudson with its molten glow. At home Gabriella would have savored such a night. She would not have been hurrying with fearful backward glances. And there was no need to do so now either, she told herself firmly, ordering herself to stop trembling. Just the same, she kept to the edge of the sidewalk, well away from the building line.

Gabriella Constante, nineteen years old, gentle, sheltered, thought longingly of San Juan and of what had been left behind —the narrow, painstakingly restored house not two blocks from La Fortaleza, her room with its own balcony overlooking the harbor. When she went out into the street, every face she saw was familiar and had a name. In this city she felt herself nameless and faceless. But the most important thing Gabriella had left behind, more important than the sum of all the rest, was Enrique. In a year she would go back and marry Enrique. A year was not so long to

1

wait. Enrique hadn't wanted her to come to New York with her parents; he'd wanted her to stay behind and marry him right away, but papa would not give permission. Papa said Enrique must get his degree and have a job. Gabriella had pleaded, she had wept, but she could not defy her father. And Enrique had not asked it of her: neither of them had been brought up to even consider such a thing.

The drastic drop in Puerto Rico's tourist trade was the reason for the family's move. Pablo Constante Morales had trained in the government-instituted school for hotel employees back in the early days of Operation Bootstrap. His first job had been as busboy at the Caribe Hilton when it stood starkly alone on the jutting point of land between the old city and the new, when there were no tourists, just businessmen stopping over on the long trip to Latin America—before jets. The erection of such a luxury hotel was a gamble for both the government and its financiers. With the shutting down of Cuba as an American playground and the de- velopment of jets, the pleasure-seekers were diverted to Puerto Rico. The island prospered, and so did Pablo Constante. He was tall, exceptionally so for a Puerto Rican, good-looking, and he learned fast. He was also determined to stay out of the cane fields. He rose from busboy to maitre d' at the supper club of the Don Quixote, one of the finest in the long line of luxury hotels along the Condado gold coast. He acquired a suave manner, knew how to handle the help as well as the customers. Then, when it seemed as though it would never stop growing, the tourist trade dwindled. With shocking abruptness, without advance notice to the guests, much less to the employees, the Don Quixote announced it was closing. One typically brilliant morning, at the height of the season, the guests came down to discover not only that there was no breakfast but also that they would be required to vacate their rooms that very night. Other hotels closed, and masses of specially trained Puerto Ricans had no jobs. Pablo Constante was too old now for the cane fields; besides, the sugar trade was hurting as much as the hotel business. He had to go where the work was, and he took his family with him.

The metal cleats on Gabriella's heels echoed sharp and lonely in the empty streets. She wished now that she'd let Luisa and Raul see her home. Raul had turned up unexpectedly at the church to see Luisa, and Gabriella had felt very much in the way. They'd got on

2

the subway together, but Gabriella insisted there was no need for them to get off at her stop and walk her the few blocks to her home. After her repeated assurances that it was still early, only eleven thirty, that there would be plenty of people around, that it was only a short way, they had agreed.

Gabriella had first noticed the pale young man with the dark curly hair and blue eyes outside the subway entrance. She was a pretty girl, accustomed to being admired. The young man followed the three of them down to the platform, and she was very conscious of his presence while they waited for the train. After a while she became uncomfortable, for his look was not the innocently cheerful leer of boys who watch girls, but sly, suggestive. She turned away and was glad that Luisa and Raul were too wrapped up in each other to have noticed. Then the train came, and he got on another car, and Gabriella thought that was the end of it.

But when she got off, so did he. For an instant their eyes met; then he moved ahead with the crowd, preceding her up the stairs, through the exit turnstile, and out to the street.

When Gabriella emerged, he was standing on the corner looking around uncertainly as though to get his bearings. She didn't know what to do. There was no policeman around. Even if there had been, what could she have complained about? "Officer, please, I do not like the way that man looks at me. . . ." While his back was to her Gabriella walked quickly away.

She had gone just over a block when she sensed him behind her. She'd kept on going till she reached the Drive, and then, when she'd looked again, he was gone. He could have turned off into one of the side streets or entered a building along the way, whichever

tion. *Tonta, vanidosa!* Gabriella Constante chided herself and at the same time swore she would never again be out alone at night.

She certainly hadn't expected the streets to be this deserted. There was no traffic at all and only one man up ahead on the other side of Riverside Drive leaning on the embankment wall and looking out toward the river. He was tall, slim-hipped, and broad-shouldered, and he carried his jacket slung over one shoulder like . . . like . . . Gabriella felt a strangling in her throat. He stepped out of the partial shadow of the trees into the moon's yellow spotlight. The crests of the crimped dark curls were bronzed by it,

3

and the pale blue eyes gleamed as though they were lit from within. It was he. There was no doubt.

Gabriella remained fixed where she was, watching as he walked to the edge of the sidewalk checking for cars before crossing. He moved on a slant, right shoulder down and leading . . . as though he were sliding, sliding around a corner or into a half-open door. . . . How had he got ahead of her without her noticing? He must have entered the park at Seventy-ninth and then moved parallel with her but behind the wall. *Santa Madre de Dios!* What should she do? Scream? Would anyone come if she screamed? Would it at least frighten him away? Or would it serve as an excuse for him to accost her? He was just about to cross Riverside Drive while she was ready to cross Eighty-third Street. She lived just on the other side and a quarter of the block up. If he crossed first, he'd be able to cut her off. Gabriella ran across the intersection.

She didn't hear the screech of brakes behind her or the yelling of the outraged driver.

By the time she reached her doorway she was gasping for breath; the stitch in her side had her doubled up; her heart was pounding. She had no idea whether the man had crossed over, much less whether he was anywhere near, and she didn't want to know. Using both hands, she pulled on the heavy glass door and entered the building vestibule. The inner lobby door was always locked, day and night, and now Gabriella sobbed with weakness and fear as she fumbled precious minutes away looking for the key in her purse. When she had it at last, her hand was shaking so badly she could hardly fit it into the lock. Then it jammed. She felt the current of warm air on her back as the outer door opened, yet though the floor was stone, she heard no footsteps. But Gabriella didn't need to hear his footsteps to know that he was there.

Madre de Dios, ayudeme!

The key turned then, but as Gabriella pulled at the knob, a hand was placed over her mouth and an arm encircled her waist, pulling her body back against his. With one foot he kicked the door open and then shoved her inside. He hardly broke stride as he half carried and half pushed her ahead of him. Past the dimly lit lobby he steered her toward a dimmer passage that led to the back stairs, almost as though he knew exactly where to go. With one hand still tight over her mouth, he dragged Gabriella up to the first landing and in one movement threw her down to the cold cement and was on top of her. Her arms were pinned; her legs kicked uselessly. The smell of his lusting sweat was sickening; her stomach heaved in the need to empty itself. The sweat of his hand was trickling down into her throat. She must get that hand off her mouth! His weight was completely on her, yet somehow she managed to free her right arm. She clutched at his wrist, trying to pull his hand off her mouth, but all she managed to do was tear his shirt-sleeve.

At that he grabbed her hand and twisted. She was strangling on her own screams.

"Don't do that!" he hissed.

He was breathing heavily now. His blue eyes were opaque and showed no reflections as they looked directly into her eyes. "I'm going to take my hand away, but if you so much as open your mouth, I'll smash your head to a pulp on these stairs. Understand?"

She was so completely immobilized that she couldn't even nod; she could only stare anxiously back into those blue eyes and blink.

He was satisfied. He took his hand away. She remained silent.

Pain brought Gabriella back to consciousness. She concentrated on the pain, on its intensifying then diminishing, using it to keep from thinking back to what had happened. The pain was a refuge from the remembrance. But finally the pain subsided. Feebly, Gabriella pulled herself over to the corner of the landing and propped herself up to a sitting position. She felt as though her insides were leaking out on the cold stone floor. She made an attempt to straighten her clothes. When she realized her panties had been ripped and felt the greasy slime on her body, she began to whimper.

At a quarter of two in the morning, as he was returning from work, Pablo Constante heard the weak moaning from the direction of the back stairs and went to investigate. He found his daughter incoherent and carried her upstairs in his arms like a baby.

Norah Mulcahaney was awakened by the ringing doorbell. She had been sleeping restlessly, yet the homely, familiar sound in the middle of the night became alarming. At first she was confused

5

and thought it was the downstairs bell. The building's speaker system was permanently out of order; as often as the management repaired it, vandals ripped it out of the wall again, so there was no way of finding out who was down there or what they wanted. Norah glanced at the luminous dial of her bedside clock—at 2:20 A.M. she wasn't about to answer. Probably it was a prankster or a drunk looking for a hallway in which to sleep. Norah lay still in the dark and wondered how long it would be before whoever it was gave up and tried another bell or another building. She just hoped it wouldn't disturb her father; he had enough trouble sleeping these nights. . . .

But the ringing continued with a steady, patient, determined rhythm, and as Norah became fully awake, she realized that it was the apartment doorbell that was ringing. She jumped out of bed instantly, turned on the light, reached for her robe, and ran out into the hall. Her father was already there.

Frowning, Patrick Mulcahaney put a warning finger to his lips and limped cautiously toward the front door. Her father was sixty-seven years old, had a bad left leg, and had recently been showing frailty beyond his years. Norah was a detective attached to the Fifth Homicide and Assault Squad recently promoted to second grade, but danger at their front door was for him to face. Norah had no intention of challenging that right.

"Who is it?" Patrick Mulcahaney called in a firm voice.

"Pablo Constante. From downstairs in 3H, Mr. Mulcahaney."

Norah could offer a little guidance, though. She put a restraining hand on her father's arm. The Constantes were new tenants; she hadn't met them, but he had. "Make sure," she whispered.

He nodded and slid the peephole cover to one side.

"I'm sorry to disturb you at such an hour," Constante said. "It is an emergency."

There was no trace of an accent, but Mulcahaney nodded again, indicating that he was satisfied. Nevertheless, with the caution that has become instinctive to everyone in every big city, he kept the chain on as he opened the door.

"Is he alone?" Norah asked.

"As far as I can see." Mulcahaney now turned on the hall light, unhooked the chain, and admitted their neighbor.

Norah had not expected such a fine-looking man. He stood

6

erect, bearing himself with a pride of heritage. He wore tuxedo and black tie. They were his working clothes, she assumed, since she'd been told that Constante was a captain in one of the fine hotel supper clubs. He held his arms rigidly at his sides, fists clenched. The pulse in his temple throbbed.

"Thank you," he said to Mulcahaney but instantly looked to Norah. "It was in fact your daughter I wanted." He paused. "Detective Mulcahaney?"

"Yes. What's happened, Mr. Constante?"

She was barefoot, light-blue robe with ruffled lace edging hastily pulled together, long brown hair so dark it could be called black tumbled over her shoulders, face still soft and relaxed from sleep. Seeing her like that, Constante hesitated. He shook his big head, his shoulders slumped the slightest bit, and he sighed—the help he needed and had come to find was not within this young woman's ability to give. Having disturbed their sleep, though, he owed father and daughter an explanation. So he spoke out of courtesy and with as much restraint as he could manage. "It is my daughter, my Gabriella. She has been . . . attacked. . . ."

Though she had not met the parents, Norah had met Gabriella Constante. The girl had come soliciting used clothing for a church charity drive. Norah had collected what she could spare, and they'd talked. She'd found Gabriella Constante shy, but eager; intimidated by the city, yet anxious to fit in and to make new friends.

"When and where did it happen?"

"I don't know exactly when, but it happened here, in the building."

The fact that Norah Mulcahaney assumed that he knew he had their sympathy and didn't waste time encouraged him. He took a second look at the young woman detective and saw a steady competence in her blue eyes and firm determination in the set of her square, overly prominent jaw. "I found her on the back stairs . . . a short time ago . . . as I was coming home from work." He tried to match Norah's detachment, but the memory of the condition in which he'd found his only child was too much for him.

"I suppose she's home now?"

Constante could only nod.

7

"All right. I'll throw some clothes on and be right down. You don't have to wait if you don't want to, Mr. Constante." She started for her room.

Constante was relieved. For one blessed moment the bitter weight of despair and the deep responsibility for the step he had decided on shifted to this self-possessed young woman. "I'm really sorry to trouble you at such an hour, Detective Mulcahaney. I know I should have called the police station. . . ."

Norah had in fact wondered why he hadn't; then she had reasoned that he had sought her out because he knew her father and therefore thought she would be likely to take a personal interest. "It's all right, perfectly all right. I understand."

"No." Before he had been reluctant; now Pablo Constante was anxious to explain. "No, I don't believe you do. It is not possible for me to go directly to the police. You see, the child is . . . deeply disturbed, in shock. She will not speak to me or even to her mother. She surely would not speak to a stranger. In fact, a policeman, a *man* asking the questions that must be asked might make her condition worse." For just a moment the depth of his distress was evident, then he continued. "Her mother doesn't want me to report the attack at all. She wants to let it go, to try to forget." Anger overcame him, swelled, and brought temporary relief. "I cannot do that. I want this . . . animal found. I want this . . . this . . ." He had to resort to his native tongue. "*Maldito! Pérfidio! Puerco sin vergüenza!* I want him to pay for what he has done to my innocent child. So we thought of you, Detective Mulcahaney. My wife and I, we thought of you."

So now Norah knew exactly what the nature of the attack on Gabriella had been. A quick look at her father showed her that he too understood it had been no purse-snatching or mugging. "Have you called a doctor?" she asked Constante as gently as she could.

"No."

"You must, right away. It's important for several reasons. First, for Gabriella's health—to make sure there are no internal injuries or . . . any other problems. Also, so he can give corroboration."

"Corroboration?"

Norah bit her lip; she didn't like having to say it right out to the girl's father. "Of the sexual nature of the attack." She hurried on.

8

"Was she beaten? Does she have external injuries, any bruises, say?"

"No."

"The doctor will check her over and give her something to calm her." For Constante's sake Norah was remaining impersonal, but while she spoke, she imagined Gabriella's state and she could have cried. "Do you know a doctor? If not, I can . . ."

"Thank you, but I do know someone."

"Why not call him while I get dressed? You can use our phone."

"The telephone's in here." Patrick Mulcahaney ushered Constante into the living room. "Here's the phone book in case you need it. I'll . . . uh . . . just go and put some coffee on." It was a tactful way of giving the stricken man privacy.

In her room Norah threw on slacks and a shirt, twisted her long dark hair into a tight knot at the nape of her neck. She took a quick look in the mirror and decided to take the extra seconds to apply lipstick and a dab of powder—the more normal she appeared, the more assurance she could give Gabriella and Gabriella's mother. From Pablo Constante's terse words she gathered that Mrs. Constante was almost as deeply shocked as the girl. The lipstick on, Norah grabbed her purse, which contained her ID and service revolver, and presented herself in the living room.

Constante had completed his call and was sitting beside the phone waiting. When he saw her, he jumped to his feet. "Dr. Lopez is on his way."

"Good." Norah called toward the kitchen, "Dad! We're going."

Patrick Mulcahaney came hurrying out. He didn't like Norah's job; he considered police work dangerous and dehumanizing. While he had to admit that so far it seemed not to have affected her natural tenderness and compassion he was afraid that the constant association with criminals and with the seamy, sordid side of life must ultimately affect her. At the least it must result in bitterness and disillusion. Of course, he had never observed her actually at work, and granted that this was a special situation, dealing, as it did, with a neighbor, for the first time Patrick Mulcahaney saw Norah not as his daughter but as a police officer and was impressed. He was also proud that a man of Constante's strength and

9

self-reliance should come to her in his need and that she was equal to it.

"I've put the coffee on." He was telling her he would be waiting when she got back. For these two, who seldom displayed their deep affection, that would normally have been enough. Now, most uncharacteristically, Patrick Mulcahaney leaned forward and kissed his daughter's cheek.

Norah blinked for a moment. Usually she would have urged him not to wait up for her. All she said was, "Thanks, Dad."

2

The bare ceiling bulb shone harshly in the empty living room of the Constantes' apartment. It was a large room sparsely furnished with cheap modern furniture, Danish style, secondhand. Constante, with his innately aristocratic bearing and his well-cut evening clothes, didn't seem to belong there. They had just entered when Norah heard a door close softly somewhere in the back, and Mrs. Constante joined them. She didn't seem to belong in that tawdry atmosphere either. Nor was she what Norah had expected Constante's wife to be. She was short, plump, and dowdy in her too-long black dress. Her black hair was liberally streaked with gray, her face sallow and tear-stained, her dark eyes sunk into crepy hollows. But she came forward and extended her hand with welcoming grace.

"Thank you. Thank you so much for coming to help us, Detective Mulcahaney."

Her accent was heavy, but her voice sweet, and in spite of her distress she made Norah feel that she was honoring them. Norah revised her opinion: she was exactly the wife for Constante. She was also a fortunate woman, who was allowed the dignity of aging naturally, a woman not forced to diet or to dye her hair in order to compete with some young secretary in her husband's office or with the contrived image of a housewife on TV commercials. It occurred to Norah that it must have been very painful for this gracious woman to leave a home lovingly created and come to this brutal city. And now to have this happen. . . .

"How is Gabriella?" she asked.

"A little more calm, I think."

"May I speak with her?"

"Could it not wait till morning?"

"*Ofelia!*" Constante chided.

"The sooner I get the facts, the better, Mrs. Constante."

"*Pablo . . . porqué debemos hacerlo? Porqué?*"

"*Ya está decidido, querida.*"

With a barely audible sigh but no further protest, Mrs. Constante motioned to Norah to follow and led her to a closed door at the end of the inner corridor. Her hand on the knob, she paused to look anxiously at Norah. "Gabriella has refused to speak of what happened, Detective Mulcahaney."

"I'll be as gentle as I can, Mrs. Constante. You can depend on me."

"I believe so. *Gracias*, thank you." She lowered her eyes and stood aside, indicating that Norah should go in alone.

One dim light burned on the night table beside the bed, a single bed up against the far wall. The girl lay on it with her back toward Norah, and she didn't move. Norah took a moment to look around. In addition to the bed and night table the only other furniture was a small bureau, an old-fashioned sewing machine, and a low chest. Except for the chest, which was a fine, dark, polished mahogany, everything else, like the things in the living room, was secondhand.

"Gabby . . ." Norah called softly, but the girl gave no indication that she heard. "It's Norah Mulcahaney, Gabby. You remember me; we had a long talk the other day." Still no reaction. Moving quietly, Norah took the single chair from in front of the sewing machine, moved it to the bed, and sat down. She waited. Gabriella Constante didn't move.

The clock ticked. There was no other sound for a long time.

"Go away," Gabriella muttered into the pillow.

"If you really want me to go, I will," Norah said and waited. Gabriella burrowed further.

"You're going to have to talk about it sometime, Gabby."

"Why? Why am I? I don't want to. I'm not going to—ever!"

She was still lying face down, her words still muffled. "I don't have to."

Norah didn't dispute it. "You saw him; you got a good look at him. You could give a description that would help us catch him."

"What good would that do? It wouldn't change anything."

"It could save another girl."

"I don't care about any other girl."

"Don't you? I'm sorry you don't care, Gabby. I'm sorry the girl he molested before you didn't care either, because if she had, maybe he wouldn't have been out on the street to attack you."

Another few moments passed, and then Gabriella turned on her side, but still facing the wall and away from Norah, and began to cry softly. Norah made no move to touch her or comfort her. Finally Gabriella turned over on her back. Her dusky oval face was swollen with crying, and there were red patches that looked like a rash, but there were no bruises or any other indication that she had been struck about the head. There might be marks on her body, of course, that neither her father nor mother was aware of, but the doctor would discover them in his examination.

Gabriella sniffed. "What do you want to know?"

"To start with—a description of the man."

"No."

"Why not, Gabby? Why not?"

"If I tell you, you may find him, and then everybody will know. I don't want anybody to know."

"There's no need to be ashamed. What happened wasn't your fault." The girl turned her head toward the wall again. "If he'd attacked you to steal your purse you'd give me a description, wouldn't you?"

"It's not the same."

"No," Norah agreed. "But . . ."

"You don't understand. It's . . . Enrique. Once he finds out that . . . that I'm not . . . that I've been used . . . he won't want me!"

So that was it! In describing her life in San Juan, Gabriella had dwelled at length on her fiancé and on all his attributes. In these permissive times it was almost a shock to discover the old standards still honored. "Enrique will know that it was through no fault of yours. He'll comfort you and cherish you." Gabby only cried harder. Norah leaned over and put a soothing hand on the girl's

12

heaving shoulders. Just how innocent and naive had the nuns at *Sagrado Corazón* kept their girls? "Once you're married, Enrique will find out. It will be much more difficult to explain then."

Gradually Gabriella stopped sobbing. She sat up in bed. "I'm afraid. I'm afraid he might come back."

"We'll see to it that he can't hurt you or anybody else for a very long time," Norah promised.

Gabby took a deep breath. "He had brown, wavy hair, frizzy, and blue eyes . . . the whites were yellowish. He had a cold; his nose dripped. . . ."

The description so far was as much emotional as factual, but Norah let her continue the catharsis.

"He was very strong; he dragged me up to the first-floor landing with one hand while he kept the other over my mouth. When he threw me down, I couldn't move." She shuddered, and the tears brimmed in her eyes again.

"Try not to think about that part of it; just concentrate on what he looked like."

"I've told you. That's all I can remember."

It was time to give her a little help. "Was he young or old?"

"Oh . . . medium . . . about twenty-five."

"Short or tall? Fat or thin?"

"Tall and . . . well, not really thin, but more thin than fat . . . And strong." She came back to that as though not sure that Norah had heard it the first time.

"Good, that's good. Now let's see if we can't round out the picture a little. How about the shape of his face—broad or narrow?"

"Narrow, with a low forehead and an extra-long chin with a cleft and cheeks sort of sunken."

Norah was pleased that the image was so clear in Gabby's mind and sorry too, for she realized it would be a very long time before the girl would be able to erase it. "Did you notice any kind of scar or identifying mark?" Gabby shook her head. "During the struggle, were you able to mark him in any way? You have long nails; did you scratch his face?"

"You said I didn't have to talk about that part of it."

"Just this one thing, Gabby; it's important."

"No."

Norah backed off. Ultimately she would have to go into the details of the assault, but this was not the time. For now she would continue to dwell only on the events surrounding it. "Where did he come from? What I mean is, was he already inside the building, or did he follow you in from the street?"

"He came up behind me and grabbed me as I was opening the door."

"Did you notice whether he'd been following you from any distance? Or did he jump out of another doorway as you passed, or what?"

"He followed me from the subway."

That surprised Norah, but she took care not to show it. "You noticed him? When, exactly?"

"When I got off the train?"

"He was on the same train with you?"

"Not in the same car. You see, he was outside the subway entrance when we came up—Luisa and Raul and me. That is my friend, Luisa Alvarez, and her *novio* . . . ah, boyfriend, Raul Martín. Luisa and I had been at Santa Teresa's sorting and packing the clothing . . . you know. . . ."

"Yes." Actually Norah had wondered what a girl as carefully nurtured and protected as Gabriella Constante had been doing out alone at close to midnight. She hadn't asked the parents, not wanting to add to their grief by suggesting they'd failed in their responsibility. "Were they supposed to see you home?"

"Luisa was. But then Raul turned up . . . he was waiting for her outside the church. I could see he was disappointed I was along; he wanted to be alone with her. So we got on the subway together, but I would not let them get off with me at my stop. I assured them I would be all right. It was not their fault."

"But you had already noticed this strange man watching you."

"But I didn't know there was anything bad in it! He would look at me; then, when I would catch him, he would quickly turn away, then look again till our eyes met, and then he smiled. I thought . . . he was admiring me!"

A common enough experience, one Norah herself had often enough. "And he didn't get on the same subway car with you so naturally you weren't expecting him to get off at the same stop."

"No, I wasn't." Gabriella was grateful for Norah's understand-

14

ing. "It made me nervous, but he went up the stairs ahead of me. When I came up to the street, he was standing on the corner looking around, but by the time I reached Riverside Drive he was gone. I didn't see him again till I reached Eighty-third."

He might have been stalking her right from the beginning, or it could be that their getting off at the same station was a coincidence—Norah couldn't see that it mattered. Gabby was considerably calmer now, so Norah decided to try again to question her regarding the actual assault. It was true that Gabby was inexperienced yet instinct should guide her. "Did he do anything or force you to do anything that was . . . unnatural?"

"No."

Thank God for that. Norah blushed along with Gabby. "During the struggle were you able to mark him in any way?" she asked for the second time.

For a moment it seemed that Gabby was going to seek refuge in tears; then unexpectedly her face cleared and she answered, "I tore his shirt . . . the sleeve of his shirt."

He'd get rid of the shirt; even if he didn't, no one could prove how a shirt came to be torn. "Could you have scratched his arm?"

"I don't know. I could not see. He had a . . . what do you call it . . . a drawing on his arm."

"A tattoo?"

"Yes, he had that on his arm so I couldn't tell whether I had scratched him. Also, he pulled his arm away too fast."

Norah was excited. "A tattoo is the best kind of identifying mark, Gabby. What was the design?"

"He pulled his arm away," she repeated. "He was very

Naturally he hadn't wanted her to get a good look at it. "Never mind. Once we get a suspect, any kind of tattoo on him will be highly significant. Do you remember which arm?"

"I don't want to talk about it anymore. Please. Please!"

Norah got up. "You've done very well, Gabby. Thank you."

A cautious knock sounded at the door, and Mrs. Constante looked in. "The doctor is here," she whispered to Norah.

But Gabriella heard and opened her eyes wide in alarm. "I don't want any doctor. I don't want anybody to see me or touch me. Tell him to go away. *Mamá, por favór, no lo quiero, no lo quiero.*"

15

The type of medical examination to which she was about to be subjected could be traumatic for a young girl no matter what the attendant circumstances, so Norah was matter-of-fact about it. "It's for your own protection, Gabby." She hesitated, wondering again just how naive the girl was. "For Enrique's protection too. You wouldn't want to pass an infection on to him, would you?"

Mrs. Constante gasped, but Gabriella simply nodded her acquiescence.

At the start of the gynecological exam Norah left the room; she felt she could spare Gabriella at least that much humiliation.

Norah was the only one who drank the coffee that Mrs. Constante had prepared while they waited in the harshly lit living room for Dr. Hector Lopez to finish. Pablo Constante paced and smoked; Ofelia Constante sat on the edge of the worn and stained couch straining for any sound from her child's room. No one made any pretense of conversing. The mother was the first to catch the opening and closing of Gabby's door. She rose instantly and went to meet the doctor.

"Todo está bien, señora. Consolese."

Hector Lopez was a middle-aged, middle-sized, balding man with a full, round face. He wore rimless pince-nez glasses, and he spoke with professional calm, but the sympathy he offered the anxious woman was very real and very personal. "She appears to be all right," he added in English for Norah's benefit.

"Appears?" The father seized on the word and in two strides was standing face to face with Lopez.

"A figure of speech, *amigo*, only that. Aside from a long welt behind her right shoulder and another along the buttocks apparently caused by the pressure of the stair edges there are no external injuries. Internally . . ." he said, sighing. "I will not deceive you—she has been much abused, but nature is a good healer. I have given her an injection of penicillin . . . purely as a precaution, you understand." He paused. "Emotionally . . . well, it has been a most violent shock for her. It is my responsibility under the law to question Gabriella, but as I understood that you had already elicited the details, Detective Mulcahaney, I did not overly press the child." He waited for Norah's confirmation.

"I did speak with her, Dr. Lopez, and she gave me a very clear description of the man who assaulted her and general details of the attack.''

"Good. That is a good thing that she is able to speak of it. However, Gabriella did ask *me* a question that is significant. She asked me if I could repair the damage.''

Mrs. Constante groaned and turned to her husband and was drawn into his arms.

"I had to tell her I could not.''

"She's ashamed for her fiancé, Enrique, to know,'' Norah explained.

Lopez nodded. "I thought it might be something of the sort.''

"Enrique will marry her, I can assure you,'' Constante announced.

"I am sure he is a fine young man and will remain steadfast,'' Lopez said, hastening to calm Constante's agitation. "However, the sooner he can personally reassure Gabriella, the better.''

"He is in San Juan, a student at the university. I will call him and tell him he must come immediately.''

"Good. Very good. I have given Gabriella medication to make her sleep. I think, señora, you should take something also.'' The doctor opened his medical bag.

"Thank you, but I do not require . . .''

"Do as the doctor advises, Ofelia. You must rest while you can, for you will need much strength during the next few days.''

The room was very still. Lopez appeared about to add something. He looked from the anxious parents to Norah and, instead of speaking, bowed his head and rummaged in his bag. Mrs. Constante held out her hand and accepted the tablets he shook into a small envelope for her.

Having closed the bag, Lopez hesitated once more. "There are one or two technical matters that I should discuss with Detective Mulcahaney. Is there someplace . . . the kitchen perhaps. . . ?''

"Please stay here, Doctor. If my wife is no longer needed, she will retire, but I will see you out when you are finished.'' Constante pointed. "Just knock on that first door.''

Lopez nodded, then waited till Constante had helped his wife into their bedroom. Once they were gone, he seemed released of a heavy constraint and sat down. Norah sat too and found to her surprise that she too was relieved by their going.

17

"As I indicated, there is no doubt that Gabriella Constante has had sexual relations," Lopez stated. "The hymen was ruptured, and there has been considerable bleeding. I am prepared to so testify. I don't know how familiar you are with the law governing rape in the state of New York. . . ."

"Only in general terms. I've never handled a rape case. I work out of Homicide."

Lopez looked at her more closely, shook his head, sighed again. "Unfortunately I have had considerable experience in such cases. While the law has become somewhat less rigid recently in the requirements for establishing rape, the more corroboration one can show, the better. I know Gabriella Constante—she has been under my care for a minor menstrual irregularity so I can not only state that she was a virgin but also am prepared to testify to her character and background and the traumatic damage caused by the assault. As to showing force . . . the clothing she was wearing if torn and bearing blood or spermatic stains would be helpful. I suggest that you collect everything she was wearing before her mother mistakenly throws it into the washing machine or even discards it."

"Yes, I'll take care of that right away."

"Well . . ." The doctor got up wearily. "That is all we can do for the moment. Here is my card, Detective Mulcahaney. Call me at any time for any help you may need."

As soon as Lopez knocked, Pablo Constante came out of the bedroom. The two men walked together to the front door. It seemed to Norah that Lopez was troubled, wanted to speak, and as before decided against it. Shaking hands, he grasped Constante's upper arm in a firm *abrazo*. Was it an expression of sympathy based on their ethnic tie, or was it encouragement for the ordeal that the doctor knew through his own experience was just beginning? In the first flurry of activity Norah had given little thought to the ordeal that lay ahead for Gabby. Rape complaints, she knew, were generally messy, hard on the victim, difficult to prove. Surely in this instance, with the excellent description of the assailant and the doctor's prompt attendance, there wouldn't be any trouble. Still, Norah wondered whether Lopez might have advised his compatriot against making the complaint if Norah hadn't been there. Was that what lay behind Lopez' hesitation?

"I'll be leaving too, Mr. Constante," Norah said as soon as the doctor was gone.

"I can't thank you enough, Detective Mulcahaney."

"Norah, please. What are neighbors for?" She too now hesitated, wondering if he realized the difficulties ahead. "You do understand that I won't be personally in charge of Gabby's case? We're in the Fourth Detective District here, and I work out of the Fifth. I'll have to turn over the information to the local . . ."

"But I understood . . . I thought . . ." Constante was upset. "I explained when I went up to your apartment that Gabriella would not speak to a stranger, most particularly that she would not speak to a man."

"I understand that. I intend to make a full report, and I'll include everything she told me tonight, and I'll ask that she not be interviewed again until absolutely necessary. But she will have to sign a complaint. And when the man is caught, she will have to make the identification. She'll also have to appear at the trial."

"You think he will be caught?"

"I think there's a good chance of it."

"Then Gabriella will do what is necessary."

Since she herself believed that the complaint should be made, that was as far as Norah went with her warning. "One more thing, Mr. Constante. Will you get me the clothes that Gabby was wearing tonight? Everything she was wearing."

Pablo Constante's pale face turned livid. "I'll get them," he said.

3

Norah was between shifts. She had planned to sleep late, finish the housework, then go shopping for a new dress for her date with Joe. Joe Capretto and Norah Mulcahaney had known each other for more than two years. They'd met when she was a rookie working out of the policewoman's pool and had been assigned to one of Sergeant Capretto's homicide cases. She'd made detective largely because "Cap" had given her the chance to show what she could do. They'd dated casually, off and on, but lately the dates had become more frequent and, Norah thought, more serious. She based that not only on Joe's manner but also on her father's attitude toward him.

Joe was handsome, Latin, and a bachelor still at thirty-nine . . . or was it forty? He was dark, medium height, and somewhat stocky—constantly waging the battle between the *pasta* and *vino* and the bathroom scales. His broad brow and prominent nose formed the classic Roman profile, and when he smiled, which he did often, he displayed a dentist's delight of even white teeth. He worked at his job with efficiency and dedication, neither glamorizing what he did nor downgrading its importance. Norah admired and respected him and . . . that was it.

Her father made no secret of his disapproval of "the Sergeant," as he persisted in calling Joe. According to Patrick Mulcahaney, the Sergeant was a playboy who would never settle down.

"He's not the marrying kind. I know his type only too well. I don't want you hurt, sweetheart!"

"I understand the situation, Dad."

"Then why do you go on seeing him? What's the point? You're wasting your time."

"I like Joe. He's a good friend. We enjoy each other's company."

The ritual exchange.

Norah always disclaimed any romantic feeling toward Joe. The truth was that she agreed with her father that Joe would never settle down and that was why she'd been careful, very careful, not to let herself care about him. Besides, she wasn't his type. Norah wasn't sure what Joe's type was. Considering how close they'd been during these two years on the job, it was surprising how little she really knew about Sergeant Capretto's private life. He had seven sisters and was the only son. The sisters were all married, but he still lived at home. Norah had never met Signora Capretto, but she assumed that the signora was as determined to keep her son single as her father was to get his daughter married. Norah wondered if Joe had ever been serious about any girl and if so what had happened.

The point was that recently Patrick Mulcahaney's attitude toward the Sergeant had mellowed. Norah traced the change to a talk the two men had while Joe was in the hospital. He and Norah had been working on a homicide connected with a housewives' prostitution racket. A stray bullet from Norah's gun had caused Joe's injury, and that she was responsible had deeply distressed her father. She didn't know what they'd said to each other that afternoon, but since then, Mulcahaney had been less critical of Joe. Maybe Joe's announcement that he was going out for lieutenant had something to do with it too.

The announcement had certainly surprised Norah. For more than twelve years Joe Capretto had been a detective sergeant and seemingly content. She knew that he'd been studying for the lieutenant's exam off and on in a desultory fashion. Suddenly he'd decided to take the test and had passed at the top of the list. Now he'd been called to take the command course. It meant going back into uniform with no guarantee that he would get out of it and into the detective division again—in fact the likelihood was against it. Back on the uniformed force he'd be making less money as a lieutenant than he was now making as a sergeant of detectives. Joe's logic was that with the continuing reorganization of the department, with new squads being formed on what seemed almost a weekly basis—crime prevention, community service, pickpocket, and confidence, all were relatively new—the opportunity for a detective command would never be better. It was also the only route to ultimately even higher rank.

So tomorrow, when Norah went on the four-to-midnight tour, Sergeant Joseph Antony Capretto would be reporting to the Police Academy for a regulation school day. They wouldn't be seeing each other for a while. That made tonight's date special.

But Norah didn't sleep late after all. Though she'd got back to bed after four, she woke at the usual six thirty. She'd called in her report the night before, but she wanted to get right over to the Eighty-second Street station house and talk personally to the detective who would be handling the Constante case, and he'd be going off duty at eight. She would have preferred to be able to turn the case over to a man just coming on, fresh, without too much other business on his mind.

She had to settle for Detective First Grade Sam Vickers.

Vickers' desk was near the window, and when Norah entered

the squad room, he was sprawled in his chair smoking and staring at it, not through it, because it was too dirty to see through. She made a quick, practiced appraisal—mid-forties, sandy hair turning gray, one hundred and seventy pounds, height—hard to say while he was sitting—make it just about six feet. His face was pale with too many lines too deeply etched unless she was badly misjudging his age. He looked as though he exercised too little, and he certainly smoked too much—the ash tray on the edge of his desk was full, the dirty edges showed it had been emptied several times, and also his brown eyes were tearing from the haze he was blowing up around himself.

He looked around. "Detective Mulcahaney?"

"Yes." Evidently the desk sergeant had called from downstairs.

From a pile of papers Vickers pulled out what she assumed was the Constante complaint sheet. "Something to add?"

"Not exactly. I thought maybe I could clarify a few points."

"What points?"

"The situation generally."

Vickers raised both eyebrows, but extracted a scratch pad and a stub of pencil from the same pile in which he'd filed the complaint. "Shoot."

So Norah got right to it. First she explained how she'd been brought into the case. Meticulously she detailed Gabriella's background and her emotional reaction to the attack. She underscored the girl's reluctance to talk about what had happened—her shyness and her shame.

Vickers nodded. "Sure. They all feel like that. But she's going to have to talk about it. She's going to have to tell her story two, three times anyway. Lucky if it's not more."

Norah licked her lips. "Yes, I know, but . . . what I had in mind was . . . if you could put off your own interrogation for a while, work on what I'm giving you till she has a chance to recover."

Vickers shrugged. "Sure. Sooner or later though . . ."

"I know." Norah was disappointed. She had expected . . . well, if not sympathy or concern, at least some interest. She continued what amounted to a verbal report, using her notes for reference. Vickers asked no questions, made no comments even

22

when she was finished. "I'd be glad to type up my notes for you," she offered.

"Not necessary, Detective Mulcahaney. I get the picture."

"How about the description of the assailant?"

"Got it." Vickers indicated the scratch pad, which as far as Norah could see was covered with nothing but doodles.

"Here's Dr. Lopez' card in case you want to contact him."

Vickers took it and tossed it to the top of the pile. "Right."

"The victim's clothing for the lab . . ." Norah held up the plastic bag with Gabriella's things in it.

Vickers shoved some papers aside to make space for it. "Right. You've turned everything over in A-1 shape, Detective Mulcahaney."

There seemed nothing more to say. Norah got up, hesitated, made one last try. "I'd be grateful if you'd keep me advised of developments. It's not that the Constantes are particular friends, but they are neighbors and they did come to me."

"Right."

"Well . . ." She still waited for some comment, opinion, some indication of how Sam Vickers intended to proceed. "What do you think? What are the chances?" She had to ask.

"You haven't given me much to go on."

Norah gasped. "You couldn't get a better, fuller description!" she exclaimed indignantly. "Even without the tattoo!"

"It's almost too good."

That set Norah back, but only for a moment. "She's not making it up if that's what you're thinking. She spotted the man outside the subway; she had plenty of time to observe him while she thought he was trying to pick her up."

"OK." But Vickers sounded and looked skeptical. "What I meant was that a description isn't much good unless you know where to look."

"You must have a list of known sex offenders," she responded. "You can check the description against that, for starters. How about other rape complaints? You could look for him in the area where previous attacks have taken place." Norah was too angry by now to care that she was outlining routine procedure.

"We have had a heavy incidence of rape cases during the past

23

four months," Vickers admitted. "We picked up the perpetrator five days ago—redhead, bad acne condition, thick glasses. He's been arraigned and indicted and is awaiting trial."

"Does that clear up everything on the books?"

Vickers nodded.

"How about checking the other precincts?"

"These guys usually operate within their own neighborhood."

"He did pick her up on the subway, remember, so we don't know what neighborhood he comes from. He could be wanted in another precinct."

"It could also be a first offense. There has to be a first time, you know."

Norah frowned. "The way he did it—the way he shoved her into the lobby and then hauled her around to the back stairs . . . it looks like a well-established MO."

"Maybe."

"How about the girl's clothing? Could be the lab will turn up something useful from them."

Vickers took a deep breath. "You know the kind of evidence the lab will turn up—corroborative, very helpful once we've got a suspect, but not much use in tracking him down."

"You never know."

"I know that Sherlock Holmes stuff is great in books and on TV, but it doesn't pay off in real life. So unless you have some other suggestions . . ." He indicated his desk.

There was plenty of work piled up there, all right, Norah acknowledged, but he certainly hadn't been doing any of it when she walked in. Though she fumed inwardly, Norah had learned to moderate her indignation, or thought she had. "I'm not trying to tell you how to do your job, Detective Vickers," she began placatingly. "It's just that . . ." She paused. She had got over her need to prove herself to each new person with whom she came in contact and to justify her right to be a detective. The promotion to second grade had something to do with that, but so did the day-to-day routine and the fact that she was equal to it. She could work now buoyed by inner confidence and no longer need the bolstering of others' opinions. Still, Vickers was sloughing her off. She wasn't interested in his reasons; she didn't even care; but she

24

would not let him slough off the case. "I get the feeling, Detective Vickers, that you're not interested."

"Oh, I'm interested, all right, Detective Mulcahaney," he answered with the same cool formality. "I'm interested in every case that comes across my desk." Again he made that vague gesture toward the litter of accumulated reports and flyers. "There's just nothing about your case that makes it special."

Norah's blue eyes narrowed, her lips turned in, and her square Irish chin was thrust forward. "It's special to the victim."

"Sure. Every piece of paper here represents a complaint or a report on a complaint, and every one is special to somebody. I'm sorry, but I can't bleed for everyone."

"I'm not asking you to bleed, just to care a little."

"I care, Detective Mulcahaney; believe me, I care. I care about every old doll who lets the mugger take her purse without resistance, then gets knocked down and beaten up anyway. I care about every old boy dozing in the sun who gets his guts stomped out for laughs. I care about the kid knifed on the school recreation grounds because he won't give up his dollar lunch money for tribute to some gang, and the college co-ed killed for bus fare—all the money she has on her. I care that the new generation has no sense of morality, that young hoodlums are roaming on the lookout for thrills—shooting up, drinking up, raping, just out to get their jollies. I care, but what can I do about it?"

"I'm sorry."

"Sure." Vickers shrugged. "Forget it."

Norah could have added that there was no point to being a cop if you weren't willing to chip away at crime conviction by convic-

she returned to the case in hand. "I admit I've got a personal interest in this. I saw Gabriella Constante right after the attack." Norah groped for a way to express her feelings without being melodramatic. "The girl suffered a severe shock, came close to a breakdown. I . . . I just don't want the case to be filed away."

"I'm not going to file it away." Vickers looked hard at her. "I assume you're familiar with the New York State rape law."

"To some extent. I realize that aside from the marks of the stairs across her back and buttocks, she suffered no external injuries; on

25

the other hand, she did undergo a medical examination within the twelve-hour limit after the assault—even though that's no longer mandatory. The panty hose in that bag are torn and stained. Not that it matters, but Dr. Lopez will testify that in his opinion she was raped. As far as we're concerned, that's it, isn't it? The rest is up to the jury."

"Right. I'll give it my best shot, Norah."

He had a nice smile; too bad he didn't use it more often. Norah was satisfied. She got up and held out her hand. "Thanks, Sam. Oh . . . Maybe you should talk to Luisa Alvarez and her boyfriend. Maybe they spotted the suspect on the subway platform and noticed something Gabby Constante missed."

"Right, right. It hadn't occurred to me."

Norah flushed. "Sorry."

"I told you I'd give it my best shot." He'd stopped smiling, and he didn't sound optimistic.

4

Norah found the perfect dress for her date. It looked like a Pucci, but of course she couldn't afford a real Pucci. This had the same sort of marvelous coloring, though—a rust background with soft blue and violet whorls in the border that brought out the color of her eyes. It also had a silky texture that she found delicious against her skin and that made her feel slithery and provocative. She was experimenting with accessories when her bedroom phone rang.

"Sam Vickers, Norah. Sorry to bother you at home, but you did say you wanted to be informed."

"Oh, yes, Sam, sure. What's up?"

"Just talked to the lab. . . ."

"That was fast."

"Yeah, well, I've got a buddy over there owes me a favor. Anyhow, maybe there is something to this Sherlock Holmes stuff after all. Seems there was a stain on Miss Constante's panty hose—besides the blood and semen, that is. Engine grease."

"Engine grease . . ."

"Don't jump to conclusions. It could be he was working on his own car."

"If he has a car, why was he riding the subway?"

"Because his car broke down and he couldn't fix it."

"If that's what you thought, you wouldn't have called me. He works in a garage."

"It's possible. Only, people who work in garages usually wash up before going home."

Norah thought fast. "It was late, well after eleven when Gabby spotted him at the subway entrance. Supposing the garage closes at eleven; he might have cleaned up and been actually leaving when a customer drove up. Could be he agreed to serve the customer, got the grease on his hands, but couldn't be bothered unlocking the washroom. How about that?"

"Possible. Do you know how many gas stations and garages there are in Manhattan?"

"All we care about is how many there are around the Broadway and Sixty-sixth entrance to the subway, right? We'll make a list and divide it up and. . . ."

"No."

"I know you have a heavy load. I just want to give you a hand, Sam, that's all. If I spot him, I'll call you right away, naturally. I won't talk to him. I won't go near him."

"Well. . . ."

"You're on the twelve to eight; how can you do any canvassing? We don't want to let it go till you change tours, do we? You'd have to work on your own time."

"If you don't mind working on your own time, why should I? I'm not that crazy about legwork. We'll divide the territory."

Norah flushed slightly because he'd known that she was working the same tour as he. So he'd taken the trouble to find out. Well, good. It meant that he was interested in the case, and the more interested and the shrewder Sam Vickers showed himself, the more Norah's confidence in him grew. The main thing was that he'd agreed to let her help. She got right down to business. "First we have to define the area we're going to canvass. It would be within walking distance of the subway entrance. The stop below is Fifty-ninth and the one above it's Seventy-second—so let's say the boundaries are Sixty-second to Seventieth as the north and south. For the east and west . . . well, the park and the river. I'll go through the Yellow Pages and pick out . . . no, we'll split it geographically with Broadway as the dividing line. You take the east, and I'll take the west. OK, Sam?''

"There are a lot more garages west of Broadway,'' Vickers observed mildly. "There's a regular row of them on Tenth and Eleventh avenues.''

"Oh? Well, we can switch if you want to. You take the west.''

"No, you keep it. I just wanted you to know that I realize what you're up to.''

"I'm not up to anything, Sam.''

"The hell you're not!'' Samuel Vickers chuckled and hung up.

Norah was excited. The description Gabby had given of the assailant was so clear in her mind it was as though she had a photograph of the suspect. She was convinced that he did in fact work in a garage or service station. That being so, she had every expectation that within the next couple of days he'd be picked up. She'd purposely stayed away from Gabby and her parents to give them all a chance to recover, but maybe, in view of the new development. . . . No. The best medicine for them all would be the arrest and conviction of the attacker, but it was just as well not to get their hopes up too soon. Norah was itching to get started. If she hadn't had the date with Joe, and if he didn't have tickets to the opera . . . Forget it. Joe was a real opera nut; he wouldn't even consider . . .

The result of Vickers' call and her subsequent scheming was that when the doorbell rang, Norah wasn't dressed. In spite of the fact that they were getting along so much better, Norah wasn't inclined to leave her father and Joe alone together for too long: you never knew which might accidentally ignite—her father's Irish temper or Joe's Italian pride. So Norah rushed the makeup; forgoing the new hair style she'd created, she settled for the usual plain knot at the nape of the neck with just a couple of curly wisps pulled out around her ears for softness. Yet when she appeared, the effect was gratifying.

Both men stopped talking to look at her. Joe went to her and took both her hands in his.

Meeting his intent gaze, Norah thought that he was looking

particularly handsome himself in his good navy suit. The weight loss, which Joe teasingly attributed to the terrible hospital food, had sharpened his profile and had cleared the flab from his middle.

"Sorry I'm late."

"It was worth it."

"Is that all you're going to put on?" Her father broke in and pointed to the black velvet stole she'd snatched up at the last minute.

"It's a warm night."

"I'll give her portal-to-portal service, Mr. Mulcahaney," Joe promised.

"Don't be too late." Mulcahaney grimaced and pursed his lips. Damn. He hadn't meant to say it; he'd promised himself he wouldn't; it had just slipped out.

The opera was *La Bohème*. The prima donna not only looked the part but also could act it, and Norah found herself unexpectedly moved by her death scene. Being Italian, Joe couldn't have cared less about her looks or acting ability as long as she could sing—and this Mimi was a little thin in the top register. But he was delighted by Norah's reaction.

"I told you you'd enjoy it."

They left the State Theater, passing the small formal park in front of the Vivian Beaumont and coming out at the back on Tenth Avenue and Sixty-fifth. The car was parked on Eleventh and Sixty-third. As they got in and Joe turned on the ignition, Norah glanced at the fuel gauge.

"You need gas."

"I've got half a tank."

"There's a station just two blocks up." She nudged her chin in that direction. "You might as well get some."

"Why?"

"Why not?"

"Why do you want to go to that gas station?"

He knew her too well. She sighed. "I'm looking for a suspected rapist. He could be working at one of the garages in this area. I thought as long as we were here, we . . ."

"No. This is a date. Besides, that station's closed."

"Is it? There's another one just . . ."

29

"Sure, and one beyond that, and then another, and another. Don't you ever quit?" He laughed, but he was also a little annoyed. "I told your father I'd get you home early. I'm just getting on his good side; I don't want to spoil it."

"It won't take but a couple of minutes. The victim gave a good description; I'll be able to tell right away if . . ."

"Since when are you working on a rape?"

"I'm not—officially. I'm just helping out on my own time."

"This is my time. Ours. Or at least I thought so. Does Lieutenant Felix know?"

"Not yet. I was going to mention it tomorrow."

"Then it can wait till tomorrow. You know I think your father may be right and you are too wrapped up in the job. Don't you ever think about anything else?"

"Sure."

"For instance? Do you ever think about me?" Under the teasing there was a serious undercurrent.

"Of course."

"What? What do you think of me?"

The fluorescent streetlight made his dark face appear sallow and intent. "I like you, naturally, and . . . I respect you. You're a fine police officer and a good friend."

"Is that all?"

Norah felt hot and cold by turn, shy and eager, totally unprepared. "I enjoy being with you—obviously, or I wouldn't go out with you so much. We have a lot of fun together." It was the best she could manage.

"We do, don't we?"

He had moved from under the wheel and was sitting close to her. Turning in the seat so he could face her directly, he placed his hands lightly on her shoulders and kissed her full on the mouth. It was not the usual, casual goodnight kiss, but firm, long, tender. At first Norah resisted, but she couldn't for long, didn't really want to . . . It was Joe who finally broke it off.

"Think about me some more, Norah, during these next six weeks. Take the time for it, will you?"

He moved back behind the wheel and started the car.

The next two days, Norah, along with nineteen other detectives of the Fifth Homicide and Assault District, was assigned to canvassing the neighborhood in which a schoolteacher had been slain the day before. They were looking for the man who had last dated her or for someone who had seen him or might even know him. That meant ringing every doorbell of every apartment of every building as well as inquiring at stores, offices, and bars in the area. Norah found it neither onerous nor boring—you never knew what was behind the next door or who would give just the one piece of information that could break the case. She was thinking about lunch when the superintendent of the building she was in came looking for her with a message. Sam Vickers was trying to get in touch. She called from the super's apartment.

"I've run into a snag," he told her.

His admitting it was surprising enough, his open agitation completely out of character. "What is it, Sam?"

"I called your Lieutenant Felix, and he says it's OK for you to drop what you're doing."

"For what, Sam?"

"Oh. I didn't tell you, did I? I got our man. Picked him up last night."

"You did?" She hadn't expected it so soon. She was elated. "That's terrific. Congratulations." And confused—why wasn't Sam gratified? "Where did you find him?"

"At a garage on Broadway and Sixty-ninth."

Not the one she'd wanted to stop at that night with Joe—not that it mattered.

"His name is Earl Dana, and he fits the description, including a tattoo on his left forearm."

"So what's wrong?"

"The girl won't come down to make the ID!" Sam exploded his rage and frustration. "She absolutely refuses. I went over to the apartment, and she burst into tears when I asked her to come with me. When I tried to explain, she ran out of the room."

"Did she understand that it's not a face-to-face. . . ?"

"Sure," Vickers interrupted. "I got as far as telling her they'd be in separate rooms and he couldn't possibly see her. She just kept repeating she was afraid. Hell, he's got no previous criminal record and no psychiatric history either. He's clean. Unless she makes a positive ID, we can't book him."

"How about her family? Did they try to reason with her?"

"They did, and it was some scene, believe me. Her fiancé, Enrique Ferrer, is up from San Juan, and he did his best too, but she just got more upset."

"Do you want me to go over and talk to her?"

"You don't have to. She finally agreed to attend the lineup if you go with her. Will you?"

"Naturally. I'd be glad to, Sam; you know that. When do you want us?"

"Now, right away, as soon as you can make it. I can't hold this guy forever."

"Hang loose, Sam. I'm on my way."

Gabriella Constante was dressed and waiting. She looked awful. Her small face was pinched, her normally glowing dusky skin yellowed, dark shadows under her eyes. To Norah she seemed, if anything, in worse shape than she'd been four nights ago just after the attack. She'd been brooding, of course; that was one reason. Possibly she was still partially under sedation; that would account for her apathy.

Before leaving, Norah looked inquiringly to Pablo Constante, expecting that either he or Mrs. Constante or the fiancé might be planning to accompany them. Constante shook his head.

"She wants only you."

Ferrer, a nice-looking slimmer and younger version of Constante, seemed embarrassed. He stood to one side effacing himself as much as possible and watching Gabby fixedly. Gabby didn't even look in his direction.

"We won't be long," Norah said and, putting her hand on Gabby's elbow, gently guided her out of the door.

During the short taxi ride she made no effort to talk to the girl. Any wrong word might put her off. She had agreed to go through with the ordeal, and for the moment that was enough. When they arrived, though, Norah stopped for a moment on the sidewalk before entering the station house. Sam had said he'd tried to explain the procedure, but how much in her distraught state Gabby had grasped before running out of the room was questionable. Quietly Norah went over it once more.

"You'll be going into what appears to be a hallway between two

32

rooms. There'll be a one-way mirror along one wall. You'll be able to see through it, but nobody on the other side will be able to see you. Several men will be lined up, and all you have to do is pick out the man who attacked you. Now, I repeat, Gabby, you'll be in different rooms. He won't be able to see you or even know that you're there.''

Gabby frowned. She said nothing.

''Gabby? Do you understand? You'll be in no danger at all.''

''Suppose I don't see him? Suppose he's not there? I mean, suppose Detective Vickers got the wrong man?''

Norah felt a moment's panic. Was Gabby planning to deny recognizing the suspect? Was that why she'd finally agreed to come down? ''If he's not one of the men in the lineup, then you have to say that,'' she replied calmly.

Gabby nodded, satisfied.

''And then the man will be released, and we'll have to go on looking.''

''You mean . . . I might have to come back here another time?''

''Probably.''

''But . . .''

''Let's hope that Detective Vickers got the right man the first time.''

They went into the station house.

As soon as he walked out, Norah knew him. Earl Dana fitted the image she'd formed from Gabby's description, but Gabby, standing beside Norah, said nothing. She stiffened as though she were afraid that any unconsidered movement might be interpreted as recognition. Would she admit knowing him, or would she deny it?

mately the same height and build and coloring—the law required it—yet there was no doubt in Norah's mind that the third in line was the assailant. She kept watching that third man. Under the harsh lights calculated to reveal every uncompromising detail as mercilessly as a mug shot, scrutinized by an accuser whom he could not see, the most decent citizen tended to appear unsavory, shifty, evasive. This suspect managed to appear less furtive than most.

Facing that one-way mirror, most also tended to avoid looking directly at it, shifting their eyes in every other possible direction; a few aggressive ones stared belligerently, as though they could see straight through it, threatening their accuser. The third man found refuge in a vague, unfocused gaze. He seemed not to know how he had got there or what was going on. Yet he had dressed for the occasion with care in a worn but freshly pressed gray suit, clean blue shirt, and conservatively striped tie. His brown curly hair had been carefully wetted down, and either he had shaved very closely or he had a very light beard. He was in an almost shy way surprisingly good-looking—he shouldn't need to go out raping strange women.

When it was his turn, he stepped forward obediently, presented his left and right profiles as ordered by the officer on the other side, and his meekness reinforced the impression of helplessness. The hypocrisy of it was maddening.

Norah waited till he had stepped back and the other men in the row had each come forward to be individually inspected. "Well, do you see him?" she asked.

Still Gabby didn't answer.

"Do you want to look at any of them another time?"

"No!"

"Well?"

Gabby sighed. When she answered, her voice was so low Norah had to lean close to catch what she said. "The third, the third from the left."

"Are you sure?" She searched the girl's face. "You'll stand by that?"

Gabby turned her lips in and nodded.

"Good."

Out on the street the daylight seemed extra bright and Gabby more nervous than ever. Norah tried to cheer her. "It wasn't so bad, was it?"

"No."

"Then what's the matter?"

Gabriella Constante sighed heavily and shook her head.

"You did what you had to do. Your mother and father will be proud of you, and so will Enrique."

"No."

"Why not?"

"Back in San Juan, Enrique was so anxious for us to get

34

married. He did not want me to come away to New York, but papa said it had to be so. He would not give his permission for me to stay behind and marry Enrique. Papa wished Enrique to get his degree and find a job first. I had to obey papa." Tears welled in Gabby's large brown eyes. "Now I would marry him no matter what papa says, but Enrique does not even mention it."

So! Norah's sympathy overflowed for both of them. "But, Gabby, dear, he wouldn't bring it up at a time like this. He probably thinks you're too upset. . . ."

"He doesn't want to marry me because . . . because of what happened."

"Then why did he come? Why did he drop everything to fly out to you?"

"Because papa ordered it."

"Oh, Gabby . . ."

"You saw yourself how he stands over to one side! He hasn't come near me. He hasn't touched me!"

"Maybe he thinks you don't want him to."

"Oh?" Clearly this was a new consideration.

"Have you given Enrique any indication that you want and need his love? That you want his arms around you? That you are looking for the comfort and consolation of having his arms around you?"

Slowly Gabby shook her head. "I was waiting. . . ."

"Maybe he's waiting too."

When Gabby and Norah had first met, there had been the beginning of friendship, but it had been stunted by Norah's official position. Now, dropping all constraint, Gabby seized the policewoman's hand. "Oh, Norah, do you think so? Do you really think so?"

"Yes. Yes, I do."

Gently she disengaged herself so she could flag a passing cab. Norah wished she was as sure as she'd sounded.

5

By the time they got back, Gabriella Constante was looking much better—her color had improved; she was less tense. Her parents noted it instantly and reacted with obvious relief. Her mother took Gabby into her arms. Pablo Constante, much moved and not ashamed to show it, looked over the heads of mother and daughter to Norah.

"It was the one?"

Norah nodded.

He turned to his child. "*Bien hecho, niña.*" As Mrs. Constante let her go, he took Gabriella into his arms.

As before, Enrique Ferrer remained in the background. Naturally he was upset by the despoiling of the girl he intended to marry; any man would be—a Latin, Norah supposed, more so than others. Surely he would forget about it. Gabby hadn't wanted either Enrique or her parents with her at the lineup because she must intuitively have sensed that it would be easier for them if they did not have the memory of the actual man to erase. There was still the grand-jury hearing, but he would not be present there. They could hardly avoid seeing him at the trial, though . . . but at least by then Enrique would have gone back to San Juan. Norah watched anxiously as Gabby stepped away from her father and turned expectantly toward Ferrer.

The two young people were silent for several moments.

"*Bien hecho, querida,*" Enrique Ferrer echoed what the father had said, still making no move.

Gabby's eyes sought Norah's, and she nodded encouragingly. Gabby swallowed, took a tentative half step toward Enrique. . . .

It was enough. "*Mi alma!*" He swept her into his arms. Norah imagined it was the first time that Gabriella Constante and Enrique Ferrer had embraced in the presence of her parents. They didn't seem to disapprove.

Quietly Norah slipped into the hall and let herself out.

The next time that Gabby faced Earl Dana, it would be in the open without the protection of a wall and a one-way mirror. Though the trial was not likely to attract much attention, she would still have to get up on the stand and tell her story in front of judge and jury, attorneys and witnesses. She would have to undergo cross-examination—a humiliating, no-holds-barred examination by the defense. Though a seasoned policewoman, Norah herself would consider it an ordeal. She wondered if people realized the cost to a woman, any woman, of exposing the intimate details of her violation in public? She was relieved that Gabby would have the loving support of her family and her fiancé.

Norah returned to the canvassing in the case of the teacher homicide. The break came through one of the other nineteen detectives on the job. The resulting flurry of activity led out of state and resulted in the apprehension of a suspect forty-eight hours after the commission of the crime. This caused the commissioner great pride and permitted him to cite the cooperation among departments as having brought about such a speedy conclusion. Norah was by then working on the homicide of two men whose bodies had been discovered in the debris of an apartment house fire but who had died earlier of gunshot wounds. This time her job was to reconstruct the background of the victim who had been renting the apartment. David Link was working on the past of the other man living with him—apparently in a homosexual relationship.

Detectives Mulcahaney and Link were seldom assigned together. Lieutenant Felix, commanding the squad, preferred to pair each with a more staid officer who would dampen the exuberance that was their common trait. In this instance the case was being "carried" by a sergeant and their work supportive and under his direction. Of all the men on the squad, David was the one Norah felt closest to—after Joe, of course. Both she and Link had been appointed before reorganization of "the bureau," which is the detective division, when Homicide North and South had jurisdiction over the entire city and was the most elite of assignments. They had been the two rookies and the two youngest members. It could have caused rivalry between them; instead it created a bond. Now they worked on their reports at adjoining desks and shared a companionable silence in the empty squad room.

A phone rang. They both looked up. It was the phone on Joe's desk.

David sighed. "I'll bet it's that same dame. I've told her half a dozen times that Joe's not available. Maybe she'll take it from you."

Norah got up, stretched, and crossed the room while the phone continued to ring. "Homicide and Assault. Mulcahaney."

"Oh. I wanted to speak to Sergeant Capretto."

"Sergeant Capretto is temporarily detached from duty. Can I help you?"

"No, thank you. This is personal. When will he be available?"

"Not for several weeks."

"Where could I reach him?"

The woman had one of those low, scratchy voices that were supposed to be seductive. "I'm sorry, I can't give out that information."

"But I'm a friend of his, an old friend. He's expecting my call."

Really, Norah thought, then why don't you call him at home? Joe's home number was unlisted, naturally, but if she didn't know it, then she couldn't be such a close friend. "Would you care to leave a message?"

"If you can assure me that the message will finally get to him . . ." she started testily, then switched to charm. "Thank you, yes. Just tell him Helen Scott, Helen Iverson Scott called. I'm staying at the Aylward, suite 507."

"All right, Miss Scott. I have that."

"Mrs. Scott."

"All right, Mrs. Scott. I'll see that Sergeant Capretto gets your message."

"Thank you, Miss . . . uh . . . Mulcahaney, was it?"

"Detective Mulcahaney."

"Oh. Thank you, Detective Mulcahaney."

"She's been calling four or five times a day for the past three days," David informed Norah when she hung up. He pointed to the assortment of bits of paper stuck along the sides of Joe's blotter all with the name Scott scrawled in various handwritings. Norah added her own notation without comment. David gave her a long look. "She sounds sexy."

Well, he knew, as the other men did, that lately she and Joe had been seeing a lot of each other. It was no secret. Norah hadn't stopped to think about it, but there was probably plenty of speculation about them. She knew David was teasing her; still, she couldn't help a sudden flare of jealousy.

"Sounds to me like she smokes too much." Norah turned aside so David wouldn't see her flush. She was surprised at her own reaction.

But David didn't have to see. "It doesn't look like Joe's much interested. After about the fifth call I got fed up with taking messages and decided to contact him at home and pass on the info. Evidently he hasn't got around to returning her call or she wouldn't still be pestering us here, would she?"

That eased Norah considerably, but she couldn't say so. "I'll remind Joe the next time I talk to him."

Before that could happen, however, she was subpoenaed by the district attorney to appear before the grand jury in the Dana hearing. Though Norah had not been officially connected with the case, she had known that as the first police officer to interview the complainant, she would surely be called. She was worried about Gabby, so before going upstairs, she rang the bell of 3H. It was a completely recovered, even radiant Gabriella who answered, threw her arms around the policewoman, and pulled her inside.

"Oh, I am so glad to see you! If you had not come, I would have gone looking for you to tell you the wonderful news and to thank you. Because it is all due to you and to your good advice. You were right, Enrique only seemed distant and remained silent out of consideration for my distress, just as you said. It was a misunderstanding. But it is over, and we are going to be married. As soon as possible. Papa has given his permission."

"Gabby, that's wonderful! I'm so happy for you."

"The wedding will be in San Juan. Enrique has already returned to find an apartment for us near the university. We have not yet set a definite date because . . . well, you know, because of the hearing and all that. It is one of the things I need to consult you about, Norah. Both Enrique and Papa want me to see it through. Now that it has been scheduled . . . well, would the following Saturday be all right? It should be over by then, don't you think?"

Her dark eyes were shining, her dusky skin glowing; she was as different from the frightened, shamed girl lying in her bed with her face to the wall as it was possible to imagine. Norah hated to cast any shadow on her happiness. "The hearing shouldn't go for more than a day, but there will still be the trial, and it might be a very long time before that comes up."

Gabby brushed Norah's words aside impatiently. "Yes, yes. I discussed that with Enrique last night over the telephone—he has already called me long distance three times . . . very extravagant. . . ." Her whole being was filled with the joy that she was worth so much to him. "He says it could be many months before the case comes to trial, and he thinks that we should be married in the meantime. I could return when I am needed." She waited with just a tinge of anxiety. "That would be permitted?"

"I don't see why not."

Gabby nodded with the satisfaction of one who never really had any doubts. "We would like you to be present at our marriage, Norah, if you would honor us. We are both so grateful to you, Enrique and I; you brought us together again. I would like you to be my . . . *madrina* . . . maid of honor."

"Oh, Gabby, that's very sweet. Thank you for asking me. I'd love to, but I don't know if I could get away."

"We would pay for your trip, of course, and if you would not mind staying in the home of Enrique's parents . . ."

"I couldn't let you pay for the trip, but . . ." Norah considered rapidly reviewing the possibilities. She had some time coming. She could combine the wedding festivities with her vacation. Why not? A week in the sun! She'd never been to Puerto Rico or any of the Caribbean islands or anywhere outside the continental United States, for that matter. The more she thought about it, the more eager she became. Maybe her father could go along. It would do him a world of good. If Gabby, or rather Enrique, could find them rooms in a guesthouse, they could swing it. "Let me talk to the lieutenant, OK?"

"*Ay si! Seguro*. Norah, I am so happy."

"Now, nothing's settled, but . . . we'll see." Norah's blue eyes were as bright as those of the bride to be. "You must get someone else to be your maid of honor, though. . . ." Norah realized she was already thinking of the trip as arranged. "Just in case at the last minute something should prevent . . ."

"No. We want you. We will count on you. If anything happens and you cannot come, then there will be no other maid of honor."

Patrick Mulcahaney reacted to the idea with a flurry of activity. As soon as Lieutenant Felix, Norah's commanding officer, gave his OK, Mulcahaney started getting ready. He collected travel folders; he went to the library and took out books on Puerto Rico; he consulted those of his friends who had been there: from all these he compiled a list of things to do, places to go, and restaurants to try that would have taken at least a month to get through. Norah was delighted. Lately her father had not been well—he'd lost weight, tired much too easily—but what really worried Norah was that he no longer took an interest in the activities that had formed the structure of his days. He still went for his usual two-hour walk regardless of weather, but she suspected that he took plenty of rest on park benches along the way. He admitted to no longer working out with the weights at O'Flaherty's Gym, and Norah had it on good authority that his beer consumption at Houlihan's was way down. But he remained active at the local Democratic Club and could still hold his own in any argument. Thank God! For when the day came that Patrick Mulcahaney could no longer argue, he would surely be dead. Like all true Irishmen, Mulcahaney considered debate a primary sport and was ready to take either side of a moot question. But the fierceness had gone out of his dialectic; he rationed his passions. Look at the way he now tolerated Joe! Seeing her father eager, revitalized, Norah was overjoyed. As far as she was concerned, on this score alone the trip was already a success.

She herself was drawn into the wedding preparations far more than she had expected. Gabby was constantly either on the phone to her or having Norah down to the apartment for consultations. She wanted an opinion on everything—the gown, the gowns for the bridesmaids. The guest list. Though Norah didn't know the people involved, she was nevertheless asked to help make the choice on whether to invite great-aunt Sofia, whom everybody loved, when it also meant asking cousin Alberto, the little sneak! What should be served at the reception? One hundred odd details that Norah would once have thought silly and inconsequential now absorbed her. She had not realized how intricate a supposedly simple family wedding could be. The synthesis of it all was expressed one day when Gabby took her new friend into her bedroom with its cheap, secondhand furniture and opened the lid of the one fine piece brought from home—the mahogany chest. Inside, carefully layered with tissue, was her trousseau. There were piles of delicate, lacy, personal things and household linens too—towels, sheets, tablecloths—handmade, hand-embroidered, which Gabriella Constante must have been working on and putting aside for years, well before she'd even met Enrique Ferrer. Now she was making her own wedding dress—the lustrous satin was draped over the sewing machine. Times had changed, Norah reminded herself; nobody did this anymore. Nevertheless, she was touched, and if she hadn't understood before how much the marriage meant to Gabby, she certainly came closer now.

These exclusively feminine preoccupations were a new experience for Norah Mulcahaney. When she was twelve, her mother had died. Her father never even considered remarrying. He had intended hiring a housekeeper, but at the beginning he'd put it off because doing the chores had seemed important to the grieving child, because she'd taken such pride in her ability to keep house for him and the two boys. It had been a kind of therapy for her. Once the pattern was set, it had been hard to break. So at a time when other teenagers were giggling together, discovering boys, Norah was marketing, cooking, cleaning, learning how to balance the household budget. Then, just as she was getting ready for college, Patrick Mulcahaney's leg was mangled by a crane. It was only his ferocious will that had kept him from becoming a cripple for life. College was postponed, then given up. Norah stayed home and continued to keep house for her three men till in due course her brothers married and moved west. Mulcahaney, feeling guilty about the years of her devotion, had been the one who had insisted that Norah get out of the house and find herself a job. What he'd really intended was that through the job she find herself a husband. He had not counted on her joining the police department. Seeing his daughter at last behaving like other girls, he was overjoyed. As far as Patrick Mulcahaney was concerned, on this score alone the trip was already a success.

Joe Capretto's pleasure in it was somewhat less enthusiastic. "You'll be back in time for my graduation?"

"In plenty of time," Norah assured him.

"Mama is already planning the menu for the celebration." He grinned deprecatingly. "The whole family is turning out, the girls

42

with their husbands and children—a mob. I thought you and your father . . . if you could stand it?''

It was the first time Joe had asked them to his home. "We wouldn't miss it, Joe.''

As the time of the grand-jury hearing drew near, Norah noticed signs of nervousness in Gabby. Her mind would wander from what had heretofore been wholly fascinating matters of wedding etiquette. She would quite suddenly grow pale, sweat breaking out over her brow and along the fine, barely perceptible hairline above her upper lip. Well, it was to be expected. After her session with John Cootes, assistant DA in charge of the case, Gabby returned more confident. She seemed impatient to get the thing over, as though it was the final unpleasantness to be surmounted before she could enter a state of permanent bliss. It was as good an attitude as any. Norah was careful not to disturb it.

6

On her way to the grand-jury chamber Norah caught sight of Gabby and her parents beside the water cooler in the corridor. She assumed that Gabby had already testified. Cootes would have taken her through her story sympathetically. There would, of course, have been no challenge in the form of cross-examination, since the purpose of the hearing was merely to establish that a crime had in fact been committed and that the suspect charged was indeed the likely perpetrator. Therefore Dana would not have been present for a confrontation. It should have been relatively easy for her, yet Gabby sat holding the paper cup in her hand and staring sullenly at the floor. Her olive skin was sallow, her full lips were turned inwardly into a thin, straight line, her shoulders hunched as though cringing against a series of blows. The Constantes stood protectively on either side of her, not knowing what had transpired and therefore not knowing what to do for her. Ofelia Constante's eyes were red as though she had been crying, but she was not crying now, for she would not add to her daughter's distress by crying in front of her. Her urge to take her child into her arms and comfort her was so palpable that Norah could sense it from a distance. Pablo Constante was the only one of the three who saw Norah. Fine leonine head high, he threw her a look that said that he too wept, but inwardly, for the shameful ordeal to which his daughter had been subjected; at the same time it indicated his pride in her courage and the grim expectation of her vindication. Norah went in.

She gave her testimony concisely and impartially as she'd learned to do. Cootes was skillful and drew from her all the points she would have liked to make herself if she had been telling her story freely, including the deep emotional shock in which she'd found Gabby. Dr. Lopez of course would offer the primary evidence relating to the victim's condition and to the fact that she was a virgin. Norah was also encouraged to tell about the encounter at the subway as recounted to her—this to serve as the groundwork for the later interrogation of Luisa Alvarez and Raul Martín. It was not usual to have corroboration both for penetration and identity; it was a strong case. Norah left the hearing confident.

Stepping back into the corridor, she got a shock. The suspect, Earl Dana, was coming straight toward her! She stopped short; for a moment their eyes met—his mild, confused, helpless as in the lineup. Then he passed on. Of course, he didn't know her. The man with him, though, the suave, meticulously groomed, elderly man steering Earl Dana toward the witnesses' waiting room, gave Norah a quick, shrewd scrutiny. Did he know who she was? She knew him—Edwin Wallingford, the attorney. Wallingford was experienced and expensive, of a stature far beyond the requirements of the case. What was he doing here anyway? The suspect was not required to appear. In fact, he could appear only at his own specific request, and if he did so, he in turn had to waive immunity. And the attorney would not be permitted to accompany his client into the hearing room, though he could remain available in the anteroom for his client to duck out for advice as needed. Dismayed, Norah watched Edwin Wallingford and Earl Dana enter the waiting room. What was Wallingford up to?

She had plenty of work to do. She had only today and tomorrow to finish her current assignments and get what she couldn't finish into some kind of shape so that David Link could take over.

Wednesday she was to have a farewell dinner with Joe. Thursday afternoon she and her father, along with Gabby and the Constantes—the wedding party—would be taking the 2:30 P.M. Pan Am flight to San Juan. The wedding would be on Saturday.

As the day progressed, Norah's concern over the presence of Dana and his expensive lawyer at the hearing increased. Wallingford was too big a man for this kind of thing. She couldn't imagine what had induced him to take the case. Well, of course, money, what else? Plenty of money. What she meant was that she hadn't supposed Earl Dana would be able to raise that kind of cash. Evidently he had.

She didn't get home till nearly nine that night. The temperature had dropped unexpectedly, and Norah, wearing only a light suit, was still shivering as she entered the apartment. "Hi, Dad," she called out, enjoying the indoor warmth. "Sorry I'm late; so many last things to do. Hope you didn't wait dinner," she said as she entered the living room.

Her father was sitting in his usual chair in front of the television, but the set wasn't on. The travel brochures were spread out on the table beside him, but he wasn't looking at them either.

"Dad, what's the matter? Are you all right?"

Patrick Mulcahaney's face was set, his jaw clamped so tight the pulses at his temples throbbed. "It's off. It's all off."

The sense of impending disaster that Norah had refused to acknowledge all day now overwhelmed her. "What's off?"

"The wedding, the trip, everything. The jury refused to indict."

"What?"

Her father picked up the newspaper from the table beside his chair and handed it to her. It was folded to page three, and on it was a picture of a beaming Edwin Wallingford surrounded by reporters and photographers as he strode triumphantly down the corridor outside the grand-jury chamber. The caption read: EDWIN WALLINGFORD WINS AGAIN. Though the great man had not set a foot in the jury room, Norah grudgingly admitted that the statement was nevertheless basically correct, for he had masterminded Dana's appearance, and he had coached him in his testimony.

"Constante called about an hour ago," Mulcahaney told Norah. "Gabby's hysterical. She's threatening to kill herself."

45

"My God!"

For once he didn't reprimand her for using the name of the Lord. "They got hold of Lopez, and he's put her under sedation." Tears of anger and frustration filled Mulcahaney's eyes.

Norah went back to the paper. The picture was large but the accompanying story brief. It gave a résumé of the crime, of Dana's apprehension, his voluntary appearance before the grand jury, and its refusal to indict. That the case was given such prominence was due to Wallingford's importance, certainly not his client's, and Norah strongly suspected that Wallingford's office had alerted the reporters and photographers to be present. The article ended with Wallingford's quoting a statement of Julia Heit, criminal appeals lawyer with the Legal Aid Society: "I have a very uneasy feeling about any defendant being sent to jail solely on the testimony of one eye-witness, the victim."

To which Wallingford sententiously added his own comment that his client's predicament was a vindication of New York State's much-maligned rape law. The law had protected his client in what might otherwise have resulted in a gross miscarriage of justice.

Norah nearly gagged. At least the reporter had had the taste not to make any comment on that! She tossed the paper aside and strode to her bedroom to use her phone. Mulcahaney followed and stood in the doorway while she dialed.

She called Cootes, but couldn't locate him. She called the precinct, but Sam Vickers was off duty. She tried his home.

"Sam!" Norah was relieved to get him; she couldn't have held in her shock and anger much longer.

"I was just going to call you."

"Sam, what the hell happened?"

Mulcahaney didn't object to that either.

Vickers was tired and dejected and sounded it, but Norah, usually so sensitive to moods, didn't catch it. "I can't believe this. I just cannot believe it. What happened, Sam? How could they *not* indict? My God! The doctor examined the girl . . . what . . . three hours . . . after the assault and testified that she'd been violated. She gave a perfect description of Dana. And it wasn't just her description; Luisa Alvarez and Raul Martín identified him. Two corroborating witnesses, Sam!"

46

"They identified Dana as the man they saw on the subway platform, and they testified that he appeared to notice Miss Constante. They couldn't say that he was the one who later followed her and attacked her."

"I realize that, but . . ." Norah stopped. "Surely the jury couldn't think that Gabby willfully and maliciously described an innocent man?"

Vickers sighed heavily. "It's worse than that. The identification wasn't challenged."

Norah held her breath. She knew what was coming, yet till the last moment, till Sam Vickers actually said it, she kept hoping it was not so.

Vickers sighed again. "Dana admitted having sexual knowledge of Miss Constante. He claimed she consented."

Norah groaned. She should have known; as soon as she saw Dana going into the witness room, she should have guessed.

Her father took a step forward. "What? What does he say?"

Norah waved him off to indicate she was listening.

"Dana claimed she gave him the come-on outside the subway station and then again down on the platform."

Norah exploded. "That's ridiculous! That innocent, naive, *straight* girl? All anybody has to do is look at her to see she's not the type. . . ."

"What? Type for what?" Mulcahaney wanted to know.

Norah put her hand over the mouthpiece. "Dana testified that Gabby consented." She removed her hand and spoke to Vickers. "How about Dr. Lopez' testimony? He assured me that all the signs were consistent with forcible rape. He didn't go back on that, did he?"

"No, but the girl was a virgin, so naturally there would be some tearing of tissues under any circumstance."

"Oh, God!"

"There was just too much against her."

"I don't see that," Norah persisted. "On the contrary . . ."

"There was no evidence that she resisted," Vickers countered. "If there had been external injuries of any kind—contusions, abrasions . . ."

"I suppose if she'd had a broken jaw, they would have believed her," Norah commented bitterly.

47

"It would have helped." Vickers wasn't being facetious.

"He threatened to smash her head against the wall, Sam! According to the 1972 revisions of the law, a threat of grievous injury is supposed to be enough."

"Sure, if you can get the jury to believe it. It was her word against his."

"OK. So when you interrogated Dana after the lineup, he insisted that he didn't even get off at Seventy-ninth Street, much less that he noticed or followed Gabby. He claimed he got off at Eighty-sixth Street and then went straight home. Didn't Cootes bring that out?"

"Sure, and Dana very humbly admitted lying. He said he was afraid that what happpened between him and Miss Constante would be misconstrued."

"You've got to be kidding."

"The jury bought it. I say again, Norah, if she could have marked *him* in some way—scratched him, gouged him, bit him . . ."

"She tore his shirt." Even as Norah reminded Sam of it, she knew as she had at the beginning that it was no proof of resistance.

"What really clinched it against Miss Constante was the testimony of her two friends," Sam continued. "Both Luisa Alvarez and Raul Martín not only noticed Dana at the subway but also were aware of the byplay between him and Miss Constante. They were very much aware of the fact that though he didn't get on the same car with her, he kept watching her from the next one. They'd intended seeing Gabby home, and suddenly she told them she didn't want them to bother."

"She explained that, Sam. She was being considerate, trying to save them trouble, trying to give them more time to be alone together."

"The impression they got was that she wanted to get rid of them."

"They said that?" Norah was incredulous.

"Actually, they tried very hard to avoid saying it—which is what made it so damning."

"But why should they avoid trying to say it? It wasn't true!" Norah groped. "They're her friends; they know Gabby; they

48

know she's not the type to pick up a man on a subway platform. . . ." She groaned. "Unless . . . Wallingford got to them and planted the doubt?" Wallingford. Of course. He was worth every cent Dana had scraped up for his fee.

"However it happened," Vickers went on, "the doubt was there and all too obvious. The jury sensed it immediately. One of the panel asked directly if either of them suspected that Miss Constante might be trying to lose them so she could meet Dana after they got off the subway."

"And they said yes? I don't believe it. How could they turn against her like that? How could Cootes let it happen?"

"By this time it was out of Cootes' control. The entire jury focused on that point, and both Luisa and Raul were finally forced to admit that they couldn't be *positive* that Miss Constante and Dana were not setting up a rendezvous."

"And that was good enough," Norah commented bitterly.

"I have to tell you that my own first reaction when you turned the case over to me, Norah, was that the girl had given Dana the come-on. I'm sorry, but it was only because you believed in her so strongly that I decided to reserve judgment. After I interviewed her myself and talked to her parents, I believed in her too. Unfortunately that belief was based more on her background than on facts."

And that was why Vickers had appeared antagonistic at the beginning.

"Miss Constante's entire testimony was turned against her by Dana's version of what happened," Vickers continued. "He contended that he took her getting rid of her friends as encouragement. He claimed that if she'd changed her mind once out on the street or if she'd been at all frightened, she had plenty of time to call for help between Seventy-ninth and Eighty-third streets. He even explained the harshness with which he treated her by admitting that at the very last moment she did have qualms, but that by then he was so aroused that he couldn't stop, and so he was somewhat rougher than he meant to be. . . ."

"Somewhat! He covered just about everything, didn't he?"

"He showed no animosity toward the girl for bringing the charges. He said he understood why she claimed rape. He understood that once her father discovered her on the stairs before she'd had a chance to pull herself together and get home, she really had no choice.''

''But that's not right!'' Norah was appalled at this final hypocrisy. ''Gabby was lying half conscious on those back stairs for nearly two hours before her father found her. If she'd consented, there was plenty of time for her to recover herself and get into the apartment before her father returned from work.''

''According to Dana, it didn't happen till close to one thirty.''

''And how did he account for the time between the pickup —which was established by Luisa and Raul—and one thirty?'' Norah asked bitterly.

''He says they took a walk along the river and did some preliminary smooching.''

''That's a lie! I don't believe that. There has to be a way to show him up on that at least,'' she pleaded.

''I have to tell you that Dana made a very good impression on the jury. He admitted everything in a very straightforward manner. He took all the blame for his part of it. Then he said he was sorry, sincerely sorry for it.''

Norah remembered the dazed and hurt look in Earl Dana's blue eyes as they passed in the corridor. Oh, yes, she had no doubt that he had been extremely effective in his well-coached and well-prepared appearance. She also remembered Gabby—head low, sullen, defensive. ''And Gabby didn't.''

''I'm afraid not. All the arguments in her favor—her upbringing, the nuns' school, the strict morality of her parents' code—all of these made Dana's claim that she panicked in the face of her father's discovering her condition more credible. Cootes recalled Miss Constante and asked her about the alleged time lapse and the alleged walk in the park. She denied it and then became hysterical. She refused to answer any more questions at all . . . and that was it.'' Vickers paused. When Norah didn't speak, he said, ''I'm sorry.''

''Yeah. Sure. Well, thanks, Sam . . . for everything.'' Norah hung up. She looked at her father. ''They just didn't believe Gabby.''

Mulcahaney had followed the gist of the conversation. He was

50

pale. "They turned it around. They made that poor girl into a criminal."

"That's it." Norah sat down on the edge of her bed.

There was a long pause.

"Well?" her father demanded at last. "What are you going to do about it?"

"What can I do?"

"I don't know. That's what your job is all about, isn't it?"

Norah went downstairs to the Constantes' apartment and rang the bell.

"It's me, Norah," she called through the closed door.

Pablo Constante let her in. He looked devastated. In the living room Ofelia Constante sat on the shabby sofa, hands folded in her lap, eyes vacantly staring. She didn't even acknowledge Norah's presence. Everywhere there were evidences of the anticipated journey—new suitcases stacked in a corner, the wrappings and ribbons for the simple gifts for the wedding attendants in San Juan, gifts Norah herself had helped to select. Airline tags were scattered on the coffee table ready to be filled out and affixed to the new luggage.

"Where's Gabby?" Norah asked.

"In her room," Pablo Constante answered.

"May I talk to her?"

"Her door is locked. She will not open it to anyone—not to her mother or to me."

"She must open it, Mr. Constante. She can't be permitted to sit alone in there. . . ."

"They have branded my daughter a liar and a whore!" he exclaimed, no longer able to contain himself. His wife looked up at the cry and moaned aloud.

"Don't say that; don't think it." Norah looked anxiously from one to the other. "What the grand jury said was not that they didn't believe Gabby, but that there is no case in law against Earl Dana. That's quite different."

"They did not believe her," the father repeated. Then, his dark eyes blazing, he added, "They preferred to believe a pervert."

51

"But *we* believe her," Norah insisted. "*We* know that she told the truth."

"Ah . . . if only we could convince Gabriella of that."

"We have to keep trying till we do."

With that, Norah turned and strode directly down the hall to Gabby's room. She had no idea what she was going to say. The last time she'd been in the room was when the bride had shown herself in the finished wedding gown. She had helped Gabby take the gown off and pack it carefully in its own special box, with generous layers of tissue paper in the folds. She could visualize the girl in there now surrounded by all the reminders of what was to have been the beginning of her joy, and she wanted to cry. Instead, she thrust her chin forward and knocked.

"Gabby, it's Norah. May I come in?"

No answer.

"Gabby, please let me come in and talk to you. We all believe you—your mother, your father, me, and Detective Vickers too. We know that every word you said was true."

There was no indication from inside the room that Gabby had heard.

Norah tried a little tougher approach. "You can't change what Dana did to you. It was terrible, but it's over. We're all sorry, and we want to help you, but before we can help you, you have to help yourself." Norah paused. "Earl Dana raped you; that's past. It won't be Earl Dana who destroys your future—you're doing that yourself."

Behind her there was a sharp gasp—Mrs. Constante, who had come up while Norah was pleading.

Pablo Constante was there too. He put an arm around his wife. "That is the truth, *mi alma*. Norah does right to speak it."

"And we're not through, Gabby. We're not licked; that was only the first round. We're going to show up Earl Dana for what he is. Between us, Gabby, we can do it. I know we can. Don't give up. I want to help you, and I will."

They all heard the sounds of bedsprings creaking, then footsteps. Ofelia Constante raised her head from her husband's shoulder and looked hopefully toward the door as it opened.

Gabriella stood on the threshold, her dark eyes sunk in their sockets, the skin rimmed in gray. She stared at Norah. "Leave me alone," she said, her voice ancient in disillusion. "I do not want your help. You told me that all I had to do was to describe the man, and I did it. Then you said I had to pick him out at that lineup, and I did that too. I wanted to forget, but you would not let me . . . you would not let me. So don't come here anymore, Norah. Don't ever come here again."

"Don't blame Norah, *querida*, blame me," Constante intervened. "It was at my request that she came to talk to you. I was the one who wanted . . ."

"What does it matter? What does it matter who or how it all came about?" The mother began to whimper.

The pleas of her parents didn't even cause Gabriella to look at them. Without change of expression she turned her back and closed the door quietly but firmly on them all, then locked it.

But not before Norah had had a look inside. The room was still festive with the wedding litter. The beautiful wedding dress that Gabby had so lovingly sewed and so carefully packed was spread across the bed. It had been savagely torn into tatters.

7

Norah had made her decision. As the lieutenant was not available the next day, she continued doggedly to clear her desk and prepare to turn over all pending cases to David just as though she were still to go on vacation. At five, when she was ready to leave, Joe Cannelli walked into the squad room.

He was wearing his blues and looked handsome and rested. "Hi," he called cheerfully. "All set for the big trip?"

She'd forgotten about their date! In another couple of minutes she would have been gone. "The wedding's off, Joe, and so's the trip."

"What happened?"

"Well . . ." His phone rang. "You might as well take it yourself; it's probably that Mrs. Scott. She hasn't stopped calling."

For a moment Joe hesitated as though he were going to make

some excuse, then, frowning, he went to his desk and picked up the receiver. "Homicide and Assault, Sergeant Capretto." The frown deepened into a scowl. "Well, I'm sorry you had so much trouble reaching me, Helen. . . . Yes, I got your messages." He glanced down at the various bits of paper decorating the edges of his blotter. "All of them. I've been intending to call you back, but I just haven't had the time. How are you? Good, that's good. What can I do for you, Helen?"

Norah walked over to the window and busied herself with comb and lipstick—not that the light was any better there, but she didn't want to be obviously listening.

"I certainly do intend for us to get together, Helen, and I'll call you as soon as I'm free. You're still at the same number? Good. Then as soon as I . . . Tonight?" He paused. He glanced over at Norah, who became very preoccupied with her appearance. "Sorry, I'm busy tonight." Then he added almost defiantly, "I have another date. . . . I never break a date; you ought to know that. . . . Sure, some other time. I'll be in touch." He hung up, but it was a minute or so before he focused on Norah. "That was an old college friend. She's back in New York after . . . oh, fifteen years."

"If you want to see her tonight, Joe, it's OK. As long as I'm not leaving tomorrow, we can have dinner anytime."

"If I'd wanted to see her, I had plenty of chances to get in touch with her, didn't I? So. Fact is, she's split up with her husband and is looking for a shoulder to cry on. She'll find one soon enough. Looks to me like you've got a few problems yourself tonight."

"I could use some advice."

"That's my specialty. Come on, we'll have a couple of drinks and you can tell me about it."

In their usual booth at Vittorio's cocktail lounge Norah presented her defense of Gabriella Constante. Arguments she hadn't even been consciously aware of forming sprang like fresh troops to be thrown into the battle.

"If it wasn't rape, if she'd consented, would she have given such a precise description of Dana? Of course not, because she wouldn't have wanted him found. In fact, why did she have to mention the sex part of the attack at all? All she had to tell her father was that she'd been mugged. He would have accepted that without question."

"Maybe she figured he'd be able to tell it was more than a mugging. Or maybe she reasoned that the doctor would discover it," Joe suggested.

Norah kept her voice low, but it trembled with intensity. "I don't think they would have called a doctor. As it was, I had to suggest it to the Constantes. I had to tell them it was necessary."

"OK, I'll go with you on that part of it."

But Norah had to get it all out, all the inconsistencies and contradictions. "Next, why mention spotting Dana at the subway entrance on Sixty-sixth and then again when they came out at Seventy-ninth? Wouldn't it have been a lot simpler just to say he sprang out at her from nowhere?"

"Maybe she realized that her friends, Luisa Alvarez and Raul Martín, had spotted the byplay between her and Dana so she felt she had to explain it. She would hardly have expected that her testimony would count against her."

Norah set her jaw. "If she hadn't mentioned it, they wouldn't have. It makes me so damn mad! If somebody calls in and says his television set has been stolen, we don't require him to prove he had a television set. We don't imply that maybe he gave it away. We take his word, and we investigate. But we don't take a woman's word when she claims she's been violated. Oh, no! We insinuate all kinds of motive behind the charge. We require her to *prove* it; we shame her; we treat her like the criminal. We put the victim on trial."

"That's the law, and you know the reason. . . ."

founded charges by vindictive women. That's Victorian. Today a woman making that charge has suffered the worst kind of abuse—psychological as well as physical."

He'd never seen Norah so aroused. He said nothing, partially not to further excite her but also because he agreed with her.

"I'm going to nail Earl Dana," Norah said. It was a plain, flat statement. "I've got next week off, and I'm going to use every minute to investigate him—every place he's ever been, every move he's ever made. I just don't believe that this is the first time he's raped a woman. Maybe there's no record on him because no woman ever made a complaint before. Or maybe there is a complaint against him under another name. I know one thing—whether or not Earl Dana ever committed rape before, he will certainly do it again. It's not a one-time offense." She hit her closed fist on the table, and the cocktail glasses jumped. "Nobody seems to have thought of that part of it. Or maybe nobody gives a damn about that part of it."

Joe put his hand over her fist. "Take it easy. Now. Let's assume that you get Dana either on a previous offense or that you catch him the next time he attacks a woman. It won't change the verdict in Gabby's case."

"One of the big things in his favor was that he has no previous criminal record, Joe." Norah fixed her blue eyes on him. "If I can prove that he has committed a similar offense, the credibility has to shift to Gabby. At the least she'll regain confidence in herself; she'll feel that she's believed by her family, her friends, and by Enrique. She'll be able to pick up her life again."

She stopped, but Joe knew Norah wasn't finished. He signaled the waiter for a refill. "What else?"

Norah waited till they were served and the waiter had gone. "The Constantes are Puerto Ricans."

Joe sighed. "I think you're out of line on that. I don't believe that had anything to do with the jury's decision."

"Maybe not, but I just wonder what the Constantes are thinking. They behaved like decent, law-abiding citizens. It cost Gabby a lot to make a public display of herself, and it wasn't easy for her mother and father either. Then they get kicked in the teeth for it."

"Because of the law, not because of their nationality. Maybe you should concern yourself with a change in the state law. There are several groups working on it; look them up; join them."

"OK, I might just do that. But first I'm going to get Earl Dana." She took her hand away from Joe and brought the fist down hard.

Gently Joe unclenched it; then, when he had her hand open on the table, he covered it with his. "Now, Detective Mulcahaney, you listen to your sergeant. You are emotionally involved here, and . . ." He hurried to forestall her protest. "I don't blame you. This is one time I don't blame you. The girl is a neighbor, and she's become your friend. But you must not let your feelings swamp your good sense. You must not turn yourself into a vigilante."

56

"Is that what I sound like? I'm sorry." Norah picked up her whiskey sour and sipped. Her contrition didn't last long—it never did. "I'm entitled to a certain amount of indignation, though, not only as a police officer who sees a criminal turned loose but also as a citizen over a miscarriage of justice." She paused, took a deep breath. "And as a woman," she added. "As a woman, I care very deeply about this case," Norah finished quietly. Even a month ago she could not have made that admission. Having made it, she felt infinitely better and freer than she had felt since making detective—no, since joining the force.

In acknowledging that being a woman could and actually was influencing her attitude, Joe considered that Norah had cleared a major hurdle toward an accommodation between herself and her profession. He was excited by it and respected her for it, but he knew better than to compliment her. Not yet. She would, he was sure, remain defensive for a while longer. "OK, but in my opinion your best bet would be to leave it to that new Rape Analysis and Investigation Squad. You've heard of it.?"

"I want to do this myself. You're right about staying objective, though. From now on, it's no personalities and all business, but *my* business, Joe."

"*If* the lieutenant says so. Have you asked him?"

"Not yet. But why shouldn't he OK it?"

Joe shrugged, spreading his hands in a gesture Norah knew very well and that was one of the few typically Italian things he did. He didn't really know of any reason why the lieutenant should turn her request down; he was merely reminding her of the possibility. "So now drink your drink and let's go in and eat or we'll be having

Norah put the case firmly aside—she was learning how to do that too. Yet as she grew livelier over dinner, Joe became in his turn subdued. By the time they were finished and ready to leave, he was most uncharacteristically preoccupied. He said very little on the drive home. It occurred to Norah that she'd shown little interest in him, how things might be going for him at the academy—even at home. She tried to draw him out, but he resisted till she too lapsed into silence. When he parked in front of her house, he turned off the ignition, but instead of coming around to open the car door for her, he stayed where he was.

He regarded her in the glow of the streetlight. "You feel a lot better now, don't you?"

"Yes, I do. Thanks for letting me unload. And thanks for straightening me out. Everything you said was right."

"We're good for each other. We understand each other; we can talk. We share the same interests."

"Even the opera."

He didn't smile. A nerve twitched in his left cheek just under the eye. Even if she hadn't noticed that, Norah would have been aware of his nervousness. Joe—nervous!

"So why don't we get married?"

Norah was stunned. The only thing she could think of to say was: this is so sudden, and she wasn't going to say that not only because it was so trite but also because it wasn't strictly true. Well, partially it was true. She had been half expecting, half hoping, yet afraid to hope.

"A couple of weeks ago on our last date I asked you to think about me. What I meant was for you to think about us. Have you?"

Norah temporized. "I didn't expect you to bring it up again so soon. . . ."

"To be honest, sweetheart, neither did I. I meant to wait till I got my new assignment. That was the whole idea behind my going for the higher rank. You must have guessed."

"No."

"Hell, Norah, I plugged along for twelve years as a sergeant. Why else would I suddenly get an attack of ambition? It wasn't just to stay ahead of you, Detective Second Grade Mulcahaney." He grinned briefly. "I know I said assignments are a lot easier to get at this particular time, and that was certainly contributory, but the real reason is that your father made me see sense. A man should have a relatively safe job and some kind of prospect before he proposes marriage. So—a lieutenant doesn't get shot at quite as often as a sergeant and he certainly makes more money. As to the future, I'll do my best on that—a wife and children are big incentives."

So the mystery of her father's change in attitude toward "the Sergeant" was solved. His grudging tolerance was the result of

Joe's assurances that his intentions were honorable. She should have guessed; she could have if she'd let herself.

"As I started to say," Joe went on, "I meant to wait till I got the new orders, but then tonight I thought—we've waited a hell of a long time already. So how about it, Norah? Will you marry me?"

In the half darkness Norah suddenly smiled. "I thought you'd never ask."

He pulled her to him.

"No, wait . . . I mean . . . I really did mean that I didn't expect you ever to ask. I've been half in love with you since the first time we met. Do you remember?"

"Sure."

"I'm not talking about the Emerson case. Before that."

"A year before. On the sweep of Times Square when they turned out practically the whole department. You were a rookie, very inexperienced and trying like crazy to cover it."

Norah flushed.

"You wore your skirt absolutely regulation length, where the other women wore it much shorter, and you had your hair pulled back real tight and severe . . . but you were the sexiest-looking of them all."

"I was?"

"Maybe I fell half in love then too, only I didn't know it. I'm not as smart as you." He leaned toward her again.

Again she edged back. "Well, that's the point. I've spent over two years putting you out of my mind; it's kind of hard now to go the other way."

"Sure. Sure." Joe sighed. "I brought it on myself. OK, so I took two years to wake up, so now you're entitled to some time. But not equal time, Norah, please, not two more years."

She should have been elated. A proposal, any proposal, is supposed to be a triumph for a woman; even if she's not interested in the man, it's considered a compliment. Certainly Norah was interested in Joseph Antony Capretto. What was wrong, then? Was it as she'd said, that she'd had to wait too long for the declaration? Lying in bed with the lights out and watching the reflection on her wall of the big electric signs across the river on the New Jersey Palisades as she so often did when she couldn't sleep,

Norah knew the real answer. Joe had not said he loved her. He'd talked about their compatibility. He'd admitted that he might have fallen half in love with her at their first meeting, but even that was more or less forced out of him. Joe had proposed marriage as though he were talking himself into it.

Why did he feel he had to talk himself into it? Norah closed her eyes, but the tears trickled from beneath the lids. Why should he ask her to marry him if he didn't really love her? He hadn't explained the timing of the proposal to her satisfaction either. With a shock Norah realized that she was examining Joe Capretto's motives as she might those of a suspect in a case! Her father was right: the work was no good for her. When the skepticism of her job carried over into personal relationships, then maybe it was time to quit.

But not till she'd vindicated Gabby.

James Felix was one of the youngest men to reach the rank of lieutenant. That was nine years ago. For five of those years his work had been almost exclusively as operations officer. He still itched to get back on the street. It was why he'd never gone out for captain, reasoning that he had a better chance of getting back into action at the lower rank. Unfortunately for him, Jim Felix was just too good at what he was doing, understood and handled men too well to be permitted to stray very far from his desk. Having married an actress who was endearingly independent, charmingly stubborn when she believed herself in the right, and dangerously courageous, he also understood the lone woman in his command. So now he leaned forward, rested his left elbow on the desk, and cupped a chin almost as prominent as Norah's in the palm of his left hand. Fixing his green eyes steadily on Detective Mulcahaney, he let her state her case.

He listened without comment until she indicated she was finished. "So." He raised his chin from his hand, leaned back in the swivel chair, tilting it from side to side. "Did you know that a new squad has been formed with the express purpose of investigating just this kind of thing?"

"I've heard—Rape Analysis and Investigation."

"Right. You want a temporary transfer? That way you wouldn't have to use up your vacation time."

60

Norah had come prepared to argue to get the lieutenant's permission; she hadn't expected anything like this. "I don't mind using my own time, Lieutenant." The reaction was instinctive; the reasons for shying from a transfer took shape afterward—there would be adjustments to a new command, new procedures, but most of all there was the possibility that the assignment might become permanent. Norah didn't want that. She liked what she was doing now. She liked the variety and the unexpectedness. The job was . . . loose, left plenty of room for initiative. "I understand their function is purely investigative."

"So is ours, when you get right down to it," Felix pointed out. "We turn over our evidence to the prosecutor's office, don't we?"

"Let me take the week, Lieutenant," Norah pleaded. "If by then I haven't come up with anything new, and you still want to transfer me . . ."

"I don't want to transfer you at all, Norah; I need you right here, but as the squad exists, we can't bypass it. It boils down to how important this is to you."

She met his eyes directly. "I have to do it, Lieutenant."

He nodded. "That's what I figured. Well, I'll have to clear it with Lieutenant Wilburn, but if it's OK with her, then it's OK with me."

An hour later Norah reported to the small, dingy, paint-peeling office on Centre Street. She was proud that she had made it as a detective—a woman in the company of men, equal by reason of ability. The Rape Analysis and Investigation Squad was composed entirely of women and headed by a woman—would they resent her? Would she be able to work with them? To be relegated to a squad whose principal function appeared to be follow-up interviews of rape victims, backtracking the work of other officers at that, seemed almost a demotion. That was pure snobbishness; Norah knew it and tried to suppress it, but it persisted.

A few minutes with her new commanding officer eased some of the qualms. Lieutenant Lee Wilburn was a petite blonde, young, pretty, and all business. She shook hands with Norah, then waved her to a chair.

"We're glad to have you with us, Detective Mulcahaney. Lieutenant Felix has filled me in on the background, and we've

61

agreed that this should be considered a special assignment. Therefore, you won't be required to take on any of the regular duties of the squad. You'll work your own hours, not any specific tour—I'm sure I can rely on you to put in a full day."

"Yes, ma'am. Thank you."

Lieutenant Wilburn smiled. "You'll work out of this office, of course. If you need help, we're here to give it. We want you to succeed, very frankly because if you do, it's going to reflect on us; it's going to make us look good. Now, Lieutenant Felix speaks very highly of you, which is why you're being given this latitude, but he also warns me that you have a tendency to uh . . . unilateral action. That's out. I don't want anything to happen that is going to brand this squad as emotional, unstable, or unprofessional. Some of the recently formed squads have already been disbanded. That is not going to happen to us. We fill a very real need, and we have a deep responsibility to the women of this city to succeed. I would like you to remember that during the course of your investigation."

"Yes, ma'am."

"In the future we hope to be able to take cases from the incident right through the courts, but for now we are exactly what our title indicates: Rape Analysis—meaning the determining of whether rape has in fact been committed—and Investigation—that is, tracking down the perpetrator, period. So while I'm not putting any strings on you, Mulcahaney, I want to be kept advised of your progress. Understood?"

Lieutenant Felix must have passed on Norah's implied opinion of the squad's limitation. She flushed slightly. "Yes, Lieutenant."

But Lee Wilburn didn't seem to hold it against her. Turning her chair slightly so she could more comfortably cross her legs, she asked informally, "What are your plans?"

"Well, the first thing I'd like to be able to do is to refute the suspect's claim that he and Gabriella Constante spent two hours in each other's company before the incident occurred. If I could find a witness who observed them entering the building and who could testify that the time was eleven thirty or thereabouts, as Miss Constante states, it would certainly undermine Dana's credibility." Norah knew she was letting her personal involvement show, but then Felix had surely passed that on too.

Her new commanding officer nodded. "It was a hot night, and it could be that somebody was sitting by an open window for air. The thing is, if the witness knew and recognized Miss Constante, he would have stepped forward by now. If he didn't know her, we'd have a hard time getting identification that would stand up. According to the complainant, the streets were deserted, but as she was under considerable stress, it's possible that there was somebody around and that she may have a peripheral memory of it. If you take her back over the ground . . ."

"She won't talk to me, Lieutenant. She's in shock over the verdict. She's broken off her marriage. She blames me."

"I see. I'm sorry. Well, maybe if one of the other women approached her, unofficially, as though by accident meeting her in the supermarket, say, or better yet in that park by the river near your house. What do you think?"

Norah was impressed that the lieutenant was so well informed. "It's worth a try."

"Good. We'll wait a couple of days, though, give Miss Constante a chance to pull herself together. Meantime, work on Dana. Since he appears to have no previous record, analyze his MO; you may be able to pick out past victims from that. All rape complaints are being funneled in to us, but as yet we have no back files, so you'll have to go through ACCB. Most rapists work within a narrow area, close to home, so to speak, so once you uncover even one similar incident in the central records, you can go on to the precinct of origin and probably come up with several more."

For the first time since making detective Norah felt herself being treated neither preferentially nor condescendingly, neither as brilliant nor backward, but simply as a police officer on a level with other police officers. In that spirit she had no hesitation in disagreeing. "I think that would be a very useful procedure if we were looking for a suspect, Lieutenant, but as we already have him, I think it would be more productive to study him directly—his background, how he spends his time, his friends and associates."

"You have a point," Lieutenant Wilburn agreed. "All right, go to it, Mulcahaney, and good luck."

8

The Broadway Garage wasn't particularly large—six pumps. Though relatively new, the slickly modern pump design indicated it, signs of neglect were already apparent—deep grease stains in the cement, trash bins overflowing, chrome surfaces scummy. Earl Dana hadn't come on duty yet; Norah had skipped lunch to get there early enough so she wouldn't run into him. Of the two attendants there, one, young, thin, with a bad case of acne, was apathetically dunking a tire in a tub of water to check for leaks; the other, in his mid-forties, short, lumpy, with a recessed forehead and platter lips that gave him a startlingly simian look, was leaning on the fender of a bright yellow Pinto staring inside the hood as though he wished someone would tell him what was wrong with it. Norah walked up to him before she noticed the small, plastic-encased card pinned to his chest pocket that proclaimed he was —Frank Gerard, Manager.

"Good afternoon, Mr. Gerard." Norah held out her hand. The manager was surprised and then instinctively reached for the rag hanging out of his back pocket before accepting. He might as well not have bothered; more grease came off the rag than he'd probably had on his hand to start with. Fleetingly Norah thought of the grease that had rubbed off on Gabby's panty hose and had been the initial clue that led to Dana's apprehension. Not that it mattered; they were past that now. She introduced herself and showed her ID. "I'd appreciate it if you could spare me a few minutes."

Gerard glared, as though by offering her hand, she'd somehow misrepresented herself. "For what?"

"I'd like to talk to you about one of your employees."

"Yeah? Which one? As if I didn't know."

"Is there somewhere we could talk privately?"

"No, miss, there isn't. I've already said all I'm going to say about Earl, which is that I don't know nothing about him or about what he does in his off time. He was a good worker. He showed up regular, on time, and sober. He didn't make waves. What more could you ask—nowadays?"

"*Was*, Mr. Gerard?"

"Yeah, was. He quit. Thanks to you."

"I don't understand."

"What's to understand? He quit. Walked out, just like that. No notice, no warning. You know how hard it is to get help nowadays? Let alone a licensed mechanic? And one who's willing to work nights? I put in ten hours myself as it is; hell, I can't stay here at night too. So now I have to shut down at six. You know what that means in terms of money?"

"I'm very sorry."

"Sure. What good does that do me?"

There was no use pursuing that. "When did Dana quit?"

"Yesterday. Came on at three like usual, worked till close to five, then suddenly barged into the office and told me he was through." Gerard jerked a thumb toward a small building with a plate-glass front so dirty it wasn't possible to see through to the inside. "Took off his uniform, collected his money, and left."

"Why?"

"Why? Because he couldn't take the stares and smirks and cute remarks, that's why. In the last week we've had the cars lined up to buy a dollar's worth of gas so they could gawk at the kid."

Kid. Earl Dana was twenty-six years old.

"It's a shame what you did to him. You branded him for life, you and that . . ." Gerard had to delve into the vocabulary of his generation. "You and that *bimbo!*"

"Mr. Gerard, the jury refused to indict Earl Dana. The case against him was dismissed."

"Great! You want to stand by the pumps and tell that to every sensation-hungry jerk that drives in? I mean, you have no idea. . . ! Since Earl's picture was in the paper along with the hotshot lawyer

mean, did you have to say where Earl worked? Give this address? You had no right to do that, you know; you had no right to print the address of my station."

"The police didn't do that. The press . . ."

"Whoever. They shouldn't give out that kind of information. It's not fair."

Norah didn't answer because privately she agreed.

So Gerard's indignation flourished. "Once a man's been accused of a thing like that, he's never going to shake the stigma. He's marked for life. You tag a man a thief, murderer, rapist—just because you put an 'alleged' in front of it and then later say, 'Oops, sorry, our error,' that don't make it right. It's a damn shame. A boy like that . . .''

Now he's a boy, Norah thought, getting younger and more sinned against by the minute.

"Anyhow, you said the case was dismissed, so why do you keep hounding him? You've forced him to quit his job; probably he'll have to change his name."

Oh, yes, Norah thought, probably that too.

"And what did he do that was so terrible anyway? He laid the girl. Who pays any attention to that kind of thing nowadays? There's no morality anymore. Look at the magazines, what they print and sell on every street corner. And the movies! God, the movies!"

Norah's own indignation smoldered. "I'm not here to discuss morality, Mr. Gerard, or what Earl Dana did. . . .''

"So why are you here? What do you want?"

"Just a look at Earl Dana's employment application."

"Why?"

"Routine."

Pouting distended Gerard's platter lips into an even stronger reminder of man's ancestry. "I suppose you'll keep hounding me until I show you, so come on." Abruptly he turned and strode into the office fronted by the dirty glass. Here all efforts at maintenance had been given up—it was filthy. The manager rummaged through a file drawer on top of a battered desk, selected a card, and handed it to Norah.

It was one of those standard personnel forms that could apply to any business and that are designed to make the applicant feel inferior with its long column of spaces to be filled in. On Dana's card most of them remained blank. His home address and telephone number were there, but Norah already had those. Under previous employment he had given one reference—another gas station down in the Village. Length of employment there just over a year—an adequate record according to Mr. Gerard's standard. She supposed he hadn't inquired too deeply into the rest of Dana's past either.

"Did Earl Dana happen to mention why he quit the other station?"

"Didn't like the neighborhood. Too many queers."

Well, well. "That's it, then, Mr. Gerard. Thanks again." She didn't offer to shake hands this time.

"Uh . . . Officer. . . ? Listen, I'm sorry I came down so hard on you. I realize it's not your fault what happened, I mean. I mean, you're just doing your job."

"That's right."

"No hard feelings, OK?"

"None."

"So . . . uh, like I said—help is hard to get nowadays and I pay good money. Maybe you know somebody, doesn't have to be a licensed mechanic, that would be too much to hope for, but . . . you know, somebody willing? So long as he shows up sober and keeps his hands out of the till. I'd appreciate it."

"If I hear of anybody . . ."

"Just tell him to mention your name." The harassed manager squeezed out a smile; it didn't come easy. "If you say he's OK, that's good enough for me."

Granted that Gerard was biased and self-serving, nevertheless his attitude had taken Norah by surprise. The more she thought about it, the more indignant she became. Probably it was as well to have this early reminder that not everybody was going to share her outrage and that not everyone would be falling over himself in eagerness to help. She was still thinking about Gerard when she noticed with dismay that Earl Dana's name was missing from the roster of tenants in the vestibule of the converted brownstone in which he was supposed to be living. She did take into account that one of the name slots was blank, that he might have removed his name as a precaution against uninvited callers. She punched the bell marked *E. Bateman, Super*.

A harsh buzzing indicating the door latch was being released sounded almost immediately. Norah entered a gloomy, narrow hallway. For a rooming house it wasn't bad. The carpet was faded but apparently more as a result of unprofessional cleaning than of wear; the walls were streaked by inexpert washing. At least someone was trying. At the back a door opened and a woman peered out.

"Are you looking for me?"

"I'm looking for the super."

"That's me. I don't put my full name out because . . . I figure it's not a good idea the way things are. I advise my lady roomers not to do it either—avoids a lot of trouble. Actually I own the building. What can I do for you?"

Norah identified herself, stated her business, and was eagerly invited inside.

E. Bateman had a soft pink and white face, coarse gray hair carved into wide waves and glued into permanency by lavish applications of hair spray. Her hips were too broad for slacks, but she wore them anyway, along with a too-tight white shirt patterned in little red hearts. "Sit down, uh . . . Officer . . . Detective . . . What do I call you? I never met a woman policeman before." She smiled ingratiatingly.

It was at least an improvement over Gerard. "Officer or Detective, whichever you prefer."

"Detective." E. Bateman savored the title. "Isn't that just great! Of course I knew they had women detectives, but I thought they mostly did work like filing and such. I didn't think they really got out and . . . detected. I'm really impressed. So sit down, Detective Mulcahaney; make yourself comfortable. How about coffee? I was just going to make myself a cup."

"Thank you, Mrs. Bateman?"

"Miss. Miss Elizabeth Bateman."

"I never say no to coffee, Miss Bateman."

"Good. Good. Won't take me but a minute." Elizabeth Bateman fluttered pudgy, rough, strong hands, continuing to admire Norah. "Excuse the looks of the place; we had a regular flood up in 3A and I was so busy—what with getting hold of the plumber, they're never available when you need them, then helping clean up afterward . . . well, I just haven't got around to doing my own work."

"I know how it is." The place was, in fact, immaculate.

"You do?" The landlady seized on this indication of affinity. "You do your own housework?"

A talker, Norah thought, sighing inwardly; she was going to be hard to turn off. Still, these lonely women who chattered compulsively had sharp eyes and sensitive ears; they didn't miss much that went on around them and were more than willing to tell it if you

68

could steer them to the right subject—and keep them on it. Norah wished now she hadn't been so quick to accept the offer of coffee—it would only drag out the session.

"But here I am babbling away and holding you up from important business, I'm sure. I'll get the coffee." Perhaps she'd sensed Norah's impatience; at any rate, the landlady ducked quickly into the kitchen and was back with the coffee much faster than Norah could have hoped for. "How about some Danish? I could run out. The bakery's on the corner, wouldn't take more than a couple of minutes. . . ."

"No, thank you, no really. I do have a heavy schedule." Norah asked her questions straight out because this witness would provide all the circumlocution herself. "I've come to inquire about one of your tenants, Earl Dana."

"Ah . . ." Without so much as taking a sip, Elizabeth Bateman set her cup aside, letting Norah know that she had expected just this and was gratified that she'd been right. "I'd be glad to tell you anything I can, Detective Mulcahaney. That was a shame what happened. Earl Dana was a very nice young man—pleasant, polite, didn't cause any disturbance in the house—fact is, you hardly knew he was here. Clean too, not like some of them these days. Not that I'd have any of those hippie types in my house. It's not the long hair and the beards, Detective Mulcahaney, but they don't look like they ever took a bath. What's wrong with being clean?"

It was what everybody who mistrusted hippies said, but Norah was interested only in Miss Bateman's use of the past tense regarding Dana. "When did he leave?"

detective knew he was gone. "Yesterday afternoon he left, suddenly, very suddenly. He didn't give notice. Of course, his rent is paid till the end of the month; still, I would have expected . . . We were very friendly, you see. I thought of him as, well not as a son, he was too old, but as a younger brother." She smirked. "Well, what happened was that he went to work as usual yesterday afternoon around two thirty, and a little after five . . . I just happened to be looking out the window, and I saw him coming up the street. He was walking fast, and he looked terrible, gaunt, shaky, like he'd been sick. He was in the house and up the stairs to his room before I could get out into the hall and ask him what was the matter. I was wondering whether I shouldn't go up, you know, just to make sure he didn't want a doctor or anything, but by the time I'd made up my mind he was back down again with his suitcase." Miss Bateman sighed. "He turned in his key and said he was leaving."

"Did he give a reason?"

"Oh, he didn't need to. You have no idea what that young man was going through, Detective Mulcahaney. We never discussed it, naturally, but I could tell. I would never have brought the subject up myself except that, well, it seemed too bad after it was all over and he'd been exonerated for him to feel that he had to leave the neighborhood. So I just sort of tried to tell him that the worst was over, and he turned red, wouldn't look at me, wouldn't say a word. I felt bad for him."

And disappointed too because he refused to confide. "Did he have any friends, any visitors?"

"If you mean did he bring girls up to his room, the answer is no. I don't allow that kind of thing."

"What did he do with his time?"

"Not much. The hours he worked were kind of restrictive, don't you know? He slept late, cleaned his place—kept it real nice—did his marketing and such." She shrugged. "Did a lot of running, what they call jogging, around the neighborhood. Had one of those sweat suits. Got back in time to fix himself lunch and went to work."

Not much of a life, Norah thought, if that's all there was to it. "What time did he get in at night?" Then, for the sake of tact, she added, "Have you any idea?"

But Miss Bateman was too eager to confide to notice any implication that she was nosy. "I never go to bed before the eleven-o'clock news, and he was usually in by the time it was over. Sometimes not, but then he'd gone to a late movie; he always told me about it the next day."

Made a point of telling her, no doubt. "Did he leave a forwarding address?"

"No."

"Didn't he make any arrangement about his mail? Ask you to hold it for him maybe?"

70

"He didn't get much mail, just the junk stuff, nothing personal."

A real loner. So now there was the additional problem of tracing him. "I see." Norah took out a card, scribbled the phone number of her new office on Centre Street, and handed it to Miss Bateman. "If you should hear from him, I'd be grateful if you'd call me."

"Why? Why do you want him? It's all over, isn't it? I thought it was all over."

It was a plaintive cry suggesting something beyond curiosity. Before Norah could make the standard reply, the woman answered herself.

"Nothing's wrong with the girl, is there? She's not sick . . . or anything?"

She was referring to VD, but whether she thought Gabby had caught it from Dana or passed it on to him wasn't clear. "No, she appears to be all right on that score."

"Good. That's good. Don't think I don't sympathize with the girl, Detective Mulcahaney, I do. It was sad for both of them. These young people—they're really not any different than we were; things haven't changed all that much. I'm not excusing Earl; I just think there's a mutual responsibility. He followed her, and she kind of led him on—a kind of flirtation, don't you think? Then they got carried away and went a little further than either of them had intended." She sighed. "It happens. It happens like that."

"Sometimes."

The woman's pink and white face became flushed; her thin lips trembled; her eyes were turned inward on a past vision. "If parents only realized that restricting a girl makes her so much more

opportunity . . . It's not right to blame the girl; she really can't help herself." The vision faded, and her color returned to normal, her mouth setting into a grimly disapproving line. "She shouldn't have brought the charges, though. It wasn't right for her to do that."

Of course Gabby hadn't wanted to bring the charges; she'd done it at her father's insistence, and Gabriella Constante had been brought up to obey her father. Norah walked slowly and thoughtfully toward West End Avenue. Miss Bateman was a lonely

71

spinster to whom Earl Dana, a single, reasonably attractive young man, had taken the trouble to be kind. That plus a similar encounter in her youth made her view the incident with romantic bathos. Yet her interpretation was the same as that put forward by Dana. It set Norah to reexamining Gabby's reaction. She had gone into hysterics; she had locked herself up in her room; she had savagely torn her wedding dress. She had not denied it.

Norah was shaken by her doubts. Had Gabby encouraged Dana? Certainly Dana's behavior both before and after the grand-jury hearing couldn't be faulted. He had gone about his normal business, tried to resume his normal way of life until . . . until yesterday afternoon. Earl Dana's behavior had been consistent and right till the moment yesterday afternoon when without warning he'd quit his job, when without notice he'd given up his room, when he'd disappeared.

Norah smiled; then laughed out loud. Crossing the avenue into the sunshine, she was so elated that she nearly hailed a passing cab. She remembered in time that she couldn't reasonably put it on the expense sheet, so she dropped her arm and hurried toward the bus stop. The bus would get her back to the Broadway Garage nearly as fast.

Mr. Gerard had stepped out for a bite to eat. Norah hesitated. She could wait for him or . . . she studied the young attendant with the acne-pitted face. His name was embroidered on the pocket flap of his coveralls. "I'm Detective Mulcahaney, Bill. I was here earlier talking to Mr. Gerard."

"Yeah, I know."

He was curious; good. "It's about Earl Dana. There are a couple of points I still need to clear up." She appeared to hesitate. "Maybe you could help me? That is, if you were around yesterday afternoon when he quit."

He shrugged. "I was around."

Norah smiled encouragingly. "Could be you noticed something Mr. Gerard didn't."

Bill stared down at the grease-stained cement, tracing the outline of the spot with the toe of his work boot. "Like what?"

"Like what suddenly made him decide to quit."

"How would I know? He didn't tell me."

72

"But something must have happened," Norah half insisted, half cajoled. "As I understood it, he showed up for work as usual and then after a couple of hours he marched into the office and said he was through. Did he get a phone call? Did somebody come to see him, talk to him?"

"Nope. I was inside having coffee." Bill gestured toward the office. "A car drove up, and Earl started to service it. The next thing I know he's coming through the door and he says to me, 'You take that'; then he turns to Gerard and says, 'I quit.' Just like that. We both thought he was kidding."

"And did you take care of the customer?"

"Yeah, sure. He had the pump running—I couldn't just leave it."

Norah held her eagerness in check. "Was it one of your regular customers?"

"Never saw her before in my life."

"Could you describe her?"

"Hm . . . blond, old . . . maybe forty. Had some kind of white fur coat."

"White?"

"Well, a real light color. She was driving a '74 Impala, cream puff." He was on sure ground there.

Norah beamed at him. "I bet you noticed the license."

"Well, no, ma'am, I didn't. I'm sorry."

He really was, and of course it had been too much to expect. "I suppose that means she paid cash?"

He frowned over that. "I don't think so. I think she used a credit card. Gee, I can't be sure, but it seems to me that I did take the license down. I'm sure I did, but I can't remember what it was."

"But you've got the receipt, haven't you? It would be on file."

"Well, yeah but . . . I don't know her name. I mean we're supposed to check the signature, and I did but . . . it didn't register, if you know what I mean."

"No reason why it should have," Norah assured him. "What do you say we go through the file? Maybe if you see either the name or the license number it might come back to you."

But it didn't. The day's stack of vouchers was too big, and there was no way of narrowing it down according to the time because there was no time recorded on the slips, and they weren't kept in

73

order of receipt either. Only a few of the slips were signed by women, but some were signed with only a first initial, and these couldn't be eliminated. Even if the printed charge name were a man's, his wife could have been using the card. So Norah copied them all, and when she was through, she had a list that covered both sides of two pages of her notebook—business at the Broadway Garage was a lot better than manager Frank Gerard had been willing to admit.

Norah thanked Bill and offered her hand. After a useless wiping off on the rag he took it. Norah didn't mind the grease—Bill had been helpful, and she said so. He was inordinately gratified. Norah headed back to Centre Street.

The lights were already on when she entered the small office of RAI. A chubby young woman with short brown hair and bangs sat at the lieutenant's desk. Seeing Norah hesitate in the doorway, she smiled encouragingly.

"Hello. Please, come on in. Can I help you?"

"Well, actually I was just looking for . . ."

"Someone to talk to?" The young woman got up and came around the desk. "I'm Ethel Dollinger, and I'm here to listen." She held out her hand.

Norah took the hand and smiled. "Well, thank you, Detective. . . ?"

"Officer, but call me Dolly, and sit down."

"Thanks, but I'm not, that is . . . I'm Norah Mulcahaney."

"Oh, say! I'm sorry. Listen, I apologize. I should have known. . . ." Dolly Dollinger didn't stay embarrassed long. "What can I do for you, Detective Mulcahaney?"

Her china-doll face suited her nickname, but her height and weight spoiled it. In fact Dolly Dollinger just barely passed the minimum 5'2" height requirement. According to the department weight chart based on age and height, if she was between twenty-five and twenty-nine years old, as Norah judged, she shouldn't weigh more than 136. But she did. However, she simply radiated friendliness and sympathy. Any woman coming in with a complaint would feel that wave of innate kindness and be put at ease. The lieutenant evidently considered that more important than the chart.

Norah herself felt less uncomfortable, less the new hand intrud-

74

ing because of Dolly's manner. "Hi, Dolly. I'm Norah. I've got to make some phone calls. Any particular phone I should use?"

Dolly waved. "Help yourself."

"Thanks." Norah sat at the nearest desk, shrugged out of her suit jacket, and got out her notebook. "Where can I find a Manhattan directory?"

"Bottom drawer. Looks like you're on to something."

"I hope so." Norah opened her book to the list of names she'd copied.

Stretching both chins, Dolly looked. "Take you half the night just to look up all those numbers and the other half to make the calls. Want some help?"

"Oh . . ." Norah hadn't been prepared for such ready and open acceptance. "That's very nice of you, Dolly, but . . ." She was on the verge of refusing when she realized that it would not be merely ungracious but as good as announcing she considered the case her private property. "Well," she began briskly, "these are the names of people who charged gas at the Broadway Garage yesterday. That's where the suspect, Earl Dana, used to work." She paused, wondering just how much more of an explanation she should give.

"He skipped?"

"Right." Evidently the women on the squad had been well briefed—a further reminder against retreating into what Lieutenant Wilburn referred to as "unilateral action."

"You figure one of these people showed up and scared him away?"

Again Norah was taken aback, this time by Officer Dollinger's astuteness. "A blond woman drove up for gas, and as soon as ~~Dana saw her he walked into the office and quit. He didn't even~~ finish servicing her car. So the first thing we have to determine is which of these charges was made by women—the wife or possibly daughter of the man to whom the card is issued. The next thing is to fix the time the customer drove in. But I don't want to alarm her."

"So what are you going to say?"

Norah had already given it some thought. "That I found a valuable lady's watch at the garage and am trying to locate the owner."

"Maybe hint you're looking for a reward?"

"Yes. Yes, that's good, very good, Dolly."

75

Looking over Norah's shoulder, Officer Dollinger scanned the list. "How about where you already have a woman's name? Do you want me to call anyway?"

"Yes, because we need to fix the time she was at the garage."

"OK." Without further questions or comments Dolly took the single loose-leaf page Norah handed her, got herself another copy of the phone book, and went to work.

The two women worked diligently without conversation or interruption. At five minutes after six Dolly Dollinger put down the phone, stretched, worked her shoulders with a rotating movement to ease the tightness, and groaned. She waited till Norah completed the call she was making at the moment.

"That's it," she said when Norah had hung up. "I've got three possibilities for you." She went over to Norah with the names. "Each one of these was at the station yesterday between four and five thirty. None of them lost a watch—naturally."

"I've got two," Norah said. "It's still a lot less than we started with." She sighed wearily, remained slumped for a moment, then twisted around to get her jacket. "Thanks a lot, Dolly, I really appreciate your help."

"What are you going to do now?"

"Grab a bite and start interrogating." Norah was tired but also eager; she sensed she was on the right track, and she couldn't bear to lose any time.

Dolly frowned—it hardly marked her plump, good-natured face. "Listen, Norah, I don't mean to tell you how to do your job, but . . . you know, it's after six."

"So?"

"So the husbands are home. I don't think you'll get what you're after from these women if you talk to them while their husbands are around."

In the act of buttoning her jacket, Norah stopped. "Oh. You're right. Of course. I'll wait till morning. Thanks for the tip, Dolly. You're a doll."

Norah's theory was that the woman who drove up to the gas pump at the Broadway Garage on Wednesday afternoon was one of Dana's previous victims. Whether she had come because she'd seen his picture in the paper in connection with Gabriella Constante's charge or by accident, whether she'd even recognized Earl Dana, he had certainly recognized her. Probably he'd thought she was going to turn him in and so he ran. From the five names to which the original list had been narrowed Norah selected Mrs. Catherine Mercer for the first interview. The reason she did so was that Mrs. Mercer lived on East Tenth Street and Dana had worked in that area before quitting to move uptown—because there were too many queers in the Village.

She had no idea what the best time to catch Mrs. Mercer might be—just after nine, probably. By then the husband would have left for work, and the children, if any, would have been packed off to school. The lady of the house would be having a second cup of coffee before . . . before doing whatever it was women who didn't work did with themselves all day. However, first it was important to check the precinct records to see whether Mrs. Catherine Mercer had ever registered a rape complaint. If she had, of course, things would be a lot easier.

Going through the files took a lot longer than Norah had anticipated, and she came up empty. There were plenty of complaints in which no suspect had been apprehended. For fear of missing Mrs. Mercer, she couldn't take the time to go through them trying to match these various descriptions with Dana. Later, if necessary, she could come back.

The building in which Mrs. Mercer lived was old and still dignified, though where once there had probably been a full staff around the clock it was now strictly self-service. It had a closed-circuit television installation to screen visitors. Norah stood in front of it, buzzed 12A, identified herself, and was permitted to enter.

Upstairs, at her own front door, Mrs. Catherine Mercer was resistant. "I was on my way out, Detective Mulcahaney, but I thought I should see you to save you the trouble of coming back later. I hope you'll make it as brief as possible.''

Bill, the gas-station attendant, had described the woman as blond and fortyish. Well, he was right, but he could have said a lot more. Mrs. Mercer was sophisticated, sleek, superbly cared for. Of course, Bill hadn't a look at her figure, which was marvelous and which this morning was displayed in a custom-made suede pantsuit. It was hard to imagine this self-possessed, elegant woman as the victim of a rape.

''I'll do my best,'' Norah said and waited to be asked inside.

Mrs. Mercer sighed and reluctantly stepped back. The room into which Norah followed her was as polished as the lady, and whatever it was the lady did in her spare time, it surely wasn't housework. Getting Catherine Mercer to the point was not going to be easy.

''I understand you bought gas at the Broadway Garage, a Mobil Station on Sixty-ninth and Broadway, Wednesday afternoon at approximately five o'clock,'' Norah began.

''That's right.''

''Is that the station you usually frequent?''

''No, it isn't.''

''May I ask how you happened to go there?''

''I needed gas. Sorry, I don't mean to be facetious.'' She produced a thin smile, not particularly apologetic. ''I'd been to the Met; I noticed that I needed gas, and that was the nearest station.''

''What station do you normally go to?''

''Is this about the watch somebody lost Wednesday? I had a call from some woman . . . was that you?''

''No, it was another police officer. What station do you usually use, Mrs. Mercer?''

''I told her I hadn't lost any watch.''

''There was no watch lost, Mrs. Mercer. We need to find out who bought gas at that particular station at that particular time. It seemed the best way to do it.''

''I thought the police weren't supposed to use trickery. Wasn't that what that big Supreme Court decision was all about?''

''You're referring to the Miranda case. That ruling was for the protection of the rights of suspects. We don't suspect you of anything.''

"That's most reassuring." Again that thin, tight smile. "I do wish you'd get to it, Detective Mulcahaney."

Norah decided it was her turn to answer a question with a question. "Is there some reason why you don't want me to know where you usually get your gas?"

A tilt of the beautifully coiffed head was admission that Norah had scored. "The Amoco station on Eighth Street." But only one round. "Now perhaps you'll tell me why you're so anxious to know."

Might as well, Norah thought. "We're trying to trace a suspected rapist." There was no reaction at all. "We think you may have recognized the man who waited on you at the station on Sixty-ninth Street Wednesday."

"Me? Recognize a rapist? Really, Detective Mulcahaney!"

"I didn't say that. We hoped you'd recognized the man who waited on you Wednesday as someone who used to work at the station where you usually get your gas."

"I don't pay any attention to who puts gas in my car."

"He recognized you."

Mrs. Mercer shrugged. She took a turn around the room, her back to Norah. "So?"

"Did he call you, Mrs. Mercer? Did Earl Dana call you and warn you to keep quiet?"

"I don't know any Earl Dana. I don't know what you're talking about."

"I'm sure you had your reasons for not reporting the attack. If it were a question of a single assault, then maybe you'd have the right to keep silent. But a rapist's appetite grows as he feeds it.

. . . Other women have been and will be victimized . . .

"Then go talk to them!" Suddenly Catherine Mercer cried out. "Let one of them make the complaint."

"One of them already has, Mrs. Mercer. Her name is Gabriella Constante. Perhaps you read about it?" The woman shook her head. "Miss Constante positively identified her attacker. He appeared before the grand jury and claimed consent. They refused to indict."

Catherine Mercer flinched; the expensively massaged, well-toned muscles of her face failed her, sagged, so that she looked as old as she really was. Her light, elegant voice became a harsh

79

whisper. "Much good it did her." She shook herself, walked over to the coffee table, and picked up the handbag and gloves that were there. When she straightened, she was again the assured woman she'd been when she'd first admitted Norah.

"Sorry, Detective Mulcahaney, that is all the time I can spare."

"That girl has been shamed and humiliated, Mrs. Mercer. She was going to be married, and the wedding has been called off. Her whole life is a shambles."

"Well, that's too bad. I'm sorry for her, but what can I do?"

Norah felt compassion for this strongly disciplined woman; she didn't want to add to her pain, but she also had to know the truth. "All right, Mrs. Mercer. I intend to prove that Earl Dana is a rapist. When I do, I'm going to ask him about you, and he's going to tell me—he won't have any reason not to by then. I'll see to it that you're subpoenaed and have to testify in court. Is that the way you want it? Or will you tell me now? Tell me what happened, and I swear it won't go any further. I won't make an official report."

"What use will it be to you, then?"

Norah spread out her hands and answered honestly, "I don't know. Maybe it will indicate a pattern in the way he selects his victims, the way he stalks them, or in the actual sex act—any of those things could help us to trace other victims. Maybe one of the other victims can be prevailed upon to testify."

"I'd like to help, but . . ."

"Then do, Mrs. Mercer. Tell me about it. You'll feel better."

Catherine Mercer clawed at the gloves and the handbag clasp. "My husband is a very jealous man, Detective Mulcahaney. You have to understand. We married late. There had been other men; we worked in the same office, so he knew. In fact, I married Jeff on the rebound from an unfortunate affair with one of the bosses, and he knew that too and never said a word—not then and not since. Lately, though, I don't know why, he's become very suspicious. Without reason, I swear. I wouldn't do anything to hurt Jeff; he gave me his love and trust when I badly needed both, and I'll never forget it. Maybe it's because he's had to be away a lot recently traveling. When he comes home . . . the questions he asks, the way he looks at me . . . And then he checks on my answers. I know because my friends have told me he calls and questions them about

80

me. It takes days for him to be reassured enough to . . . to come near me. God in heaven! If Jeff found out . . .''

"He won't find out from me.''

Catherine Mercer took a deep breath. She put the bag and gloves down and reached instead for the silver cigarette box. "I'm trying to stop smoking, but when I'm nervous . . . I really need it.'' She took a long, deep drag. "The irony of this is that I did notice this . . . Earl Dana . . . when he waited on me at the Amoco station down here. I thought he was very pleasant. He always greeted me with a smile and small talk and implied flattery. But I didn't encourage him; I'm not that hard up. Then when it actually happened I didn't recognize him. Would you believe that I didn't know who it was until after? Until it was over and he was gone? Would you believe that?''

"Yes.''

"That's another reason I couldn't bring myself to report it. Once Jeff found out that I knew him, no matter how slightly, he'd never believe that I . . . hadn't asked for it.''

Up to now Norah had hoped that once she got her talking, Mrs. Mercer might be prevailed upon to give evidence after all. Now that hope was just about gone. "Would you describe the incident?''

"I tried to wipe the whole thing from my mind—not only how it happened but that it ever had happened. It wasn't easy. At the beginning I couldn't think of anything else, but after a while—you think you're never going to forget the pain of it or the shame—but you do, thank God. Naturally I stopped going to that gas station. I couldn't face him again, and I didn't want him to have the slightest
excuse for coming back. So Wednesday afternoon when he walked up to my car window . . . well, I just couldn't believe it. He'd changed his appearance, of course, but I knew him.''

Norah sat up. "Changed his appearance?'' she asked. "How?''

"He used to have long blond hair, shoulder length, and a mustache. But those watery blue eyes, he couldn't change them, or those greasy hands with the blunt, splayed fingertips . . .''

That was the explanation for what Norah had noticed in the lineup and attributed to his having given himself a very close shave. His beard had been light because he was naturally blond.

81

"How about a tattoo? Did you notice whether he had a tattoo on his arm?"

"It was November. He had his overcoat on; he kept it on."

Norah sighed. "Around what time did the attack take place?"

Catherine Mercer ground out her cigarette and lit another. "The girls—I have two girls—hadn't come home from school yet, so it wasn't quite four. Do you suppose he could have known that? About the girls, I mean?" She shook her head over it, then went right on. "I'd been shopping; I had a couple of packages, and I was letting myself in with my key at the front door downstairs when somebody came up from behind, covered my mouth with one hand so I couldn't scream, and pushed in along with me. Before I knew it he had shoved me through the lobby and over to the back stairs. It was almost as though he'd looked the place over and knew exactly where to go." She was somewhat calmer. "I'm strong, I keep myself in shape with dance classes, skiing in the winter whenever Jeff can get away, and tennis in the summer, but when he threw me on the floor and got on top of me . . . I just couldn't heave him off."

"Did he have a knife or a gun?"

"No."

"Did he hit you or abuse you in any way other than sexually?"

"No."

"Were you able to inflict any injury on him?"

"No, but I tried. Oh, God, Detective Mulcahaney, you've got to believe that I tried."

"I do. I do. I'm just matching up what he did to the other young woman. Did you attempt to scream?"

"He had his hand over my mouth."

"Yes, I understand, but did he keep it there the whole time?"

Mrs. Mercer looked away. "No, but before he removed it he warned me that if I uttered the smallest sound—a whimper even or a groan—he'd smash my head to a pulp against the wall."

It was exactly what he'd said to Gabby. Certainly it was enough to stop a woman from resisting. There was one more question that had to be asked, a delicate one, and no way to lessen the embarrassment of it. "Did he display any particular fetish? Any abnormality?"

"No. Oh, no, and thank God. It was bad enough without that."

As Norah had anticipated, talking about it had brought Catherine Mercer some relief. "I had to pull myself together before the girls came home from school. I couldn't let them see me in that condition. That's another reason I didn't call the police—I didn't want the girls to know: they're at the age . . . nine and eleven, very impressionable, just beginning to understand. . . . For their sakes I washed and changed my clothes and tried to act naturally. I even remembered to collect my packages," she added wryly. "I think maybe that was the hardest part of all—having to behave as though nothing had happened in front of my girls."

Yes, Norah thought, that would have taken plenty of self-discipline and love. At the beginning she'd resented Catherine Mercer because she hadn't lodged a complaint; later that had turned to pity. Now the policewoman felt respect. She showed the victim one of Dana's mug shots. "Is this the man?"

"That's the way he looks now, yes."

"And it is the same man who raped you?"

"Yes."

"Thank you, Mrs. Mercer, you've been very helpful. I'm not just saying that; you really have. And I'll keep my part of the bargain; you don't have to worry."

Though the svelte, supremely cared-for woman had regained a large measure of her composure, she looked haggard as after an illness. Nearly a year ago she had made a decision and never wavered. Now she regarded Norah uncertainly. "I wish I could give evidence, Detective Mulcahaney. If you think it would do any good after all this time. . . ."

Norah hesitated too. Just one push, one little bit of added inducement . . . Then she sighed. "It's the identification, Mrs. Mercer. I'm afraid it wouldn't stand up. If Dana hadn't changed his appearance or if you'd noticed the tattoo . . ." It wouldn't require a lawyer of Edwin Wallingford's caliber to decimate Mrs. Mercer under cross-examination, and it wasn't fair to let her expose herself uselessly.

But she'd made the offer, and that was good. For her sake, Norah was glad she could turn her down.

The MO in both cases matched; the discrepancy was in the manner the victim had been selected. In Mrs. Mercer's case it appeared that he had spotted her at the station, taken the trouble to familiarize himself with where she lived and with her movements, and then chosen a time when she would be vulnerable and when her husband and children were not likely to be around. That Jeff Mercer had been out of town Norah considered a coincidence, though it was always possible that Catherine Mercer making small talk at the garage might have casually mentioned that he was going away. It didn't matter. What mattered was that Gabby appeared to have been a target of opportunity, the attack on her pure chance. Question: which was the habit and which the deviation?

As she turned the corner to Fifth Avenue, a stinging wind sweeping up from Washington Square caught Norah full in the face and made her eyes tear. She kept on toward the arch anyway, wanting a place where she could sit and think for a few minutes. When she'd been a little girl, her mother used to take her down here each year to a children's puppet show—a Christmas treat. The young Norah had called the Village "Little Old New York" and peopled its narrow, winding streets of neat row houses behind glisteningly painted iron palings with ladies in bustles and bonnets and gentlemen in frock coats and tall beaver hats. Not even a child's innocent imagination could transform Washington Square now. Traffic cut through the middle. The benches were broken, the water fountains vandalized, the grass trampled beyond next spring's regeneration. At least the cold wind had swept the place clean of the usual addicts and pushers, though the taint of their transactions and of all the other ugly business regularly initiated in that place remained. Norah found a bench that looked as though it might bear her weight and carefully balanced on its edge.

She reviewed the similarities between the two attacks. The scene: first-floor landing of the back stairs. No, more basic: the buildings, both large, impersonal, so that strangers coming or going would not attract attention; both self-service buildings. Neither had doormen or elevator men—that was crucial. Nowadays, of course, only the real luxury buildings could afford a full staff; still, if Dana was selecting his victims in advance, it was a prime consideration. Mrs. Mercer had stated that he seemed to know just where to take her. How had he known where the back stairs were when he shoved Gabby into the lobby? Had he committed the act so many times in the same way that he instinctively sensed the layout even though he'd never been there before?

She had to discover another victim. But Norah was becoming more of a realist. The law might have been liberalized so that it was no longer necessary to show penetration and so that the threat of force, not actual force, was sufficient. That was theory. In practice you had better show semen *and* injury. One without the other just wasn't enough, she thought bitterly. So finding another victim wouldn't be enough. It had to be one who would fulfill those two requirements and also make a positive identification.

That meant more lists, more legwork, more interviews, but Detective Second Grade Mulcahaney had no doubt it would pay off because Norah Mulcahaney was convinced that such a victim existed. Hunching her shoulders against the sharp wind, she left the ramshackle bench and headed for the Amoco station.

Paul Zoubek was the manager, a short, rotund man with thin strands of reddish-blond hair through which a pink pate gleamed and whose expansive smile was brightened by a row of gold crowns.

But of course he had time for Detective Mulcahaney! Zoubek waved a manicured hand to indicate a small battalion of his minions in overalls nearly as crisply clean as his own scurrying among the pumps.

No lack of help here, Norah noted as she accepted his invitation to enter a spotless office and took the proffered chair.

Though it was only two months since he had left, Earl Dana might already have been forgotten if not for the recent story in the newspapers, Paul Zoubek explained. He had no feelings about the incident, not for or against. He shrugged the whole thing off. It was part of the ugliness of the city that you ignored, that is, if you wanted to keep your sanity. Oh, but of course he wanted to help! He wanted to do his duty. He was always ready to cooperate with the police. The police of New York were wonderful! It was terrible the way they were treated, abused and vilified—an outrage. Unjustified. Well, in one or two instances of course . . . there are unfortunately dishonest men in any line of work, but . . . Ah yes, yes, about Dana. Well, he didn't really know anything about his private life. You see, Detective Mulcahaney, the help pretty much came and went as they pleased. Licensed mechanics particularly knew they could get a job anywhere and anytime. Drifters, really, without ambition, without any kind of goal in life . . .

Norah broke in to ask if she might see the employment records. She wasn't surprised that Paul Zoubek kept better files than his counterpart uptown; nevertheless, Earl Dana's card wasn't that much more informative. Under previous employment he again had given only one reference—a garage in Syracuse, New York. There was no time lapse of consequence between the two jobs.

"Did you check his last employer?"

Zoubek looked sheepish. "I didn't think he'd be around long enough to make it worthwhile. As it turned out, he stayed longer than most, nearly a year. He left . . . well, you can see for yourself, end of August."

"Yes. Did he give a reason?"

"Told me he got a better job. I pay good money, but . . . it's possible."

"Maybe the hours were better? What hours did he work here?"

"Three in the afternoon to eleven at night. Never complained, never tried to change to the day shift."

He'd attacked Mrs. Mercer at 4 P.M. "What was his day off?"

Zoubek waved his hands. "It varied."

"Was he a good worker?"

"Yes. Yes. He knew his business, and he didn't make trouble."

"How about the customers? Did he get along well with them?"

"They liked him. He was pleasant. I demand that from my help; I don't want no sourpusses here. It costs nothing to smile."

"Did he seem particularly pleasant or friendly with any of the women customers?"

Zoubek gaped. "I see what you mean." He was still smiling but not so easily. "I didn't notice anything like that."

He was thinking it over, though; Norah could see him at it, recalling and assessing the responses of the women to Dana. "Do you have a list of regular customers? People with charge accounts?"

Zoubek didn't like the way it was turning out. He didn't want to be the one who caused a good customer to be involved with the police—particularly when it might put the customer in a bad light.

"I keep the bookkeeping to a minimum," he explained. "It's cash or a gas-company credit card."

That was the usual way. "Still, there must be some customers who come so regularly that you know them by name."

He scowled, trying to find a way out of that one. "I told you at the start that I'm not interested in the private life of my employees. I consider the private life of my customers none of my business."

"You wouldn't mind my checking through your file of back vouchers, would you?"

"There's not much to check; I only keep them a week."

"Is that all?"

His cordiality was fading fast. "How do you think I pay for my gas?"

"The company would keep yearly records of their credit customers, wouldn't they?"

"Search me."

"Only one way to find out." Norah got up. "Incidentally, which credit cards do you honor? Not all of them, I hope."

"Just the one."

"That's something to be grateful for anyway."

Norah smiled. Paul Zoubek did not.

The assault that Norah particularly wanted to uncover had probably occurred just before Dana had quit the Amoco station, but she couldn't ignore the rest of the period during which he had been employed there. The entire credit-card operation was computerized, naturally, but the computer wasn't programmed to give the readout Norah needed, and a year's record of charges from all over New York City and the neighboring states took a long time to go through. The out-of-towners she could eliminate because it was hardly likely that Earl Dana had chosen a victim whom he would have to follow to New Jersey or Connecticut. Unfortunately that didn't shorten the job by much. Names appeared over and over again. As regular customers, these went on the list of most likely prospects, but the one-time customers couldn't be ignored either. Having checked the charges credited to the station, Norah then had to refer to the individual customer accounts. She worked the rest of the week in the company's accounting office, and at the end of it she had culled hundreds of names, and as before, there remained the ordeal of finding which of the cards registered in a man's name had been used by a woman.

From time to time as a change of pace she worked at tracing where Dana had gone. On the assumption that he was still in New York, she called gas stations, starting with the AAAA in lower Manhattan, to ask whether they had recently hired a new mechanic. By the time she got to the Elite in the Sutton Place area, she had him. She didn't do anything about it though; for the time being it was enough just to know where he was.

So aside from knowing the suspect's whereabouts, all Norah had to show for two weeks of grueling research was a new and longer list of names. No, in Catherine Mercer she at least had private confirmation that raping Gabby had not been Earl Dana's first offense. Her hope now was that one out of the hundreds of names on this list would appear on the precinct log of unsolved rape complaints. She chose the precinct files rather than the ACCB (Arrest and Crime Coding Bureau) because that was the area in which Dana had been living and working, and it was more likely that the victim would have been living in that area too. She believed that Dana not only followed the usual pattern of the rapist of operating within his own neighborhood but also had further refined it by choosing his victims from among the customers of the place where he worked.

Indian summer revived the city, and with it Norah's natural optimism, which had been considerably taxed during the long, eye-straining hours, reasserted itself. She headed straight for the precinct house. There she settled down to compile a list of the unsolved rape cases for the past year. The next step was to compare those names with the names on her credit-card list. She started with the list of those cards issued directly to women and made the match in less than an hour.

She could hardly believe her good luck. It was like checking one of those contest circulars—you did it on general principles, not expecting to find your number, and when you did find it, you kept rechecking it over and over to make sure you hadn't made a mistake before letting yourself rejoice. Of course, afterward you found out you'd won not the Trip to Europe for Two but the packet of seeds. Norah rechecked the name and address: Isabel M. Haggerty, 340 East Nineteenth Street. No mistake. According to the credit charges, it appeared that Miss Haggerty used her car during the summer months only. The first charge for the year had been made just before the Decoration Day weekend. The attack was reported as having occurred on June 18, earlier than Norah had expected and before the attack on Mrs. Mercer. According to the complaint, the assault had taken place at 11:30 P.M. as the victim was returning from the movies. The perpetrator had pushed his way in behind her to the lobby, dragged her to the back stairs and up to the first-floor landing, where he had sexually attacked her. A tremor of nervous elation went through Norah. This time she'd won; she'd won big.

She read on. The perpetrator was described as very strong, tall, thin, with long blond hair. Unfortunately the bulb on the stair landing was burned out, so Miss Haggerty was not able to get a really good look at him.

Damn, Norah muttered under her breath. Here she'd finally turned up somebody with the courage to make a complaint and it was useless because she wouldn't be able to identify Dana. It looked as though she'd won only the packet of seeds after all. *Damn!* This time Norah said it aloud, but the civilian file clerk didn't even look up—she'd heard a lot worse.

Well, so far she'd uncovered two victims who she was morally certain had been raped by Earl Dana. If she still couldn't nail him, then she'd just have to keep on looking. Not that she was giving up on Isabel Haggerty. Not by any means. From the darkness of the station house Norah stepped into blinding sunshine. You never knew, she thought as she took a deep, lung-filling breath of the crisp November air. You never knew what an interview might turn up.

The building in which Isabel Haggerty lived was exactly right—self-service, medium size, middle income. It even had a beauty parlor on the second floor, which meant that the downstairs door was open, though that would be only during the daylight hours probably. She scanned the names in the back of doorbells, but there was no Isabel Haggerty. She rang the super.

89

He was a wizened but dapper little man in a neat business suit, snug vest, striped brown and white shirt. He could have fitted right in with her father's cronies at Houlihan's except for the Alpine feather stuck in the band of his fedora—that set him a cut above in elegance.

"Oh, she's gone, miss. Miss Haggerty moved a few months back."

Shouldn't that have been noted in the precinct file? Norah wondered. "Did she leave a forwarding address?"

"Well . . ." The dapper little man appraised Norah.

"It's all right, I'm a police officer. Here." Norah showed her ID.

"Oh." There was surprise followed by respect and relief. "Oh, well . . .Well, then, you know all about it, the attack, I mean. It was a terrible thing. She just never felt safe in the building after it. She used to be a real cheerful girl, healthy, full of pep—like yourself, ma'am. But after the attack . . ." He shook his head dolefully. "You talked to her, and she didn't hear you. She was always looking over her shoulder. Real nervy. Not that you could blame her. Finally she moved."

Norah nodded. "If you could get her new address for me."

It must cost plenty to live here, Norah thought as she looked over the place to which Isabel Haggerty had fled for refuge. Money spent principally for the presence of the stolid, bored doorman and the stolid, bored elevator operator sitting on a stool beside the open elevator door while he read the *Daily News*. When she asked for Miss Haggerty, the doorman, who at her approach had automatically started for the house phone, stopped, and the elevator man looked up from his paper.

"She does live here, doesn't she?"

The doorman swallowed. Despite the fact that he stood outdoors for the greater part of the day, he had an unhealthy, indoor pallor. "No, ma'am." He looked at her oddly. "What do you want with her?"

The elevator man got up and edged over to them.

Wordlessly Norah took out her identification.

"Police!" It appeared to confuse the doorman. "Police," he repeated. "And you don't know?"

She could guess. "I'm not from the local precinct. Just please tell me what happened."

"She's dead, ma'am. Miss Haggerty's dead. Jumped out of the window. About a year ago. Just about a year ago."

10

The suicide had occurred in the Seventeenth Precinct. As Isabel Haggerty had not told anyone she was moving, the investigating detectives had no way of making the connection between her death and the rape that had occurred in the Ninth. Their report was sadly laconic.

Subject: female, Caucasian, spinster. Aged 22, height 5'4", weight 115 lbs. Brown hair, brown eyes, no identifying marks. Lived alone. Known to have been in depressed frame of mind—attested to by neighbors and fellow workers, also by her parents, Mr. and Mrs. Roger Haggerty of Huntington, Long Island.

Probably she had driven out to her parents' home on summer weekends, Norah thought; that would account for the limited use of her car. Maybe she had put it up in the family garage during the winter. Norah was concentrating on every detail and following it to its logical conclusion as much to keep her frustration and her pity in check as to get a clear picture of how it had been. According to the report, Mr. and Mrs. Haggerty had been concerned about their only daughter's low spirits, but she had assured them that she was tired and preoccupied from carrying a heavy work load—Isabel Haggerty had been a research chemist at the Sloan-Kettering Institute. Evidently she hadn't confided in them about the rape; probably she hadn't wanted to add to their worries about her, especially since the man hadn't been caught, and there was no indication that he ever would be.

The detectives hadn't gone further. There had seemed no need: depressed, frustrated, lonely girls jumping out of windows are not particularly remarkable in big cities. It was an open-and-shut case. Even if the officer carrying had known about the rape, it wouldn't have made any difference. On the contrary, Norah reasoned, it would have provided the final clincher in a direct motive.

Only she knew that Earl Dana was responsible. Morally, if not legally, he had killed Isabel Haggerty. And now Norah was more determined than ever to get him.

So back to the lists. Norah compared, called, interviewed, and got nowhere. If any of the countless women she talked to had been attacked, she couldn't discover it. Discouraged by the long, unproductive hours and days, she wasn't surprised as the month ended to be called in by Lieutenant Wilburn.

"How's it going?"

"Not good."

"Well, I have some good news. Officer Dollinger finally managed to talk with Miss Constante."

"She did?"

The lieutenant nodded. "She met her in Dr. Lopez' waiting room. Posing as a patient, she got Miss Constante to recall that on the night of the attack, just as she was running across Eighty-third Street, she was nearly run over."

"I didn't know that."

"In view of what happened afterward, it's not surprising she forgot. Anyway, Dolly rang doorbells till she discovered a witness. He heard the screech of brakes and raced to the window just in time to see the car drive off."

"He got the license?" Norah asked eagerly.

"We weren't that lucky, but he did watch to make sure that the girl who had nearly been hit was all right. He watched till she made it to the sidewalk and entered the outer door of her building, your building. That was before midnight; he's sure because he's always in bed by midnight."

"Did he see Dana follow her in?"

"No. As soon as the girl went in, he left the window. As I understand it, the assailant didn't make his move till Miss Constante had entered the vestibule between the outer and inner doors. He could have been lurking out of sight; Dolly says the window ledge is too wide for anyone much beyond the curb to be seen from above. He might even have been in sight, but with his attention fixed on the girl it's possible that Mr. Dorfmann just didn't notice Dana."

It wasn't much. "How can he even be sure it was Gabby? It was dark, and he must have been looking from several stories up. . . ."

"Three. It seems that as soon as Miss Constante reached the safety of the sidewalk after nearly being hit, she paused for a moment to catch her breath—directly under the corner streetlight. Mr. Dorfmann described her very well, right down to the dark green dress and bright red shoulder-strap handbag." As Norah said nothing, the lieutenant added, "It supports the victim's claim of the time the attack took place."

Norah nodded.

There was a fleeting satisfaction on Lieutenant Wilburn's part; then she got back to business. "The rest of the news you may not like so much. You're being taken off the case and returned to regular duty."

It wasn't exactly unexpected. "But I'm not finished."

"You have a new lead?"

Regretfully Norah shook her head. "I just can't seem to get past Isabel Haggerty," she admitted. "I thought I'd switch to Dana's background, his home, his friends, his hangouts. It was what I had intended from the beginning."

"Haven't you more or less established he's a loner?"

Once again Norah was impressed that Lieutenant Wilburn was up on everything that was happening, yet if it had been Lieutenant Felix, she would have taken it for granted. She continued to underrate Lee Wilburn for no other reason than that she was a woman, and Norah of all people shouldn't be doing that. But just because she was ashamed didn't mean she was going to give up the case without a fight. "Dana must have had some kind of life before coming to New York—parents, school friends, neighborhood or army buddies. . . ."

"Sorry, Mulcahaney, that's it. We've got other priorities, and you're needed back at the Fifth Division."

"You mean you're going to just drop it?" Norah cried out. "Earl Dana is directly responsible for that girl jumping out of the window! And he's going to attack again, Lieutenant Wilburn. You know it. You know he has to."

"We'll be on the lookout. At the first report of an assault that bears the slightest resemblance to his MO, we'll follow it up, and we'll notify you. That's a promise, Norah."

93

"He could lie low for months."

"Or he could be cured," the squad commander pointed out. "He could be so frightened by Miss Constante's charge that he'll never try it again."

"And if he isn't? If as a result of holding back he erupts into more violent attacks, into a series of them?"

The lieutenant looked grim. "We'll get him on the first one. That's another promise."

"*If* the victim reports it!" Norah shot back.

The two women looked at each other. "That's beyond our control."

"Couldn't a surveillance. . . ?"

"You know better than that." The lieutenant made her final stipulation. "We'll pay particular attention to all reports from the Nineteenth; that's where Dana is working now, isn't it? OK, we'll keep a sharp eye on the Nineteenth. That's it, Mulcahaney." As Norah got up to leave, she relented.

"You've done good work, Norah, but give us credit for some competence . . . and for caring—almost as much as you do. Trust us."

Norah could feel her embarrassment coursing through her whole body and knew that it burned in her face. "Yes, ma'am."

"Miss Constante hasn't been informed yet that we have corroboration for the time of the attack. Dolly thought you'd like to be the one to tell her."

"Yes, ma'am, thank you. Thank you for everything."

Nobody made any fuss over Norah when she walked into the Fifth Division squad room on 100th Street. The greetings were as casual as though she hadn't been away a single day. Yet every man made a point of stopping by her desk sometime during her tour. Even normally taciturn Roy Brennan paused for a few grunts and aimless remarks about the weather. It was gratifying; it made up for a lot of things; it was good to be back. She didn't have much time to loll around enjoying it, though, for she was almost immediately assigned along with David Link and Gus Schmidt to the investigation of an execution-type killing of three men that had occurred the night before in a sealed apartment.

The new case plus the familiar and comfortable way of doing

94

things wiped out some of the futility of the past month. She worked late, but when she got home, before going up to her own apartment, Norah decided to look in on the Constantes.

"Norah . . . Come in, come in." Mrs. Constante gave her the well-remembered welcoming smile.

Norah was relieved to see Gabby's mother looking so much better. Tired, and perhaps a little thinner, but otherwise normal. It suggested that Gabby herself must have recovered, and Norah felt a heavy anxiety relieved. The news she brought should cheer them even further.

"Is Gabby home?"

The smile vanished; tears sprang into Ofelia Constante's limpid eyes. "Oh, yes."

Norah took the woman's hands into her own and gave them a reassuring squeeze. "May I speak with her?"

"She is asleep."

"I have news, and I think it's worth waking her up."

"She is under sedation."

Norah was appalled. "Still?"

The mother gave in to a series of terrible, soft whimperings. "No, no. Again."

Enrique—it must have something to do with Enrique. "Didn't Enrique come? My father told me you'd sent for him."

"Yes. He has come and gone." She couldn't hold back the tears.

Norah put an arm around her. "Now, Mrs. Constante, as soon as Gabby wakes, you tell her that we've discovered a woman who admits that Earl Dana raped her. She's a married woman, and her situation was such that she felt she couldn't testify at the time. But she has admitted it to me, and she has identified Dana as the man." No use adding that the identification wouldn't hold up in court.

"There was another girl too," Norah continued. She could hardly admit this one couldn't testify because she'd killed herself. "In addition we've found a witness who saw Gabby coming home and actually entering the building at exactly the time she says she did." Norah wished that she could add that the witness had also seen Dana force his way in behind Gabby. A month's hard work seemed woefully meager recounted like this, and she couldn't blame Mrs. Constante for not being more impressed. "We've always believed in Gabby; don't you think this might help her believe in herself?'' Then she added, because she was certain that it was the core of the trouble, ''And to make Enrique believe in her?''

Ofelia Constante sniffled, wiped at the tears with the back of her hand. ''Thank you, Norah. You are a good friend. We are very grateful to you, but it can make no difference now.''

''It will. It will. Let me call Enrique. Let me talk to him.''

''It would be useless. Gabby is . . . we think . . . we fear . . . she is pregnant.''

That was a jolt. Norah had taken it for granted that along with the penicillin against VD Dr. Lopez had also given Gabby estrogen to abort pregnancy. Evidently he had not—whether because of the possible harmful side effect or out of deference to the Constantes' religious conviction was a moot question; probably he'd desisted on both counts. The easy solution of abortion would not be acceptable to them. Fleetingly Norah wondered if in the same situation she would resort to abortion. ''She may not be pregnant. Surely it's still too early. . . .''

''We are praying to the Holy Mother.''

Norah was a staunch believer in prayer, but she also believed that God helps those who help themselves. ''Have you spoken to the priest? Surely, under the circumstances . . .''

''There is no need to consult the priest. The knowledge of what is right lies in each man's heart.''

There was nothing more Norah could say or do. If Gabby had the child and then gave him away for adoption, she'd never forget. If she kept the child and raised him, he would be a constant reminder of the rape. Either way, being who and what they were, this put an end to any future for Gabby and Enrique. Norah put her arms around Mrs. Constante, kissed her, and left.

She had just put her key into the lock when her father opened the door.

''You're late,'' he said and then quickly kissed her on the cheek. The way he did it was a kind of warning and at the same time an assurance of his support. ''We called the office, and they said you left over an hour ago.''

''I stopped downstairs to . . .'' Norah noticed the ''we.'' Joe? She was glad. It would be good to see Joe. She hadn't even spoken to him on the phone for . . . nearly two weeks. Maybe if she reviewed the case with him, he might just spot something. . . .

As though he knew what she was thinking, her father shook his head. "We have a guest." Obviously he was trying to prepare her for something unexpected.

Not Joe, then. Norah raised her eyebrows and went into the living room. A woman sat on the couch.

"Good evening." She scrutinized Norah quite openly. "I'm sorry to barge in on you without warning, but I thought we should talk. I'm Helen Scott."

For a moment Norah didn't remember. "Oh, yes, we've spoken on the phone. You're Sergeant Capretto's friend."

"He's told you about me. That's a help."

"You told me when you called," Norah corrected quietly. With her shoulder-length blond hair, level gray eyes, makeup so artfully done it looked as though she wasn't wearing any, twin cashmere sweater set over man-tailored slacks, and dark ranch mink tossed in a heap on the Mulcahaney sofa, she flaunted money by seeming to belittle it. Out of her league, Norah thought, but not out of Joe's evidently. And she wasn't that much older than Norah either.

"You're precise, but they teach you that at the Police Academy, don't they?"

Norah was about to remind her that her friend, Sergeant Capretto, was taking a course at the academy, but she decided against it. "What can I do for you, Mrs. Scott?"

"Hasn't Tony mentioned me at all?"

"Tony?"

"Joseph Antony—I call him Tony."

knew you in college."

"That's all?"

"Exactly what is it you want, Mrs. Scott?"

Helen Scott produced a quirky smile that was supposed to be engaging. "You're very direct. All right, first I wanted to see you, see what you looked like. Frankly you're not what I expected. You're a lot younger, and . . . prettier." For a moment Helen Scott appeared uncertain, but it passed. "Since you don't want to say what Tony told you about me, perhaps you'd like to hear what he said about you."

97

Norah had plenty of experience in hiding her reactions, but she was totally unprepared for this, and she could see that Helen Scott sensed and savored her discomfort.

"If your father would excuse us . . ."

"No. You might as well say whatever you've come to say in front of him; it'll save me repeating it later."

Helen Scott looked from one to the other. "I didn't expect that either." She took a small gold cigarette case and matching lighter from her alligator handbag. As she lit up, she tilted her head so that a fall of blond hair undulated in the light. A calculated gesture, but for whose benefit? She inhaled, exhaled, then leaned back and gave Norah a sharp look. "Tony says you're going to be married."

Norah sat very still and avoided looking at her father. The bald announcement had surely shaken him, but she hoped he'd take his cue from her. He did.

Failing to get any kind of reaction from either of them, Mrs. Scott continued. "If that's so, there are certain things you should know about Tony and me."

Norah got up. "If he wants me to know, he'll tell me."

Helen Scott stayed where she was. "He's not going to tell you what he doesn't know or doesn't want to admit to himself. Do you want to marry a man who's in love with another woman?"

"You? He hasn't seen you in . . . fifteen years."

"Sixteen."

"You're saying he's been carrying a torch for you all this time?"

"He hasn't married, has he? Look . . . Norah . . . we went together for nearly two years. I was crazy about him, but there was another man too, a man with money and from my own background and religion. My parents preferred him, and I let them sway me. I was wrong."

"It took you a long time to find out."

"No, I found out very quickly. But we had children, and for their sakes . . ." She shrugged. "Then there was my pride. I didn't want to admit that my reasons for marrying Al were the wrong ones. I didn't want to admit it to myself. Certainly not to Tony."

Joe had characterized Helen Scott as a woman who had to have a man around all the time. He'd indicated that she was after him only because there was nobody else and that he didn't want to renew the relationship. Well, look at the way he'd been dodging those incessant telephone calls! Obviously Helen Scott didn't give up easily. Somehow she'd cornered him. She'd refused to accept that it was all over between them, so to end it Joe had simply told her he was getting married. He'd put up the ultimate defense. Norah almost smiled at the thought of Joe Capretto, suave and experienced, being cornered.

"It seems you've waited too long, Mrs. Scott. You should have married Joe when you had the chance." She couldn't resist adding, "I always call him Joe."

"Haven't you wondered why he never married?"

"I'm not going to discuss this anymore, Mrs. Scott. You've said what you came to say; now I'm going to ask you to leave."

"Just answer one question."

Saints in heaven! Wouldn't the woman ever let go? "Ask Joe."

"When did he propose? How long ago?"

Now what was she after? Norah was going to reply—none of your business. Instead, in spite of herself, in spite of loyalty to Joe, she said, "A month ago."

The quirky smile became smug. "That's exactly when I came to New York. A month and a half before that I wrote to tell him I was getting a divorce."

Just about then Joe had suddenly decided to take the exam for lieutenant. To make a future for himself and Norah or to show Helen Scott he was a success? He said that he'd planned to propose after graduating from the command course but then decided there was no point in waiting. Because of the pressure from Mrs. Scott? Norah stood very straight. "I've known Joe a little over two years, Mrs. Scott, which seems a long time to me. Maybe your arrival did give him just that little extra nudge. If so, then I should thank you." She picked up the mink coat and held it out to her visitor.

Scowling, Helen Scott took it. She looked from daughter to father and back again. "Are you going to tell . . . Tony . . . that I was here?"

"Probably."

In a gesture that dared her to do it Helen Scott flung the coat around her shoulders, picked up her handbag, and stalked out.

Patrick Mulcahaney waited till the door was slammed shut. "You might have told me."

"There wasn't anything to tell."

"You mean . . . he didn't propose?"

"Oh, he proposed, all right."

Mulcahaney's eyes lit up; he started to chuckle. "You turned him down."

"No, I said I'd think about it," she teased. "That was before I met Mrs. Scott of course."

"So?"

"So when somebody else wants what you've got . . ." She shrugged.

It was no joke to Patrick Mulcahaney. "If you ask me, neither one of you has him. If you ask me, no woman is ever going to get the Sergeant to stick his head in the noose."

11

Maybe her father was right. Norah wasn't as sure of Joe or of his motive in proposing as she'd pretended. She'd put up a front for Helen Scott's benefit and for her father's too. Alone, the doubts overwhelmed her. Suppose Joe really was still in love with the woman after all these years. Norah didn't question his honesty toward her, but she couldn't dismiss Mrs. Scott's suggestion that he wasn't aware himself of the ambivalence of his feelings. She was tempted to get hold of him and ask him outright—but if he didn't know himself . . .

She wanted to take some kind of action, but there was nothing she could do but wait it out, and that, for Norah, was the hardest of all. Brooding only increased her uncertainty, so she tried to concentrate on work. The trouble was that at this point what she was doing was routine, so she found herself reverting to the Dana case. She made herself think about it so she wouldn't think about Joe. As a result, Dana was the last thought in her mind before falling asleep at night and the first thing her mind automatically seized on at waking. A couple of mornings after Mrs. Scott's visit, as she was lying in bed savoring the last few moments of delicious warmth before jumping out into the cold room, the phone rang. It was Joe.

She was unprepared; she didn't know what to say to him. To cover it she started talking about Dana.

And Joe, sensing that she was ill at ease, put it down to the fact that she wasn't ready to give him an answer. He didn't want to appear to be pressing her, so though he knew she was officially off the case and was not inclined to encourage her to pursue it, he too was at a loss to find another topic.

"The only thing you can do is wait for Dana to make a move, Norah."

"I can't get rid of the feeling that I've overlooked something."

"Are you asking me?"

Norah was instantly alert. "Yes."

"OK. Why did Dana switch jobs? Did you ask?"

"Well, sure, naturally. That's the first thing I asked his new boss—the reason he gave."

"I'm talking about the real reason."

Norah frowned. She had never accepted the ridiculous explanation Dana had offered Gerard, the manager of the Broadway Garage, that he wanted to get out of the Village because there were too many queers! "I didn't follow it up, Joe," she admitted ruefully.

"It's the only gap I can see."

"You're right. That's it! It has to be. Something scared him. Listen, Joe, do you mind if I hang up now?"

"No, but listen, Norah . . ."

She wasn't in the mood for the inevitable cautions. "And thanks, Joe, I really appreciate this. Thanks a lot." She hung up without giving him a chance to say one more word. She threw back the covers and reached for her warm wool robe.

A wind off the river had driven a fine drift of the season's first snow into the room, and Norah's bare feet tingled as she stepped on the damp patch of carpet. She shivered as she slammed the window shut, but it was from excitement and not the cold. Isabel Haggerty had filed a rape complaint, the only one Norah had so far been able to discover, but as Miss Haggerty had not been able to see her assailant clearly, no suspicion had fallen on Dana. He had stayed on at his job in the Village, kept his same lodging. It was the girl who had moved. Obviously her suicide had been no threat to him either—if he even knew about it! When he did finally quit and move uptown, it was nearly . . . Norah ticked off the months, nearly a year later. He had moved because he was afraid. That meant another as-yet-undiscovered victim. Somebody who could identify him.

But she had been over the precinct rape reports thoroughly, matching them against the gasoline-company credit-card list, and had come up empty. Where was the loophole?

Norah stared out the window at the winter-colored waters of the Hudson. The answer was on the edge of her subconscious. . . . Even if the victim's name was not on the credit-card list and she had not been a customer at the Amoco garage but had been, like Gabby, a target of opportunity, Norah should have spotted the MO on the precinct rape reports. Unless, naturally, the rape hadn't been reported. Norah grimaced. But then there would have been no reason for Dana to run away. Then it came to her—in all its splendid and terrifying simplicity. The report was there, all right, but not under rape. Dana had progressed from rape to murder.

Quickly Norah threw on some clothes—the same outfit she'd worn the day before, a sure indication of preoccupation. She grabbed a cup of coffee and headed down to the precinct and the homicide file. She started with the end of the previous August, which was when Dana had left his job, intending to work backward. She didn't have far to go.

On the twenty-second Frances Russo—female, Caucasian, age twenty-eight, had been found murdered on the first-floor landing of the back stairs of the apartment house in which she'd lived. That took care of the scene. Her head had been smashed against the cement floor.

Norah shuddered. It was the threat Dana had used to make Gabby and Catherine Mercer submit. They had submitted. Evidently Frances Russo had not. In fact, she had put up a violent struggle. Her face had been disfigured by repeated blows of the attacker's fists. She'd inflicted some damage herself, though—the lab had removed skin scrapings from beneath her fingernails, found blood spots on her clothing that were not her own blood, and more foreign blood in her mouth. She'd been raped anyway.

The medical examiner set the time of death as between 2 and 4 A.M. No one had seen anything. Screams were heard by several of the tenants at the relevant time, close to 2 A.M., but they had been

102

dismissed as only the customary drunken brawling of a couple on the second floor rear. Evidently the police had been called once before about their quarreling, and the couple had been indignant over the interference. The night of the murder had been hot; all air conditioners in the building were going full force, so the screams were heard only faintly, and those who were even aware of them simply tried to ignore the commotion, annoyed at being disturbed rather than alarmed, and relieved when it was finally over so they could get back to sleep. Shades of Kitty Genovese, Norah thought.

The neighborhood had been canvassed for possible loiterers, records reviewed for comparison with previous rape complaints, the list of known sex offenders checked—all the routine moves. Nothing. Investigation of the victim's background was unproductive. Frances Russo lived alone. She was a nice-looking enough girl but quiet. She had no friends, didn't date, didn't frequent any of the Village hangouts. There was nothing to go on. The case petered out for lack of leads.

Norah sat back and considered. The MO fitted like the original drawing and its tracing. The only discrepancy was that Frances Russo lived in a building with doormen and elevator men. The service, however, was not on a twenty-four-hour basis. At midnight everybody went off, and the downstairs front door was locked. OK, so Dana had to know that. That suggested that he had selected Miss Russo as he had selected Mrs. Mercer and Isabel Haggerty—through the gas station. The report didn't mention whether or not Frances Russo had had a car—no reason why the investigating officer should have considered that pertinent. Norah took note of his name.

retired . . . let's see, back in September."

"Do you know where he lives?"

"Moved to California. Got himself a lush job at one of those big technological companies; can't think of the name. Security chief. Top salary *and* his pension, lucky slob. Not that he doesn't deserve it," Sergeant Perry hastened to add. "Schonbar was a real fine officer."

"Could I get his new address from the pension fund maybe?"

"Why not?" Perry had been on the desk a long time, and he was sharp. He knew everything going on in the precinct, and he knew how many times Norah had been around and why. "You got something new involving the Russo case?"

"Maybe." Norah was learning to be cautious. "A possible tie-in to a couple of other rapes."

"Yeah?" He gave her a nice, avuncular smile. "I don't want to discourage you, Detective Mulcahaney, but Art Schonbar went into that aspect pretty thoroughly, and he came up empty. Like I told you, he was a real shrewd investigator. If he didn't find it . . ." He raised both shoulders and dropped them. "Plus which there was plenty of manpower on that one. It was an ugly business with all those people hearing the screams and nobody reporting. The captain went all out to solve it. They just couldn't tie it in to any other assault."

"One of the cases I had in mind happened afterward. The other was never reported."

"Yeah?" Perry was impressed. "Why don't you go in and talk to the captain?" he suggested.

"Ah . . ." Norah looked Perry over and decided she could tell him the truth. "I was working out of RAI on these other cases I mentioned, but I didn't get anywhere, so I was told to drop it and go back to my regular job. Then I got this idea. It seems to check out, but I want to make sure before . . . you know. . . ."

Perry got it. "OK, whatever you say. Meantime, anything we can do for you down here, you just name it. That's one pervert killer every man in this division wants to get."

Before seeing Lieutenant Felix, Norah wanted confirmation that Frances Russo had had a car and had been a customer of the station where Dana worked. She still had copies of all those lists she'd so laboriously compiled, and it would be a simple matter to look and see if her name appeared there. But the lists were at home, and she was due to report for her tour at four. It would have to wait.

As the hours passed, her anxiety to check those lists grew. With it came a foreboding of danger. So far it appeared that Dana was remaining quiet; at least there had been no complaint of an assault that fitted his pattern or she would have heard from RAI. But how much longer would he remain quiescent? How much longer before need overcame caution?

"Dolly? This is Norah. I need some help. You know those lists of the credit-card customers? Will you see if you can find a Frances Russo of Twenty-two East Twelfth on there?''

''You bet. What's up?''

''I think I may have located another victim.''

''Good work.''

''Don't get excited; this one won't be able to testify either. She was killed, and I think Dana did it.''

There was a moment's silence. ''I'll get back to you.'' Dolly Dollinger hung up.

From then on, each time Norah had to leave her desk she made sure someone knew she was expecting an important message. But the message never came. What was taking Dolly so long? Could she have been called away? Then why didn't she phone and say she was busy? It was a long list; still, running it down for one specific name shouldn't take so long. It was there, the name was there, had to be, but the longer Norah waited, the less certain she became. When the phone rang and she finally heard Dolly's slightly nasal, slightly midwestern drawl, she had just about given up.

''Well?''

''There's no Frances Russo on any of those lists, Norah. I went over every page twice. I looked for any Russo at all, man or woman. I even checked through for the address: nobody in that building ever used that garage, that is, nobody with a credit card. There is, of course, the chance that she might have paid cash. You could ask.''

''She wasn't the kind of girl who would be remembered.''

''I'm real sorry.''

''Sure. Well, thanks anyway, Dolly. Sorry for the trouble.''

''I wish there were. I can't think of one other darn thing.''

Norah hung up, slid low in her chair, stretching long, slim legs out under the desk, and stared at the cracked ceiling. The squad room was quiet at that time of night and that time of year—the summer peak of violence past, the holiday bloodshed still ahead. She took a long, deep breath, held it, then noisily expelled it. David Link, hammering at his typewriter, looked up. Norah didn't realize she'd picked up the habit from Joe. David smiled but didn't comment.

Norah certainly wasn't thinking of Joe. If she had been, she would have been surprised and pleased to realize that he'd been out of her mind for nearly twenty-four hours, very good progress. What she was thinking was that if Frances Russo's name had turned up on those lists, she could have asked Lieutenant Felix for permission to bring Dana in for questioning. Without Russo's name on that list the evidence tieing Dana to her rape-murder was circumstantial. Not even that—deductive. OK, a hunch. Lieutenant Felix would label it that, and maybe he'd be right. But you couldn't overlook hunches. Hunch or instinct, whatever you cared to call it, was an important part of a good detective's equipment. A detective had to rely on instinct constantly to judge the intangibles of a case. Just how important was a certain clue? Just how credible was the witness? A good detective developed a feel—hunch. And when that was all there was, it couldn't be summarily dismissed; it had to be played out—at least until it was proved wrong. Surely Lieutenant Felix would grant her that much.

"Frances Russo could have been a target of opportunity," Norah reasoned. She had reviewed her deduction step by step for Felix. "If he's alternating between a careful selection and observation of his victim and chance attacks, then the next assault is going to be that much harder for RAI to spot," she said.

James Felix tilted back in his swivel chair, pressed his long fingers together tip to tip, and considered. "You're assuming a pattern of selection on the basis of one case—Catherine Mercer's."

"You're forgetting Isabel Haggerty, Lieutenant," Norah countered impetuously.

"No, I'm not forgetting anybody, Mulcahaney. There's no proof that Dana was the man who raped Miss Haggerty."

"No, sir," Norah agreed, chastened. "But . . ."

"You have not established a pattern of selection," he reiterated.

"How about the scene, Lieutenant? Both rapes for which we know Dana is responsible were committed on the first-floor landing of the back stairs. So was the homicide. And the threat he used against both known rape victims—that he'd smash their heads against the floor if they resisted. That's how Frances Russo was killed. We can't overlook that."

Felix was silent.

"Can we call both the scene and manner of death coincidence, Lieutenant? Do we dare?"

She'd made it a challenge, and she was a little overawed by her own temerity.

Felix let the chair swing forward into its normal position, leaned elbows on the desk, and looked levelly at her. "What do you want to do, Mulcahaney?"

"Start over. Approach the homicide as though it had just occurred, as though no previous reports exist. I want to go back to the scene, interview the neighbors, the girl's friends, the people she worked with—take the whole thing from the top."

"The case belongs to the Third District," Felix reminded her.

Norah could have argued that the case also belonged to the Rape Squad, that she'd worked out of RAI, and that RAI had citywide jurisdiction. Not long ago she wouldn't have hesitated, but she'd learned to respect procedure, though she still chafed at it. "The detective who carried the case is retired."

"So? They're still going to want one of their own on it."

"Couldn't I work along with him? Why not, Lieutenant? Why couldn't I do that?" It would be better than nothing, she thought.

While Felix weighed it, Norah fidgeted. Since this was her first experience with rape, she'd done a little homework—gone to the library, read articles by psychiatrists. The thing that had most particularly struck her was the poor response of repetitive rapists to therapy. Granted the number of cases were limited; nevertheless, the figures were chilling. Thirty-five percent of repetitive rapists under treatment were still under treatment after ten years. She would have liked to ignore those figures to the lieutenant. But the lieutenant's grim look indicated that he was well aware of the statistics—and of their implication.

"All right." Felix slapped the edge of the desk. "I'll give you two more weeks on special assignment and that's it, Mulcahaney." As he reached for the phone, Lieutenant Felix relaxed and grinned. "That is, if Captain Blake is willing to take you on."

"I didn't join the force to take orders from a woman!"

"You're the one carrying. She takes orders from you. Make sure she knows that."

"No woman's told me what to do since kindergarten."

"Anyhow, she's only going to be around a couple of weeks."

About to enter the Third Division squad room, Norah hesitated.

"She's got to be smart to pick up anything Schonbar missed."

That was a new voice joining the discussion.

"I can't stand women with brains: they act like nobody else has any."

That was number one again, the gruff voice belonging evidently to the man who was to be her new partner.

"I hear she's a looker." Voice number two.

"When you consider what we've got in the department, that's not saying much."

Norah decided she'd heard enough. She slapped the palm of her hand hard against the door frame and pushed it open with as much force as she could so that they'd be sure to hear.

Three men stood near the window, drinking coffee and smoking.

"I'm Norah Mulcahaney," she announced and looked them over as frankly as they would have her if she hadn't beat them to it. Of the three she picked out the youngest—a short, chunky, broad-shouldered, heavily muscled redhead—Captain Blake had shown great concern for her personal safety. He wore a knit pullover with a turtleneck that came right up to the end of his chin and the loudest plaid sports jacket she'd ever seen. "You must be Detective Robert Hoff." She held out her hand.

Hoff gulped and took it. "How come you knew me?"

"You're the only one who blushed when I identified myself."

The other two smirked, and Hoff's face turned an even deeper red. The freckles disappeared in the wash of red; even his wavy red hair bristled.

"Score one for the lady." Voice number two took a step forward and offered his hand. "I'm Sal Parisi."

Number three did the same. "Nate Oberlander. Glad to have you with us."

"Thanks." Norah turned again to her newly assigned partner. "In case you're wondering how much I heard, I got to the door just when you were saying you hadn't joined the force to take orders from a woman. I think it's only fair for you to know the advance info I got about you."

"From the captain?" Hoff's high color faded, and his chubby face was creased with worry.

"I can't reveal my source, but it wasn't the captain. The word I got is not to underrate you."

Parisi and Oberlander gaped.

Norah went on coolly. "I also heard that you talk loud, but you're real cool in a crisis. I was told I could count on you."

"That's score two for the lady," Parisi said and let his admiration show.

"Thank you." Norah smiled politely. "About Detective Schonbar . . . he didn't miss a thing. The possible break in the Russo case wasn't anything he overlooked but a result of the investigation of a crime committed after he retired."

"Score three for the lady," chortled Hoff. "OK, Detective Mulcahaney, what's on the schedule?"

"My name's Norah, and I was just going to ask you."

Hoff beamed. "Well, I guess we ought to start at the beginning. Go back to the scene."

"Whatever you say."

"Let's go, then." Hoff sprang forward and reached for the door.

"We're partners, so I'll open my own doors and I'll pay for my own coffee or beer or whatever. OK, Detective Hoff?"

"Call me Bobby."

12

The super escorted Norah and Bobby Hoff up to the first-floor landing, where Frances Russo had been raped and murdered. Of course, the floor had been thoroughly scrubbed, he informed the two detectives. It had been impossible to get the walls clean—they had had to be repainted; his fleshy lips curled to denote his squeamishness over the stains that had been there. Harold Jarman dressed and acted more like a manager than a superintendent. Naturally he had not himself discovered the body, he continued;

that had been Fred Grout, one of the staff, while he was taking out the garbage—a task much below Jarman's dignity. Fred had immediately rung his bell, though, and Jarman was the one who had notified the police.

Jarman disclaimed any knowledge regarding the personal life of Miss Russo or for that matter of any of the tenants. The only information he had about them was whether they were behind in their rent.

The doorman, a handsome, strapping young man, was at first glance as superior in his job as Jarman—until he opened his mouth. Then it was evident that holding doors, flagging cabs, and announcing visitors were suitable duties. He was more than willing to talk, though; the problem was to get something other than a repetition of his original testimony out of him.

Oh, sure, he remembered Miss Russo: how could he forget? Before the murder? Oh, sure, he remembered when she moved in. Well, because she hardly had any furniture. This big van pulled up and they took out—like a bed and a couple of chairs. Yeah, at the beginning she dated a lot, but never the same man more than a couple of times. By the end, say, last summer, she didn't date at all—except for the night of the murder. But they knew all about that, naturally. Frank Titus regarded Norah and Hoff respectfully.

"We'd like your slant on it, Mr. Titus," Hoff said, and Titus preened himself.

"There's not much to tell. They picked Miss Russo up at . . . like seven, in a taxi. Two men and a woman. I called Miss Russo on the house phone to let her know they were here, and she came right down."

"Had you ever seen these people before?"

"No, sir."

"Go on."

"Well . . . that's all." He appeared both surprised and sorry that he had no more to tell.

Norah helped him. "I suppose one of the men, the one who was specifically Miss Russo's date, must have got out of the cab to have you make the announcement and also to greet her when she came down. Could you describe him?"

Titus frowned. "He was an older man, too old for her. Smooth too, know what I mean? I was surprised Miss Russo was going out

110

with somebody like that. Probably her girlfriend talked her into it—the woman in the cab; *she* was in her element. I was right about Miss Russo too. I could tell when they got back that she hadn't had a good time."

Norah glanced at Hoff. "The four of them came back together?"

"Yes, ma'am, in a taxi. Her date insisted on going up with Miss Russo while the other two waited. She didn't want him to, but he wasn't going to be talked out of it. I caught him wink at the other two. I figured they'd fixed it up between them that if he didn't come down right away, they weren't going to hang around. Know what I mean?"

"And did he come down right away?"

Frank Titus grinned. "Pretty fast. But his friends were already gone."

Norah frowned. According to the postmortem, death had occurred between 2 and 4 A.M. According to the screams heard by the neighbors, closer to two. "You think he might have come back later on?"

"I doubt it, ma'am. You can kind of tell when they're still hoping or when they know they've struck out."

Hoff resumed the interrogation. "Did he appear angry?"

"He was disgusted. I'll say that."

"And what time was all this?"

"Just before I went off duty, say, a quarter to twelve."

That left a minimum gap of two hours before Frances Russo was attacked. She would hardly have been loitering in the hall all that time, so it had to be assumed that her date had seen her safely into her apartment.

"She was a nice person, Miss Russo," the doorman volunteered. "Honest. Know what I mean? A lot more attractive than she gave herself credit for being. And decent. Maybe if she hadn't been, if she'd let the guy go ahead and do what he wanted . . ."

Bright, Frank Titus might not be, but there was plenty of basic shrewdness in him—and compassion. "How soon after her date left did Miss Russo come down?" Norah asked.

Hoff sighed impatiently, and even Titus gawked because that was the point—nobody knew when or why Frances Russo had come out of her apartment to be killed on the back stairs.

"I went off duty just a few minutes later," the doorman reminded Norah.

"Was she in the habit of going out late, say, for a walk or a bite to eat or a pack of cigarettes?"

"She might run down to the deli on the corner but never after ten. Anyhow, it closes at ten except for weekends. If she went to a movie, she'd be in by eleven the latest. No walks. She was afraid. In fact, she mentioned to me that she'd like to get a dog but didn't want to be going out late at night to walk him."

Norah now showed him a mug shot of Dana. "Was this one of the two men on the double date with Miss Russo that night?"

"No, ma'am."

"Have you ever seen this man before?"

"No, ma'am."

It was the way Dana looked now, of course. He had been blond then, and the autopsy report stated that the victim had been clutching strands of blond hair. "Was either of the men on the double date a blond?"

Titus shook his head.

Hoff stood aside patiently as Norah went over it all again with the elevator man with the same lack of results.

"OK, Bobby, let's start on the tenants. Want to take the front of the building while I take the back?"

Hoff's initial enthusiasm was flagging. "I don't know, Norah. According to Schonbar's report, nobody heard anything."

"Correction—half the building heard what they thought was Mary Grogan getting beaten up by her husband."

"So now they know they were wrong."

"They knew that the next morning."

"It wouldn't have been so easy for them to admit the very next morning," Norah pointed out.

And with a sensitiveness Norah had not expected from him Hoff retaliated. "That kind of guilt lasts a long time. Assuming we can get anybody to admit that it must have been Frances Russo he heard screaming, how's that going to help?"

"I wish I knew."

Norah had suggested that she canvass the rear section of the apartment house because since the murder had been committed on

112

the back stairs, the tenants living in the back apartments would have been more aware than the others of the girl's dying screams. She had a list of those originally interviewed, but she was methodically ringing doorbells and checking the list only to see which member of each family had been the one to answer the questions. In 3D it had been a Mr. Benjamin Roche.

A woman answered Norah's ring, a young woman with black hair and a creamy skin and scowl lines already well established across what should have been a clear brow. She kept the door on the chain, peering suspiciously through the slit, apparently not at all reassured by the fact that the caller was a woman. Even after Norah identified herself, she was admitted reluctantly.

Norah consulted her list. "Mrs. Amanda Roche?"

"I was just going out." It was acknowledgment and complaint at the same time.

She'd started to get ready, having applied a heavy layer of makeup but still not changed out of slacks and sweater that were not only sloppy but also dirty—the kind of woman who doesn't care what she looks like at home but has plenty of pride outside. "Actually it was your father-in-law that I wanted to see."

"He's out."

"When do you expect him back?"

Amanda Roche hesitated. "If it's about that poor girl that got killed . . . he's already told everything he knew . . . which wasn't much."

"I wanted to go over it with him once again."

"Why? Dad was very upset about the whole business. He felt real bad about not calling the police, but it wasn't his fault—how one who heard the screaming—it woke half the building, but none of the other tenants reported it either. So why pick on him?" Her voice rose querulously.

"Did you hear the screams, Mrs. Roche?" According to the report, she hadn't.

"No, I didn't, and my husband didn't either. Our bedroom's at the front, and we have air conditioning. We slept right through. If Dad had turned on his own air conditioner, he would have been spared the aggravation. But he thinks it's unhealthy, air conditioning, I mean." She shrugged. "We've been through all this."

"Yes, I understand, and I'm sorry to trouble you again." Norah offered an apologetic smile, but Amanda Roche remained set in determined sullenness. "If you'll just tell me when you expect Mr. Benjamin Roche . . ."

Somewhere in the back of the apartment a baby cried. The young woman broke out into open exasperation. "There! You've wakened the baby!"

She'd been the one doing the shouting, Norah thought as Amanda Roche stalked out. What was eating her anyway?

The time away placating the baby had evidently also served to reinforce the mother's resistance. When she returned, she faced Norah squarely. "I might as well put it on the line, miss. I don't want you to come back and talk to Dad. I don't want him harassed anymore. He's a sick old man. That girl's death upset him. He's taken the whole thing very personally."

"I have no intention of harassing anyone, Mrs. Roche."

"Good. Besides, he has nothing to tell you." She looked at her watch. "Now, I'm sorry, but I really have to get moving."

Norah nodded. "Of course. I'll come back this evening."

Indignation emanated from Amanda Roche like an electric charge. Norah thought that if she were to reach out a finger, sparks would jump the gap between them. "Can you force yourself on us like that? Don't we have any recourse against you people? Doesn't the plain, ordinary citizen have any rights or privacy anymore?"

"I'll come back this evening, Mrs. Roche. If your father-in-law says he doesn't want to talk to me, that'll be the end of it," Norah stated quietly and left.

She walked to the end of the hall and stopped behind a jog in the wall. The housewife's antagonism was out of all proportion to the situation. There had to be more to it than just protecting an old man's emotional health. Norah was now very interested to see the old man. He'd be along any minute, because of course Mrs. Roche couldn't go until he returned—she couldn't leave the infant unattended. That explained her anxiousness to get rid of Norah. The minutes passed. No one came up in the elevator, and Amanda Roche remained in the apartment. Norah had an idea. She went to the back and rang for the service elevator.

"Is there a laundry room?" she asked the operator.

114

"Sure."

"Would you take me down, please?"

It wasn't so much a room as an alcove in the basement. The only person there was a small, sturdy, and lonesome-looking old man. He sat on a stool with a newspaper folded to the crossword puzzle on his lap; pencil in hand, he stared through the glass door of the dryer at the tumbling clothes as intently as though it were a television screen. His skin had the tight, stretched look of the very aged that erased lines and gave a false look of youth. By contrast the powder-white hair, scraggy eyebrows, and unhealthy pallor were even sadder.

"Hello."

He looked around. "Hello."

"This is a very nice laundry area. The machines look brand new."

"They were installed six months ago."

He was dispirited—well, you could hardly expect enthusiasm on the subject of laundry machines. Still, it was apparent that he was not a well man, and Norah didn't want to upset him with the bald announcement that she was a police officer. "I'm just taking a look around. My name is Norah Mulcahaney."

"Benjamin Roche," he replied.

So she'd been right—the father-in-law had been in the building all along and likely to walk into the apartment at any moment. That accounted for Mrs. Roche's nervousness—part of it. Norah smiled and held out her hand.

"Thinking of moving in?" he asked without any real interest, his handshake limp.

She nodded. "It seems like a well-run building."

"As well as any."

"How about the tenants? Nice? Friendly?"

"I guess you're not a New Yorker or you wouldn't ask." Norah looked at him questioningly. "We're no different in this building than anywhere else in the city—we mind our own business."

"I've found New Yorkers to be decent. In fact, in a crisis New Yorkers can be pretty wonderful."

"As a group maybe—individually . . . individually everybody looks out for number one."

"That's natural. But I'm sure that if I were in trouble, if I needed help, I'd get it in New York, here in this building, just as quick or quicker than anywhere else."

For a moment the old man looked at her with rheumy eyes. "I hope you never need it," he said. Then he went back to staring at the tumbling clothes.

"Actually that was one of the things I was wondering about —the building security. You see, I'm alone. A place without twenty-four-hour service is risky, don't you think?"

Roche didn't answer.

"The super, Mr. Jarman, tells me that hiring a round-the-clock staff would mean a considerable raise in rent, and that besides, it's hard to get help to work through the night." She was reaching delicate ground. "I suppose if someone really wants to get in, he'll do it no matter how many doormen and elevator men there are."

"Jarman didn't tell you that a young woman was attacked in this building not three months ago?"

"Really?"

"A man forced his way in, raped her, and killed her. Half the building heard her screams, and nobody did a damn thing. That's the kind of people who live here, Miss Mulcahaney. So maybe you should go somewhere else."

"Why didn't you call the police, Mr. Roche?"

Not only had she not asked him whether he'd heard the screams, Norah had purposely slightly underscored the *you*. He could deny having heard; he could be indignant. Instead, he dropped his head and mumbled so low she could barely catch the words. "Scared, Mr. Roche? You were scared—of what?"

"Send me away . . . old folks' home . . ."

That was what she thought he said, but it didn't make sense.

Benjamin Roche looked up, his sad eyes brimming. "I called the police once before—about the Grogans." His voice cracked, then grew stronger, and the words tumbled over one another like the clothes in the dryer. "The Grogans live right under us, in 2D. They drink a lot, and then they fight, and it ends with him beating her up. She screams; I think she screams until she drives him to hit her, and then she has a reason for screaming. Well, one night I just couldn't take it, and I reported it. By the time the patrol car came, naturally it was over. Mary Grogan had her usual black eye and

116

assorted bruises, but she wouldn't admit James gave them to her. Claimed she fell down, which in her condition wasn't hard to believe. The officer rang our bell to get me to sign the complaint—for disturbing the peace. Got my son and wife up, woke the baby . . . pandemonium it was. The Grogans threatened to sue for defamation of character. I want to tell you I wasn't likely to interfere a second time.''

"Nobody can blame you. You shouldn't blame yourself."

The old man nodded and fell silent. But he couldn't contain himself, and it burst out of him. "I knew it wasn't the Grogans! I knew it right away. For one thing, the Grogans are right under us, but these screams were fainter, coming from farther down. For another . . . I've heard Mary Grogan often enough to recognize her voice. This wasn't her. It was no drunken brawling; it was pure terror.''

No wonder he'd been brooding all this time. Whether or not his calling in would have been in time to save Frances Russo, he thought so. Norah wanted to offer some consolation; in doing so she had to drop further pretense that she knew nothing about the crime. "If the screaming wakened you, then it must have taken a while for you to get oriented, to realize that it wasn't the Grogans fighting, and by then it must have been just about over."

He wouldn't accept the easy out. "I had plenty of time. The screaming didn't wake me up. I was up—I was reading in bed.''

"I understood . . .''

"I had a towel stuffed along the crack under the door so they wouldn't see the light: I'm supposed to turn out the light at ten, get my rest, like a child! I was smoking too!" He threw up his head rebelliously. "I'm not supposed to do that either. So I heard the screams from the beginning, and they went on long enough for me to have called. I should have. My God, I should have just gone into the living room and picked up the phone and called the police. But I thought I ought to tell them. . . . I didn't want Amanda getting mad, so I knocked on their door and woke them. They said I was wrong, I had to be wrong, that it was the Grogans again. They said they weren't about to go through all that aggravation another time. I made them come into my room so they'd hear for themselves . . . and you know what? *She* smelled the cigarette smoke, and that led her to the butts—I'd forgotten to dump them down the toilet. So she started in on me about smoking in bed, and while we were arguing, the screams stopped." He paused; then, with a bitterness that would never be completely gone, he added, "While we were arguing about my smoking, Frannie died."

The tears spilled out of the old man's eyes and coursed silently down the slippery glaze of his cheeks. The distant rumble of a truck passing over a manhole cover in the street above them emphasized the silence in the laundry alcove and made Norah aware that the dryer had stopped operating. Benjamin Roche didn't notice.

"Paul . . . my son . . . he was willing for me to make the call; *she* was the one who said no. When the screams stopped, Paul took me aside and said it was all over anyway so there wasn't any point in calling. So, I gave in, and we all went back to bed. I even slept." He sighed. "The next day, when we found out . . . I wanted to volunteer to talk to the police. Again Paul was willing, but she pointed out that we really had nothing to tell, nothing that was going to do Frannie any good. 'What purpose would it serve?' she kept asking. We didn't see anything; we didn't know anything. All that would happen would be that we'd get our names in the papers, that people wouldn't understand the prior situation with the Grogans: all they'd care about would be that we hadn't bothered to make a simple telephone call. We'd be harassed by cranks. . . . Actually, Paul is a social worker, so it would look extra bad for him."

Evidently guilt nagged Amanda Roche too. Her antagonism had been not so much in defense of the old man but an attempt to hide her own culpability. At least she had the decency to feel ashamed.

"Paul said it was to be my decision, but *she* was right on that score—I didn't have anything to tell."

Her brief moment of relenting toward Amanda Roche passed, and Norah was angry again, both at her and at the old man's son. They'd made it impossible for him to do what he wanted to do; then they'd made him bear the burden of their decision. And Benjamin Roche was wasting away under it. Could it be he feared that what the young wife wanted was for him to become so bemused, so irresponsible that she would have the excuse to put him away?

"Did you know Frances Russo well?"

Roche smiled shyly. "We used to keep each other company down here Saturdays while we waited for the laundry. Sometimes we talked—about anything and everything—other times we played gin. We played for pennies and put the winnings in a kitty. When we had enough, we were going to go out to dinner and a show. That's the kind of girl Frannie was—saving her money to give an old man a night out."

Maybe there was a touch of jealousy in the daughter-in-law's feeling; maybe she resented the old man's being so close to another young woman.

"I guess by this time you realize that I didn't just walk in here by accident, Mr. Roche. I'm a police officer. It wasn't my intention to trick you, just to sort of ease you into talking. I hope you're not angry."

"I guess I knew you weren't just making conversation. I was glad to get it off my chest; I've been wanting to for a long time. I'm glad it was to a police officer. I wish I had more to tell you, more that could be useful to you, that is. But maybe Amanda is right —none of it helps. Does it?" he asked hopefully.

"Hard to say, Mr. Roche. If you don't mind dwelling on it for a little longer . . . You didn't mention whether your window was open that night when you brought your son and Mrs. Roche into your room. I assume it was."

"Yes."

"Did you look out the window at all and try to locate where the screams were coming from?"

"No. The sounds appeared to be coming from inside the building. That is, I took it for granted. . . ."

"Yes. Well, we know now where they were coming from. So you didn't go near the window at all?"

"Yes, I did. After Paul and Amanda left. See, *she'd* closed it and turned on the air conditioner to clear the smoke and the smell out, she said. I don't like the air conditioner; it aggravates my arthritis. She knows that, but she turns it on every chance she gets—says it cuts out the air pollution. Well, I turn it off just as fast—I'd sooner choke on the pollution than die of pneumonia. So the minute she was gone I turned it off and opened the window again."

"Did you happen to look out into the street? Did you notice any activity? I know you weren't looking particularly; still, you might just subconsciously have noticed something or someone."

"After ten o'clock at night there's not much moving around here, miss . . . uh . . . Officer. Two blocks over and you've got bars, restaurants, theaters, and God knows what else—it's livelier than noon. But on this block—it's like they'd dropped one of those bombs I heard about on the radio—kills the people but leaves the buildings standing and everything around on the streets intact."

"Just put yourself back into that moment at the window, Mr. Roche. Try to re-create how you felt, your exact movements as you closed it. Did it move easily? Did it stick? Was the night air fresh or still hot? Was there a moon?"

Benjamin Roche sat very still. Just the attempt to be useful was restoring him. He was not only calmer, he was recovering some of the testy determination that every old man is entitled to. "The window stuck; the window always sticks no matter how much of that sliding stuff I spray into the track. I couldn't pound on it because I didn't want *her* to hear me and come back, so I had to wrestle it. While I was trying to force it up . . ." His voice grew stronger; his eyes gleamed as the memory returned. "I did look down the street, and I saw a man crossing over from our side. I did. I remember. He was walking fast, not running, but fast . . . and there was something else. . . ." Roche closed his eyes and grimaced. "Yes! I know what it was. He was hunched forward with his arms wrapped around himself . . . like this." Roche demonstrated. "Like he was cold."

"But it was mid-July."

"That's true. Maybe it was some kind of nervous habit?"

"Could be. Go on, Mr. Roche. Go on."

Roche stopped hugging himself. "That's all."

"What did he look like?"

"Oh, Miss . . . Officer Mulcahaney . . . I can't remember that."

"Try."

He made the effort again, closing his eyes and the concentration pulling his smooth skin into cracks and crevices, but it didn't work. "It's three stories down to the street; I had my reading glasses on, and they're only good for the close-up stuff. Anyhow, the light out there isn't the best. The block committee's been agitating to get those new vapor lamps installed, but it's six months now they've been trying. I wouldn't have been able to see what he looked like even if I'd been trying.''

The man Roche had noticed wasn't necessarily the man who had killed Frances Russo anyway. Norah hesitated. Should she show him the mug shot? Could it prejudice the case later? She decided to show it. "Have you ever seen this man before, Mr. Roche? In the building or around the neighborhood?''

He studied it closely. "No. I've never seen that man.''

"All right, Mr. Roche, thank you. I certainly appreciate your cooperation.'' Norah paused. "About your daughter-in-law, if you'd rather she didn't know that we talked together, well . . . there's no need for you to mention it. I won't.''

"You won't? That's really nice of you. That's real nice. . . .'' He stopped. The color rose once more into his smooth cheeks like the most delicate watercolor tint on old porcelain. He pulled himself stiffly erect. "No. Let her know. I'm through hiding things. From now on I'm going to do what I want. I'll stay up as long as I want or watch television if I feel like it and smoke—in the living room! If she doesn't like it . . . well, I can move out; I can get a place of my own.''

Norah smiled at him. "I don't think she's going to let you do that, Mr. Roche. I get the idea you're real handy to have around.'' She gestured around her at the machines. "You take care of the laundry. I suppose you must run plenty of errands. Then there's the baby-sitting: I'm sure you're always available for that.'' Norah thought of the housewife impatiently waiting to get out for a little respite from the household drudgeries. "I don't suppose Amanda would be able to play Mah-Jongg with the girls or go on shopping expeditions or to matinees if you weren't available, would she?

And how about at night? If your son and his wife want to go out to a movie, say, you oblige, don't you? Baby-sitters are pretty expensive if you can even get one. Have you ever considered charging?''

"Charging?'' The rheumy eyes widened; they sparkled. From a low chuckle he proceeded to nice, round guffaws. "You've got a head on your shoulders, Officer Mulcahaney. Plus which you're a real nice lady.''

Norah left him to unload the dryer. As he sorted and neatly folded the clothes, Benjamin Roche was humming.

* * *

121

Upstairs in the lobby Bobby Hoff waited. "Anything?" he asked.

Norah pursed her lips. "Maybe. I'm not sure. You?"

He was sure. "Waste of time."

"Have to try."

"I know. I know. Let's go to the deli."

Norah was surprised. "The doorman said it closed at ten. She wouldn't have been going there."

"I meant for lunch."

"I'm not hungry. Listen, you eat, and I'll grab the subway uptown to Union Utilities. According to Schonbar's report, the men on the double date both worked in the same office as Russo. I want to talk to them."

Hoff looked uncomfortable. "We're supposed to stick together. Sorry, Norah, captain's orders." He saw her bristling. "Besides, a message came in for you to call Officer Dollinger. You could phone from the deli."

Dolly! The fingers of dread tapped along Norah's spine, but a thrill of excitement went through her at the same time. She forgot about being indignant. "I guess I'm hungry after all."

13

"You sure are hard to keep up with." Dolly's cheery greeting crackled with energy. "I wish you'd let me know the next time you shift districts."

"Sorry, Dolly, it just happened. I haven't had the chance. What's up?"

Dolly's tone changed. "We've had a complaint."

Norah's stomach knotted. "Dana?"

"Looks like it. The assailant followed the woman into the building, grabbed her, and dragged her around to the back stairs and up to the first-floor landing. Threatened to bash her head in if she resisted. She didn't."

"Praise God," Norah murmured. "Is she badly hurt?"

"Could be worse."

"You mean he was interrupted? Somebody scared him off?"

"No."

"Well, what? Come on, Dolly, what?" Norah was amazed to hear her friend chuckle.

"I'm sorry. It's not really funny, of course, but . . . I don't know if you're ready for this, Norah. Should I tell you? Maybe you'd rather go over and talk to the woman yourself?"

"Tell me, Dolly, just please tell me."

"She's a prostie."

"She's a what?"

"A prostitute. Would you believe it? And mad as hell about what happened to her. Called right in and demanded to have a detective go over there. Gave him a real blast too, told him her profession was irrelevant to the complaint—in just those words, I may add. Told him she knows her rights and she's entitled to the same protection as any married woman. And that's true. She wants the man caught and charged."

"Did she give a description?"

"You bet your life she did. Right down to the leather strap of the watch on his left wrist."

"Has anybody shown her a mug shot?"

"Not yet. The investigating officer had no way of knowing there was a possible suspect, and the report just came in to us. Before getting back to Detective Rand, the lieutenant wanted you to be informed."

As promised, Norah thought.

"There's a consideration here too. If we go ahead and show Miss Eva Lynn—cute name, huh?—if we show her the mug shot and she makes Rand, she's going to be hot for us to pull him in.

She's not going to be shy about going to court and confronting him either. The point is how much weight is her word going to carry in front of the grand jury?"

"Isn't his luck ever going to run out?" Norah exclaimed.

"Bound to. Our problem is, can we afford to wait? Lieutenant Wilburn wants to know how you're making out on the homicide investigation."

"We've barely started."

"Well, she says to tell you that we'll hold off on the mug shot for a while. The more corroboration that can be presented when

123

Miss Lynn goes into court, the better. In the meantime, if Dana thinks the woman didn't complain . . ."

"It's going to bolster his confidence, and the attacks may become more frequent."

"So we can't wait too long. So keep us advised. OK, Norah?"

"OK, Dolly. And . . . tell the lieutenant thanks for me."

She came out of the phone booth to find Hoff at the counter enjoying lunch. Really enjoying it. He waved to the plate beside his.

"I ordered you a hot roast beef sandwich."

She'd about decided to skip lunch after all, but . . . "My favorite, Bobby, thanks." She perched on the stool and started eating. Was it really that delicious, or was she so hungry that anything would have tasted terrific? They ate in silence. Hoff finished first.

"Pie?"

Norah was careful about her weight, but in the last month she'd lost six pounds. "Sure."

She cleaned her plate as quickly and thoroughly as Bobby. When she'd drained the second cup of coffee, Norah had to admit that she felt a lot better, even more optimistic. She rumpled the paper napkin and tossed it on the counter. "OK, on to Union Utilities."

Hoff hung back. "Norah, neither one of the men on that date was a blond."

"I know, but Frances Russo hadn't dated in months. Then on the first night she goes out she gets herself raped and killed. It seems like too much of a coincidence."

George Laighold, junior executive and junior Casanova, was aggrieved. "Now don't misunderstand me, Detective Mulcahaney. I feel terrible about what happened to the poor kid, but it's got nothing to do with me. It was just my lousy luck that I was the last one to see her alive—aside from the killer, naturally," he added hastily. "If ever I regretted anything in my life, I regret going out with Frances Russo that night."

I don't doubt it, Norah thought. Bobby hadn't been able to find a parking place but had agreed it would be safe enough for her to come on up to the Union Utilities office while he continued circling. So she was interviewing George Laighold alone in a corner of the company cafeteria, which by this hour was nearly empty.

"Frankly I don't even know why she came out with us!" Laighold continued to complain. "She was a wet blanket all night; she hardly took a drink; dancing with her was like holding a stick, and when I took her home . . . I made a pass at her, sure—what did she expect? And you know what she did? She burst into tears! Can you tie that?"

By now the last straggler had left the cafeteria to go back to work, and Norah and Laighold were completely alone. Yet Laighold took a quick look around before giving Norah a knowing wink and lowered his voice. "I don't mind a little friendly tussle; well, I expect to have to use a little persuasion. Besides, it adds spice." He smoothed back hair that was already perfectly in place, dark, with the gray so strategic it appeared painted in for maximum effect. "And the girl has her pride; she doesn't want you to think she's a pushover. But tears! Who needs it? So I left. When I got back downstairs, Sylvia and Ernie were gone. Naturally they didn't expect me to be back down that fast. The doorman couldn't get me another cab, so I had to hop the subway, but I managed to catch the eleven-fifty-nine to Brewster." Again he smoothed his perfectly ordered hair. "The other detective, whatever his name was . . . he checked that out."

Norah knew it. "You left Miss Russo standing outside her apartment door, or did you get inside?"

"If you call the vestibule getting inside, then I got inside, but that was it."

"Did Miss Russo know you're married?"

"It's no secret. I'm not that kind; I don't pretend—the girl knows exactly where she stands with me. When Russo first came to work for the company, well, you know how it is, everybody tries to make it with the new girl—kind of a competition. But she turned everybody down. At first we thought she was playing hard to get, so we kept trying. It was a challenge—you know how men are. After a while we gave up. At least I did. She really wasn't worth the effort." He must have realized how he sounded, because he hastened to add, "I don't mean to speak ill of the dead, but . . . she was pretty enough, but she had no zip. I mean, there are plenty

125

of pretty girls around, and most of them are also accommodating.''

"That's exactly the point, Mr. Laighold. Frances Russo was a shy, reserved girl, and she'd made it clear she wasn't interested in playing around. So why the change? Why should she suddenly accept your invitation?''

"Beats me. Maybe she got tired of being alone. Anyhow, you've got it wrong—I didn't approach her. Sylvia Petrie set up the date. Sylvia came to me and said how about me and Fran double dating with her and Ernie? I thought she was putting me on, but she said no, it was for real. So I said sure, why not? So why don't you go and talk to Sylvia, Detective Mulcahaney? She's on the fifteenth floor in Finance.''

Sylvia Petrie's name appeared in Schonbar's report with the notation that she had left the country the day after the homicide on a business trip with her boss and thus had not been available for interrogation. Evidently Schonbar had considered the men's testimony sufficient and hadn't bothered to look her up on her return. Norah pushed the cold coffee aside. "I'll do that, Mr. Laighold.''

"Fine. Uh . . . Detective Mulcahaney? You're not going to go out to my house and talk to my wife, are you? As I said, the other detective, whatever his name was, he already checked out the time I got home and all. He really upset Betty.''

I'll bet, Norah thought. If Betty hadn't known what her dashing husband was up to, it must have been a shock to find out. If she had known, being forced to admit she knew would have been almost as bad.

"My life's been pretty miserable these past three months, Detective Mulcahaney. Betty just doesn't trust me anymore. I mean, I can't even stop off on the way home for a drink. If I'm so much as half an hour late, she puts me through a regular inquisition. I've just about got her calmed down, so I'd appreciate it if you didn't go out and stir her up again.''

According to Schonbar, the time Laighold got home indicated that he had in fact caught the 11:59. Therefore he couldn't have gone back up to Frances Russo's apartment after the doorman went off duty. There was no need to interview Mrs. Laighold a second time. Norah just didn't feel he was entitled to that reassurance. Let him stew. "It depends on what Miss Petrie has to say.''

He shrugged to show lack of concern, but it didn't quite work.

126

"She'll say I play around. What man doesn't? But I'm cured now, Detective Mulcahaney. Boy, am I ever!"

Norah noticed the twitch at the upper corner of his mouth, the earnest look of his brown eyes. No doubt the incident had scared George Laighold, but cured him? She wouldn't put money on it.

"Who arranged the date?"

"I did," Sylvia Petrie admitted readily. "I was only trying to help."

Norah was glad Sylvia Petrie had suggested using her boss' office for the interview instead of the cafeteria—not only was it a lot more comfortable, in fact luxurious, but one more cup of coffee would have been more than she could take. Evidently the secretary could have used a cup of something, if only to wrap her hands around. She was a tall, highly polished woman, extremely attractive but at the age when the maintenance was considerable—a full-blown rose held erect by florist's wire. Her nervousness caused the fine lines to crack the perfection of her makeup. Yet Norah had the impression that Sylvia Petrie was glad to see her, because, like Roche, there was something she needed to get off her conscience.

"How do you mean—help?"

"Fran was upset because her boyfriend wouldn't pop the question."

Norah hardly believed what she had heard. She sat quite still. It was that way often—you went along asking the same questions, more or less, getting back the same answers with minimal varia-tions, then suddenly, without warning, somebody said something different, opened a whole new aspect, and from then on, everything accelerated. "Boyfriend?" she repeated, keeping the surprise out of her voice. "I didn't know Frances Russo had a boyfriend."

"Oh, yes." The sophisticated woman was too concerned with herself to be aware of Norah's deep interest. "They were ideally suited—both lonely, shy, morally old-fashioned. Fran was really impressed that he never made a pass at her. Never even went into the building with her, much less up to her apartment."

Which explained why no one in the building had ever seen

Frances Russo with him. Norah would have been willing to bet that Dana was the one—who else would have a reason for being so circumspect, so secretive? "How did they meet?"

Sylvia Petrie smiled. "It was a pickup."

"A pickup!"

"In a way. Fran took the car in to the garage to have the mechanic . . ."

"Frances Russo had a car?"

"No, no, she was thinking of buying one, secondhand, and she wanted it checked out by a mechanic."

So she had not been a chance victim. So Dana at that time was still holding to his pattern.

"The fellow who looked it over advised her against buying it. She was grateful. A couple of days later she happened to notice him in the neighborhood, and she went up to thank him."

God! Norah thought, that must have startled Earl Dana. Evidently it had also put him off—for a while, anyway.

Sylvia Petrie smiled ruefully. "At first Fran thought it was great that he kept hands off; after a while it began to worry her. She wondered whether the whole thing wasn't a little too platonic, if maybe he didn't really care for her. I told her he probably took his cue from her and that she should loosen up a little, indicate to him that she wasn't all that straitlaced. I convinced her that if she cared for him, she should let him know it. Invite him up for dinner, I said—they'd never really been alone together, if you can believe that."

Norah could.

The secretary went on. "I told her again what I'd been trying to get through to her all along—that things aren't the way mother told you: to get a man a girl has to put out."

Norah held her breath.

"She wouldn't buy it." Miss Petrie sighed. "She insisted he'd lose respect for her if she so much as hinted that she was willing to go to bed with him. So the only other thing for her to do was to try to make him jealous. I told her the next time he called, she shouldn't be so anxious to see him; she should put him off. The time after that she should tell him she had another date and have one."

"And she agreed and you set up the double date?"

128

"Right."

"And did Frances tell. . . ?" Norah caught herself about to mention Earl Dana by name. "Did she tell her boyfriend?"

"Of course. That was the whole idea. She spent the whole evening looking over her shoulder as though she expected him to turn up. It got so bad she had me doing it too. When we were outside the various places waiting for cabs, I got really nervous. I mean, I didn't want a scene."

Maybe he wasn't following her, but he certainly could have been waiting near the apartment house for her to come home. If it was Dana, he got off from work in plenty of time to have been there. Frances Russo had sensed that there was something wrong in their relationship and had blamed herself, her own reticence, her lack of sex appeal; whereas the fault lay with the boyfriend. For the moment Norah permitted herself to assume it was Dana. Maybe Dana had actually cared for her; maybe Frances Russo's unusual shyness and modesty had affected him enough so that he was trying to go straight. As long as she made no sexual demands on him, as long as she maintained the stance of purity, he was not likely to touch her. Yet he must have sensed the delicate balance of his emotions, or he would not have continued to avoid being seen with her. Frances Russo's intuition had been more reliable than her friend's extensive experience. When she went out on that double date, though, she reduced herself to the same level as Dana's other women, and he used her in the same way. Sylvia Petrie's good intentions had not really brought about the tragedy, but they had hastened it. There was no use telling her so.

"Did you catch sight of anyone loitering around the building when you dropped Frances and her date off at the end of the evening?" Norah asked.

"I wasn't looking anymore. By that time I was just relieved the whole thing was over. And I was sort of busy in the taxi anyhow."

Well, Frances Russo had been looking for him all night and could be she'd finally spotted him. It could be why she was so nervous about Laighold's going upstairs with her and why she burst into tears at his advances. She got rid of him fast but not fast enough. Dana assumed the worst. A normally jealous boyfriend might have gone storming up to confront his girl, might even have forced himself on her against her will—in the apartment. Dana would have compulsively followed his established pattern. He would have lured her outside.

The boyfriend was the only one who could have got her to go out again. Probably all it had taken was a simple telephone call to say he wanted to see her. She, thinking the ruse had worked and he was going to declare himself, would have gone out to meet him eagerly and joyously.

Where was the meeting place to be, though? In a restaurant or nearby bar? In the park? Afterward had he walked her back home, escorting her inside the building for the first time? Or maybe he hadn't bothered to meet her? Maybe he'd let her wait the lonely, endless, ever more disconsolate, sad minutes and hours worrying that something had happened to him? Maybe, finally, she was returning alone to her apartment to call the police for help for him while he waited in the shadows to spring on her from behind. She probably didn't know it was he when she was grabbed, forced into the building, dragged up the back stairs to the first landing, and thrown to the floor. When he straddled her, then she saw his face, and then she screamed. In surprise, in shock, in horror. Of course, she pleaded with him: she loved him; she couldn't believe that he would actually do what he threatened. Of course she fought, kicking, tearing at his hair, scratching, instead of meekly subsiding as all his other victims had done, because Frances Russo believed he was inflicting the jealousy she herself had purposely aroused, and jealousy is one facet of love, and maybe she thought she could cry and plead him back to reason again. And when she saw it was useless . . . of course she screamed again and went on screaming as long as she was able.

"How is it you didn't give this information to the police?"

"Nobody came around, that is, not that first day. Actually we didn't know about it till the afternoon. Fran didn't show up for work, and I did try to reach her at home, but when there was no answer, I figured . . . well, that she wanted to keep to herself. Then just before quitting time somebody, I've forgotten who, spotted the item in the late edition. I was just horrified. Everybody was horrified. The next day, I left for Europe with my boss. We covered all the major cities and were gone three weeks."

It was reasonable that Schonbar had not got to Union Utilities that first day the crime was discovered; there would have been too much to do at the scene. "You had plenty of time to call that evening."

"It didn't occur to me. I swear, Detective Mulcahaney. According to the paper, Fran was raped and killed by a stranger."

"And of course you didn't want to risk being detained, maybe having to cancel your trip."

"No, no, it wasn't that. I was just that I never thought of him as a suspect. I mean, how could he have done it? The man was undersexed; that was the whole problem between them."

"When you got back and learned the killer hadn't been found, didn't you feel you had an obligation to tell what you knew and let the police draw their own conclusions?"

Sylvia Petrie bit her lips. Her small, artfully madeup eyes framed by false lashes showed her distress and pleaded for the policewoman's understanding. "I didn't want it to get around that I'd been out on that date."

Norah stared at her. "I don't understand."

"Well, you see, well . . . I have a steady arrangement. You understand? The man is very good to me, and I wouldn't want him to find out I cheated on him. Damn it, Detective Mulcahaney, it's Alan Saxon, my boss!"

The secretary sprang to her feet and strode over to her boss' liquor cabinet, where she fixed herself a generous shot of something and drank it off. "I'd got off lucky. I don't mean to be callous, but leaving the next day as we did kept Alan from knowing. Neither George nor Ernie was about to go out of his way to tell him, so why should I? It would have been a useless sacrifice. I never met Fran's boyfriend. I don't even know his name."

Norah was stunned. "She talked about him all the time; she must have called him something—Joe, Mac, Johnny, Clarence—"

"She called him 'Buzz.' "

"Buzz?" Norah repeated in utter frustration. She sighed. "Well, did she ever describe him? Did she mention what kind of work he did?"

Now that she was reassured that Norah wouldn't be running to her boss, Sylvia Petrie was willing to ease her conscience by being as helpful as possible. "I did see him once, though, in Central Park. It was last Easter . . . Easter Sunday. My friend and I were taking a ride in one of those hansom cabs. . . ." Miss Petrie flushed.

Busy girl, Norah thought, but she wasn't interested in the men on the secretary's string.

"Actually he was my cousin. Really. Well, it was a beautiful day and very hot. Maybe you remember? It was like summer. So. There was no traffic in the park except for those horse-drawn carriages and bicycles. Fran was riding a bicycle along with a young man. We passed and waved to each other. We were both moving slowly enough so that I had plenty of time to look him over."

"You're sure this man was with Frances Russo?"

"Absolutely. They were riding side by side. Anyhow, I asked her the next day if that was Buzz and she said yes."

"Good. Can you describe him?"

"I certainly can. He was a hippie. What I mean is that he looked like one—long blond hair, mustache, like that. I certainly never thought Fran would go for that type." Sylvia Petrie was still shaken. She glanced longingly toward the bar, then settled for one of her employer's cigarettes instead of another drink.

"How about his eyes?"

"He was wearing dark glasses."

It wasn't much of a description, but what there was of it was consistent with Catherine Mercer's. "How was he dressed?"

"The usual jeans and sloppy shirt."

"Short sleeves or long?"

"Oh, one of those awful singlet things. I remember thinking it wasn't really that hot, and how unattractive men look in them unless they have a good, healthy tan and are really well built."

"He wasn't?"

She shook her head. "He was awfully thin . . . and pale. I don't mean to be sacrilegious, but he reminded me of those paintings of the ancient martyrs—bushy hair and plenty of beard, but no body hair at all. Have you noticed?"

"But this man didn't have a beard, only a mustache?"

"That's right. It was just an analogy."

"I see. Since you observed him so closely, then you probably noticed whether he had a tattoo on his arm."

"I didn't notice a tattoo."

132

"It would have been quite large, covering the entire forearm."

"No, nothing like that. As I told you, he was so white and hairless I would certainly have noticed anything like that."

Norah showed her the mug shot, but Sylvia Petrie shook her head. "I don't see any resemblance."

The buzzer sounded from the reception room. The secretary got up instantly, ground out her cigarette, replaced the used glass on the bar counter, and fixing a bright smile on her face, went to the door. She might be Alan Saxon's mistress, but it was evident her privileges did not extend to the office.

It was only Bobby Hoff.

"Good timing, Bobby," Norah greeted him. "I was just leaving."

"Great," he answered. "I just found a parking place."

14

Miss Eva Lynn's entire evening was engaged by a favorite client. He was from New Orleans, and he enjoyed taking her out and being seen with her as much as their later, more private entertainments. They'd had dinner at an elegant French restaurant. Well insulated against the cold by good food and good drink, they were strolling along Third Avenue to her place, stopping from time to time to peer into shopwindows. Michel Feraux was a generous man, and Eva Lynn knew that if she admired something suffi-

ciently, he might very well be back the next day to buy it for her.

She was thus steering him toward a favorite jewelry store that had a brooch she was interested in on display.

But before they got to the jewelry store, Michel Feraux stopped. "Say, this place is new, isn't it?"

It was a restaurant Eva hadn't noticed before. "I guess." She shrugged and tried to move him on.

"Want to go in for a nightcap?"

If he drank any more, he wouldn't remember the brooch she intended pointing out to him, but you didn't tell "Mitch" he didn't need another drink. "It doesn't look like much."

"Can't tell from the outside. Come on, a quickie. What do you say?"

She had to say yes while he was still asking. Eva Lynn smiled and gave up on the brooch, for the time being, and they went in. She'd been right, she thought, as she waited for Mitch to check his coat—it really wasn't much of a place. Ordinary. It had the usual bar with back-lit glass shelves and the usual somewhat wider dining room section at the rear. Not many customers either. In the rosy half darkness Eva Lynn squinted—she didn't wear glasses on a date. . . .

"What would you like, sweetheart?"

She was just turning around to answer when she spotted him. For a moment Eva Lynn didn't move. Then she backed up so hard and fast she rammed into Mitch. "Come on, quick, we've got to get out of here."

He followed, of course. "Eva, what the hell!" For now he was only curious.

"He's in there. I saw him. It's him. Listen, we've got to call the police."

"Who? Who's in there? What are you talking about? Police? Did you say police?" Now he was alarmed.

"Yes. Listen, Mitch. . . . I can't go back in there, because he might see me. So you go on in and call the police. Tell them they've got to get right over here, fast. Tell them. . . ." Suddenly Eva Lynn realized exactly what she was asking and of whom she was asking it. "No, no, I'll call. I'll go to the drugstore down the street and call myself. You just go back in there and get yourself that drink at the bar and wait. OK, Mitch? OK, lover? You'll do that for me, won't you? He's sitting in the back at the right-hand side of the dining room at a table for two. He's got dark brown curly hair, and he's wearing a gray suit. Please, Mitch." She gave Michel Feraux a slight shove toward the restaurant entrance; then she ran.

She was still breathing hard when her call was put through to the precinct.

As she reached for the ringing phone in the dark, Norah automatically noted the time on the luminous bedside clock. Only eleven fifteen, but it seemed like the middle of the night. She'd

134

gone to bed right after dinner, weary with discouragement and with the aches of an incipient cold. "Yes?"

"Detective Mulcahaney?"

"Yes." She pulled herself up in bed, shifted the receiver to the other hand, and switched on the table lamp.

"This is Rand at the Nineteenth. It's about that rape complaint by Miss Eva Lynn. If you don't want the whole case to break wide open, you'd better get down here—fast."

You certainly wouldn't take her for a prostitute, Norah thought as she walked into the station and got her first look at Eva Lynn. In her Emba Haze mink and bottle-green velvet pantsuit she looked like a young, upper-class matron—pretty, in a nice, well-bred way, but nothing spectacular. That, of course, was the idea. She was sitting on one of the wooden benches along the hall outside the squad room, head tilted back, and resting against the wall, eyes closed, evidently resigned to a long wait and determined to stick it out.

"Miss Lynn?" Norah asked quietly.

Her eyes opened instantly, wide, alert, and the same intense green as her outfit. "Yes."

"I'm Detective Mulcahaney. I'd like to talk to you."

She looked Norah over with considerable skepticism. "What's to talk about? I was raped. I made an official complaint, and nobody gives a damn; nobody's done anything. Well, I realize that it's not so easy to go out and find one man in eight million just from a description, but once you're told where he is. . . ! The minute I spotted him I called in and was told a patrol car was on its way over. You know how long I waited in front of that restaurant? In the cold? Half an hour! That's how long."

"I'm sorry about that, Miss Lynn."

"Sure. That helps. If a person was really in trouble . . . I mean a person could be dead in half an hour, you know that? By the time the patrol car showed up, the guy was gone. Naturally. What else?"

"I understand the suspect took a cab and you noted the license number. That was quick thinking, Miss Lynn."

"Well, thanks. Detective Rand was very complimentary too, but he's not doing anything about it."

Norah had been briefed by the harassed man. "I believe he explained to you that . . ."

"That he can't do anything till the cabby reports back to the garage at the end of his shift."

"That's right, because there's no way of communicating with him."

"And I told Detective Rand that I would wait." She uncrossed her legs and recrossed them the other way, pulled a pack of cigarettes out of a small green satin bag, and lit up.

"Till four A.M.?"

"Till whatever."

"You're assuming that the cab took the suspect home. Suppose it only took him to another bar."

"Are you telling me you couldn't trace him from another bar?"

"I don't know whether we could or not. I'm just pointing out that your wait won't necessarily be over when we talk to the cabby."

"OK." She blew a puff of smoke upward toward the ceiling.

Norah suppressed a smile. "I admire your spirit, Miss Lynn."

On the verge of making a snappy retort, Eva Lynn changed her mind. "You mean that, don't you?"

"I certainly do. Most women would have been terrified to come suddenly and unexpectedly on the man who had raped them. You acted coolly and quickly in calling the police, and you had plenty of courage to stand outside that restaurant and watch while he got into the cab and then to note the license number."

"Well . . . thanks. It cost me, let me tell you. My . . . friend, the man I was with . . . I left him at the restaurant to go and call; when I got back, he'd split. So I'm out a night's work. Probably I've lost him for good. Not that I blame him for not wanting to get involved with the police. I'm not complaining about that. What burns me is that I'm getting the runaround. Don't try to snow me, Detective Mulcahaney; I know what you're all up to, and I know why, and I'm not going to stand for it. I know my rights. If necessary . . ."

"Miss Lynn!" Norah had to shout to get through her indignation. "I'll admit that we haven't followed up on your complaint as quickly as we might have, but it's not for the reason you think." She took the now-well-worn mug shot of Earl Dana out of her handbag. "Is this the man who attacked you?"

"Yes! Yes, that's him. How did you know? How come you've got his picture?"

Norah hesitated. She'd decided that the best way to get Eva Lynn's cooperation was to be honest with her. And she was entitled to the truth. Still, Norah wasn't sure whether she should bring up the matter of the homicide. "He's a suspect in another rape case. The complaint you filed with Detective Rand was forwarded to Officer Dollinger at the Rape Analysis and Investigation Squad. Officer Dollinger noted the similarity of your description to that of the suspect in a case I'm working on as well as the similarity of the MO. So she contacted me."

"You mean . . . three detectives have been working on this?"

"Plus my partner, Detective Hoff, Captain Blake, our commander, and Lieutenant Wilburn, who heads the Rape Squad."

"I didn't realize. . . . I'm sorry. I thought . . . I thought nobody gave a damn because . . . I thought you were all probably laughing at me."

"Nobody's laughing, Miss Lynn."

The prostitute pressed her lips together and gulped. "So how come nobody showed me his picture before?" she asked, but without rancor.

"We were afraid you'd insist on having him picked up right away. We know where he is, but we'd like you to agree to let us hold off till we have more on him."

"More?"

Norah decided to go all the way. "He's also under suspicion of murder."

"Oh, God! Somebody he raped?" Eva Lynn looked sick.

"Someone who resisted. So be patient, Miss Lynn. Give us a little time. If we can't make headway, I promise we'll bring him in on your complaint."

"Take as long as you need." Eva Lynn dropped her cigarette in the sand-filled container near the bench, got up, and pulled her mink coat around her as she shivered with inner cold. "Don't you think it's kind of risky letting him stay loose? Shouldn't you warn the girl?"

"What girl?"

"I assume she was his girlfriend. I don't suppose he was taking his next victim out to dinner."

"You didn't mention he was with a girl."

"No, I guess I didn't. I should have. I was too annoyed over the delay. I'm sorry. But, Detective Mulcahaney, you ought to warn her. He's a real bastard, this guy. I've been in a lot of rough situations; I've taken abuse, all kinds, but . . . he hurt me. I mean, he really hurt me."

Tracing the girl was easy. The driver had her address in his log. He'd driven there first, waited while Dana saw her inside, then driven him home. Dana evidently was behaving normally with this girl or he wouldn't risk being seen with her. How about the girl though? How deep did her feelings for him go? Norah decided to ask around before approaching her.

Jenna Carpenter was very different from Frances Russo—gay, outgoing, with plenty of friends. She knew her way around. Her neighbors had seen her with Dana frequently in the past month. She made no secret of her feeling about him. With this kind of girl the relationship couldn't remain platonic for long. Maybe Dana had already felt the strain of the inherent demand; maybe he had assaulted Eva Lynn to relieve its tension. Up to now the attacks, those Norah knew about, had been widely separated. The time ran into months between as Dana chose and observed his prospective victim. But Eva Lynn had no car, so she didn't frequent the garage where he now worked; like Gabby, she had been a target of opportunity . . . and need. There had been no preliminary planning with her and might not be with the next victim. He was under severe emotional pressure now which would surely accelerate. How long could he be expected to remain quiescent? Weeks or days? The girl had to be warned. But how do you walk up to a young woman and tell her that a man she's been dating, perhaps getting really serious about, is a rapist—could even be a murderer?

Suppose Jenna Carpenter in turn warned Earl Dana? Suppose she told him the police were closing in? What could he really do? Well, probably he'd do what he'd done before—run. And maybe this time they wouldn't find him quite so easily. Still . . . Norah decided that Jenna Carpenter's safety came first.

The rock and roll on the stereo blasted into the hallway. Inside, Jenna Carpenter's apartment vibrated with color as it did with sound; islands of garish cushions dotted the bare floor, and giant psychedelic posters appeared three-dimensional against white walls. Money had been spent, though, and there was evidence of a certain taste, if this was the kind of thing that turned you on. The girl waved Norah in but showed no inclination to turn down the stereo, certainly not to shut it off. Norah explained that she was making inquiries about a certain Earl Dana, but it wasn't easy to be tactful while shouting.

"Well, Officer, have I got a surprise for you! Earl's already told me all about it."

Jenna Carpenter gathered the loose strands of her long, lanky blond hair in one hand, then flung it all back over her shoulder. The defiant gesture matched open satisfaction in her bright brown eyes. She was a slim, elfin kind of girl with that unhealthy look so typical of the "now" young who seemed to revel in their sickly frailty as in their arrogance. She was dressed in the same gypsy assortment of colors as those with which she had surrounded herself, challenging colors, the battle banners of the war between the generations.

"Sorry to disappoint you, Officer. . . ." And that was a put-down, because she knew the title was Detective. "Earl and I have no secrets from each other. There's nothing about him that I don't know."

It reduced Norah's careful construction for the interview to rubble. Jenna's voice was low; she spoke under the noise, but Norah couldn't manage that. Abruptly she crossed the room and switched off the player. "I doubt that."

Jenna Carpenter made a move as though to put it back on; then she shrugged. "It's a question of life-styles, yours and ours. That reached for ours, but then she got frightened and brought the charges. Fortunately the jury understood, and that was why they didn't return an indictment."

No use trying to reason with her; it would only make Jenna defend Dana more staunchly. "Has he told you about the other women he's assaulted?"

"He's told me about you!" The girl's voice remained low, but there was vehemence in it, and a slow surge of color made her indoor pallor turn feverish. "Oh, yes, he knows all about how you've been sneaking around asking questions from his employers

139

and his landlady. The charge was dismissed! You have no right to blacken his character with unfounded allegations. He could sue you. I'm going to tell him to sue you."

No use reviewing the long, careful investigation, the slow buildup of evidence. Jenna Carpenter was smart, and she'd recognize that it was all circumstantial. She'd gloat over that. Norah hesitated even about mentioning the one case she could prove—the assault on Eva Lynn. Once Jenna found out that Lynn was a prostitute . . . All that was left was the slim hope that she might shake the girl's stubborn trust in Dana enough at least to make her careful.

"Did Earl Dana also tell you what he did last Tuesday night? This past Tuesday night?"

"I think you should ask yourself why you've got this hang-up about Earl," the girl retorted. "Why are you hounding him? Examine your own motives and your own quirks. Can't you accept the fact that you made a mistake when you arrested him?"

"I wasn't the one who arrested him."

Jenna waved that off as a technicality. "Can't you stand being wrong? Too much for your ego?"

"I asked you a simple question, Miss Carpenter. Why won't you answer it? Is it because you don't know where Earl Dana was Tuesday night?"

"I didn't expect a third degree from a woman, but I guess all pigs are alike."

Norah winced. It was the first time she'd been called that, and common as the epithet was, it hurt. "Then I'll tell you where your boyfriend was and what he was doing."

"He was with me." Jenna Carpenter shut Norah off. "He was with me. It was his day off. We went to an early movie and then had dinner."

"What time did you get home?"

"Around ten thirty."

"And did he come in with you?"

"That's none of your business. All right, yes, he did."

"And what happened?"

A new wave of color suffused her face right up to the pale hairline. "He didn't rape me, if that's what you're after. Nothing happened at all. Earl is the sweetest, gentlest, most respectful man

I've ever known. He's never made a pass at me. How about that? How does that fit in with your picture of a sex maniac?''

Norah decided it was time to ease up, change direction. ''May I ask how you met?''

''Why not? It was at the Wollman skating rink. Some dumb kid ran into Earl and sent him flying into me. I fell and turned my ankle. Well, I tell you, he was so concerned. . . . He carried me inside, got my skate off, put cold towels on the bruise. Ended up seeing me home in a cab.''

''Well . . .''

''And left. And he didn't call back either, not the next day or the day after. I called him. I called him to thank him and invite him to dinner.''

''And he came?''

''Certainly he came, and the first thing he did was tell me about Gabriella Constante.''

Had he been subconsciously warning her? The effect was that Jenna Carpenter was preconditioned not to believe anything against him. Still, Norah made one last try. ''After Earl left you Tuesday night, he didn't go straight home. He followed a woman into her apartment house, forced his way in the same way he forced his way in behind Gabriella Constante, and assaulted the woman. She lodged an immediate complaint, and she has positively identified his photograph.''

For a moment Norah thought she'd got through. The girl looked shocked, but she rallied.

''I don't care how many photographs she identifies; I don't care if she identifies him in person—she's wrong. Whoever attacked her wasn't Earl. And you know how I know that?'' With another flip of the straying strands of lanky hair, defiant and proud, Jenna Carpenter answered her own question. ''I know it because if Earl had wanted or needed a woman that night or any other night, he could have had me.''

''Did you expect her to thank you?'' Dolly asked. ''Even if she did believe you, she wouldn't admit it. You can confront her with Eva Lynn, and if she really cares about him, which it seems she does, she's going to rationalize that too. She's going to tell herself that he went to another woman out of respect for her, and she's going to think the more of him for it."

"So what's going to happen when Jenna Carpenter won't permit him to go elsewhere? I have to warn her that we suspect him of murder."

They faced each other across the corner of Dolly's desk in the office on Centre Street.

"Suppose you're wrong." Dolly suggested ever so gently. "Suppose Dana didn't kill Frances Russo?"

Norah had come to Dolly because she respected Dolly's shrewdness and her professional logic and because, being a woman, she too would be extra sensitive to this problem. Actually what Norah wanted was for her friend to reinforce her own conviction that Jenna Carpenter had to be told everything. "Don't you think it's significant that he quit his job and moved to another part of the city right after the murder? That he cut and dyed his hair, shaved off his mustache? He must have had a reason."

"Another assault we don't know anything about."

"Oh, Dolly . . ."

"Sylvia Petrie can't make him as the boyfriend. She can't identify the mug shot. OK, you can get around that by the change in appearance, but she's positive the boyfriend didn't have a tattoo, and that you can't get around."

"Then where is the real boyfriend? Why didn't he come forward?"

"He'd hardly come forward if he killed her."

"Are you telling me that we're dealing with two different people?"

"Could be."

"Catherine Mercer says they're one and the same."

"So you have to decide who is wrong—Mercer or Petrie."

The thought had haunted Norah. "No, I won't accept two people. Why should the boyfriend lure Russo out of the apartment and rape her on the first-floor landing? Why should he kill her? Killing her in the particular way Dana threatened to kill Catherine Mercer and Gabby is a little too pat. Only the boyfriend could have got her out of the apartment at that hour of the night. And if you want to stipulate that the boyfriend called her and got her to come

142

out at just the time Dana happened along looking for a victim . . .''
Norah shook her head.

"All right, but you still have to get around the tattoo."

Norah frowned. "Why couldn't the tattoo be part of the change in identity, like cutting and dying his hair?"

"Far out."

"It's sure confusing us."

"Why didn't he change his name?"

"He's a licensed mechanic. How's he going to get another job if he changes his name? Besides, nobody knew his name at the time."

Dolly nodded. "OK, but how did he get the tattoo? There are no tattoo parlors in New York anymore. They were declared illegal in . . . 1963 or thereabouts."

"So he went outside New York."

"Where?" Dolly insisted. "How would he know where to go?"

Norah stared thoughtfully out the window. The light was a murky yellow—snow; that color in the sky meant snow. A cold draft seeped in through the loose window frame, and Norah shivered. She was so terribly sensitive to cold these days. With an effort she paid attention to what Dolly was saying.

"I know it's a disappointment after all the work you've put into it that you can't pin the murder on him, but you have accomplished what you set out to do. You can get him on Eva Lynn's complaint. She's going to make a strong witness, and her charge is going to be stronger because of Gabby's earlier complaint. The grand jury is bound to take that into consideration."

"That's not what you said four days ago," Norah reminded her almost absently as she watched the light shifting to a greenish cast—yes, definitely snow was on the way.

"That was when I thought we could get him on the murder rap," Officer Dollinger admitted. "Now I think we should go with what we've got. Norah? Are you with me?"

Tired, she was so tired all the time and not for lack of sleep; she was getting plenty of sleep, too much. "Sorry, I was thinking. Suppose the grand jury turns him loose a second time. And then we do get something that makes it possible to bring him in on the homicide. Any halfway decent lawyer is going to claim we're persecuting him. Some of the witnesses have even brought it up already. Jenna Carpenter wants Dana to sue. We'll lose him then for sure.''

"So what are you going to do?'' Dolly exclaimed. ''You've run down every possible lead.''

"Except one.'' Norah sat up straight, leveled her chin, and stopped staring out the window. ''I haven't run down the tattoo.''

"That's just about impossible. I told you. . . .''

"That there are no more tattoo parlors in New York—yes. You say that Dana wouldn't know where to go for a tattoo. But obviously he did know. The interesting thing is that he should even think of a tattoo. It's an unusual act, right? The average person doesn't get tattooed, but a sailor . . .'' Norah smiled, all the aches and pains and weariness forgotten. ''Thanks, Dolly. Thanks for putting it all together for me.''

15

Sailors hang around the waterfront, but New York has many waterfronts: the Battery, along the Hudson, the old Brooklyn Navy Yard area, Staten Island, Long Island, New Jersey, Connecticut—all had nooks and crannies impossible for her and Bobby Hoff to cover by themselves. The only way would be to discover Dana's particular connection to the sea. It would be simple to check with the armed services in Washington. Now that the initial excitement had passed, Norah felt cold again, aching more than ever. It was too late to start today anyway. She headed for the subway and home.

She spent a restless night alternately shivering under a pile of blankets, then sweating so that she had to throw them all off. She woke with a sore throat and a headache, and she just about tottered into the kitchen. As soon as her father saw her he ordered her back to bed.

"You're not going out of this house today.''

"It's only a cold.''

"Fine. And you're going to stay home and take care of it."

Actually she could do a lot on the telephone. "Maybe you're right."

Patrick Mulcahaney didn't like the easy capitulation. He watched with mounting disapproval as his daughter got out the phone directory, pad and pencil, and set up an office in bed. He saw the sweat break out on her forehead and glisten above her lip at even this small effort. "Do you have to do everything yourself? Don't you have any confidence in your partner?" He gathered up the materials she'd spread out. "Call Hoff."

Again Norah obeyed meekly.

If she felt as lousy as she sounded, Hoff didn't want to argue with her, but he did have reservations. "Just because he has a tattoo doesn't make him a sailor, Norah," he protested mildly.

"I know that, but it's the most direct line to checking the tattoo. If he's not a sailor, if he has no association with the sea . . . we'll have to try something else. But we ought to go for the obvious first, right?"

Hoff grunted agreement.

"The tattoo is the key to the whole thing, Bobby. I know it." Norah broke into a coughing fit. When she could talk again, she added, "I'll put money on it."

"OK. OK, sure. I'll get started. You take it easy and leave it to me."

"You'll get back to me?"

"As soon as I have anything."

Norah slid low on the pillows and almost immediately fell into a feverish dozing. She seldom dreamed, but now she drifted from nightmare to nightmare. She had not seen the body of Isabel Haggerty, the girl who had jumped out of the window, but she saw it now in her dream lying broken on the pavement. She was standing over it, looking down at Isabel Haggerty's body, but the face that looked back at her was Jenna Carpenter's. The eyes were vacant, but the dead lips moved, forming a silent word—"Pig."

She knew she was dreaming, but she couldn't wake herself up. At last she managed to rid herself of the spiteful image, and for a while the screen of her mind remained blank. Norah hadn't seen Frances Russo either, though she had studied the details and description of how she'd looked, and of course she'd seen the lab

145

photos. These now inexorably blended with the innumerable pictures of rape victims in her medical books. She saw Frances Russo lying legs apart in the classic sprawl, but the face, swollen and bruised, was again Jenna's. This time the words the dead lips formed were audible: "I love him."

Norah awoke covered with sweat. The room was nearly dark. The hands of the bedside clock pointed to four. She'd slept the day away! It took a couple of moments to recall why she was in bed and to fight down the sense of dismay and alarm that accompanies time involuntarily lost. The hoot of a boat whistle on the river brought Norah out of her daze. Bobby Hoff—why hadn't he called? She frowned at the phone, picked it up, and turned it upside down. With a sigh of exasperation she got out of bed and went into the living room to look for her father.

Patrick Mulcahaney was placidly reading his newspaper. "What are you doing out of bed?"

"Did you turn my phone off?"

"I did. We have another line, you know," he reminded her mildly.

She swallowed her annoyance. "Did Bobby call?"

"Yes. You look terrible. Get back to bed."

"Why didn't you wake me? Oh, Dad, I specifically wanted to talk . . ."

"He was the one who said not to disturb you."

She sighed. "OK, I'll call him back."

"He said to tell you that Earl Dana served in the army engineers, but that he was born and raised in Lancaster, New Hampshire. That's right near Portsmouth, he said."

And Portsmouth was, had been, a major seaport!

"He said he'd make all the arrangements for the trip and be around tomorrow at eight to pick you up. He said to tell you he'll go alone if you're not well enough."

"I'll be well enough." That meant, as they both knew, that well or not, she'd be going.

"You had another call," Mulcahaney told her as she started back to her bedroom.

"Oh?"

"Joe."

146

"Oh." Norah hesitated. "What did he want?" She didn't feel like talking to Joe right now. She'd reached the point where she was unsure not only of his feelings toward her but also of how she felt toward him. "Did you tell him I wasn't well?"

"I did." Mulcahaney sighed and passed on the message. "He wants you to call him back. He says it's important."

Flushed from the fever, Norah now broke out into icy prickles. What could it be about? Not the case; Joe wasn't up on it. Helen Scott. Mrs. Scott had had plenty of time to get to Joe. Maybe she'd convinced him that he still loved her. Maybe he did. Maybe he'd stayed single all these years not because he was waiting for the right girl but because he'd already lost her. Only Norah didn't want to hear about it. Not now. "I'll call him in the morning." She walked out of the room.

Her father stared after her. She wouldn't have time for any personal calls in the morning—they both knew that too. Though Mulcahaney had been trying hard to be fair and not to interfere, he still felt Joe Capretto was not the right man for his girl. He should have been pleased that Norah didn't want to talk to the Sergeant, but how could he be when he could plainly see that the trouble, whatever it was, was making her miserable?

If his girl really cared for the Sergeant . . .

No longer as important a seaport as it had been in early days, Portsmouth was still active as a naval base, yet there was no direct flight from New York. Though Manchester was nearer, Hoff elected to go by way of Boston because of the convenient shuttle service. There he and Norah picked up a rental car and drove the rest of the way. They arrived just before lunch. Their first order of business was to check in with the local police. The amenities observed, they were directed to the Wentworth House, a small hotel near the waterfront. From the outside the white frame building looked sadly unprepossessing as it leaned against a neighboring warehouse and gasped for breath amid the concrete and steel that had grown up all around it, but inside the gracious past lived on in the fine oak beams, wide, open fireplaces, gleaming brass and copper fixtures. They had no trouble getting rooms, yet the dining room and bar were full. The two detectives had a good lunch of Yankee pot roast, then went to work. They looked up Earl Dana's birth certificate and then drove out to the address given on the records.

Whereas the Wentworth House still battled the encroachments of change, Castle Road had long since succumbed. From a street of what must have been pleasant, middle-class homes, each with its distinctively ornamented widow's walk overlooking a fine sweep of coastline, it had slipped into an area of genteel rooming houses and was on the way down from there to becoming a slum. Number 25 wasn't any different from the rest. A young slattern in a Japanese-style robe came to the door.

Sorry, but she'd never heard of the Danas. No, she didn't own the house; she was renting. No, she didn't know the owner; she dealt through the agents, Peabody and Shane, in Manchester. Sorry, but that was all she could tell them. She wasn't even interested in why they were asking—all she wanted was to get rid of them. Norah's spirits, which had been so high when they started from New York that morning, fell at the thought of tracing back through the various buyers and sellers. Well, when was it ever easy?

First, though, they canvassed the neighborhood, and for that Norah and Hoff separated. None of the people to whom Norah talked remembered the Danas, and, like the young woman at number 25, none of them was even curious as to why she wanted to know. It was, after all, nearly thirty years ago, and most of the people who had lived in the area were gone—either dead or, like the Danas, moved away. As the early winter dark covered the present squalor of Castle Road, Norah rang the bell of the last house, the one nearest the water, and discovered a frail man lost at the edge of senility and trembling with Parkinson's disease who had not been able to escape.

"Cap'n Dana? Ayuh . . . I remember Cap'n Dana." The Down East twang gave substance to his thin voice. "Big man. Nasty temper. Ran a charter off Jenning's Wharf. Pretty little redheaded wife. Treated her real mean. Beat her up something terrible. My Alice, she used to go over there and sit with Miz Dana." The tears came. "My Alice . . ." He wheezed; his jaw trembled and went slack; spittle formed at the corner of his mouth.

"Do you know where the Danas went when they left here?"

"Didn't tell nobody. Didn't even say they was going. One day my Alice went over there with a pot of her special clam chowder, and they was gone. My Alice was the finest cook in all of New England."

"When was that? I mean, when did the Danas leave?"

The tears spilled over and ran down his sunken cheeks, collecting temporarily in the hollows beneath and then splashing out again.

"Do you remember the boy?" Norah asked. "Do you remember young Earl Dana? How old would he have been when the family moved away?"

"You should have tasted my Alice's pumpkin pie, miss. That was a treat, a real treat. Finest pumpkin pie in all of New England." He was crying copiously, but he was smiling at the same time.

Jenning's Wharf was on the other side of town from the naval base. Norah had no idea what it had been like in the old days, but it was prosperous now, made so by a small but attractive marina for pleasure craft. The sea was evening quiet. The waves lapped soothingly against the pilings, barely stirring the few boats in the water at this time of year. The moon had not yet risen. Norah took a moment to steep herself in the tranquillity. She loved the sea—to look at, to swim in, but not to sail on. As a child she'd been on a Hudson River day liner and, seeing a man vomit, had become violently sick herself. Since then she'd lost all interest in boats. The various establishments supporting and supported by the marina were mostly shuttered for the season, but some seemed closed only for the night. Norah and Bobby went back to the hotel.

The next morning was cold, raw, with a mist so thick it just missed being rain. Once again they divided up the work—Hoff to the ship's registry to check on the senior Dana's charter business and Norah back to the marina. There wasn't much more activity there than there had been the night before, but Grant's, a supply store at the foot of the wharf, was open. Well stocked, the place was also well ordered, and though there were no customers at the moment, it gave every indication of doing a thriving business during the season. At the tinkle of the old-fashioned bell over the door that announced Norah's entrance the man working at a desk in the back looked up.

"Mr. Grant?"

He was probably in his early sixties. His hair was completely gray but still thick and wavy. There was no portion of his face that was not seamed and pitted, strip-mined by the years, and yet he was handsome. He stood to his full six feet, lean and Yankee proud. He took off steel-rimmed glasses and flashed tobacco-stained but strong, even teeth that were surely his own.

"Can I help you?"

Norah introduced herself and began to explain her errand, but at the mention of the name Dana the proprietor's affability toward a customer changed into the New Englander's inbred mistrust of strangers.

"What do you want to know?"

"Anything you can tell me."

"Why?"

"How long have you been in business here on Jenning's Wharf, Mr. Grant?"

Hamilton Grant gave her a sharp look. "Going on to twenty years." His reluctance was underscored by a trace of that dry twang she was beginning to associate with the real old-timers around the waterfront.

Norah always asked the easy questions first, the ones she could ask elsewhere, knowing they would be answered for just that reason and hoping in this way to establish the habit of answering by the witness. "You don't look like an indoor man, Mr. Grant."

"Been getting my sea legs back last year or so."

Had he been sick? Norah let it pass. Having acknowledged how long he'd been in that location, Grant could hardly now deny having known the Danas.

He didn't try to deny it. "Vic Dana used to work for me. It was me sold him *Lorelei* when I couldn't handle her myself anymore. After the accident." He raised his left arm, and Norah caught the glint of metal and saw a hook protruding where a hand should have been.

Whether intentionally or not, Grant had told her a great deal more than the facts that Bobby Hoff was probably at this moment unearthing from the registry files. He had indicated that he

150

had been forced to sell the boat, that Victor Dana was not the man he would have chosen to sell it to.

"It's the son I'm interested in, Earl. Has he been back to these parts recently?"

"Earl comes to see me as often as he can. He's like a son to me. I have no one else, and neither does he. What do you want with him?"

Jackpot! He hadn't used the nickname Buzz, but he might later on. Controlling her excitement, Norah asked, "Are his parents dead, then?"

"His mother is. I don't know nothing about his father, and I don't care."

His contempt for Victor Dana was still virulent and festering. That plus what Norah had learned from the shaking old man on Castle Road regarding the violence of the Dana's family life conjured up a picture of a lonely man and a frightened boy finding solace in each other. She asked, "When was the last time Earl was here?"

Waving her to a chair, Hamilton Grant turned and went back to sit at the desk beside the window overlooking the water. It wasn't courtesy but a means of gaining a little extra time to think. "August. It was sometime in August."

He must have realized she could find out just by asking around the pier, yet he hadn't named a specific date. "Early August? Say, the first week?"

"Mebbe."

Each time he was pressed he fell into that dour accent. "Is that when he got the tattoo?"

"Please, Mr. Grant, if you're as close to him as you say, you must know that Earl is in trouble."

"What kind of trouble?"

Well, maybe Earl hadn't told him; it wasn't, after all, the kind of thing you rush to confide. Still, Grant must sense that something was very wrong or he wouldn't be so wary.

Suddenly Grant changed tactics. His coldness eased; he became almost friendly. "What kind of trouble, Detective Mulcahaney? I can't believe that Earl has done anything so bad a detective has to come up here from New York to ask questions. He's a good boy.

151

I've known him since he was nine years old. He's shy and sensitive and . . . basically decent. He's Lois Dana's son. If you'd known Lois, you'd know that her boy couldn't do anything bad.''

The earnest defense by a man whose manner up to now had been lackluster said it plainly. Hamilton Grant had cared for Lois Dana. He had loved Earl Dana's mother. ''Earl is his father's son too, Mr. Grant, and from what I've heard, Victor Dana was a violent man.''

''He was a brutal man who abused his wife and consorted with other women. But he had no influence on the boy. Earl was as frightened of him as Lois was. It was one of the reasons she tried to get away.''

''Tried?''

Hamilton Grant took a deep breath. ''Twenty years ago divorce was not the assembly-line business it is today, Detective Mulcahaney. Aside from the legal complications and the social ostracism, it was also a matter of dollars and cents for the woman. She couldn't expect more than minimal support from her husband if she willfully left him, and getting work and at the same time bringing up a ten-year-old boy wasn't so easy. Vic kept telling Lois to get out, kept showing her the door, because he knew she couldn't go. As soon as he found out that there was somebody who wanted her, who was willing to care for her and the boy—then he wouldn't let her go. He didn't want her, but he wouldn't let anybody else have her.'' In the milky light from the mullioned window Grant's pitted face seemed desolate as crumbling statuary in an abandoned garden. ''He took her away in the middle of the night. He just put her and the boy aboard *Lorelei*, and in the morning, when I went to look for them, they were gone.''

''Didn't you go after her?'' They wouldn't have been hard to trace, Norah thought; it was just a matter of tracing the boat.

Grant didn't waste time denying that he was the man who had wanted to care for Lois Dana and her son. ''Of course. And I found them. But it wasn't any use. Lois wouldn't come. She was too frightened—for me. You see, we'd already fought once, Vic and me, on the *Lorelei*. That's how I lost my arm. It got caught in the anchor chain as we struggled. Somehow the winch released, and the anchor went over the side. I was dragged and pinned against the rail. My arm was nearly twisted off. They had to make a new, clean cut. By the time I got out of the hospital my money was gone, my strength, and my means of earning a living. So Vic offered to buy the boat. I didn't have much choice. I took the money and set myself up here.'' Grant paused. ''Of course, the boy was Vic's real hold on Lois. She knew that even if he left me alone, he'd still make every effort to take the boy away from her.''

Grant was silent for a while. Maybe he was thinking back; maybe he was considering how much more he should tell Norah. ''We kept in touch. That is, Lois and the boy wrote; I couldn't answer because he checked the mail. After Lois died, Earl left his father and came to me. Vic must have known where he went, but he didn't care; he'd never cared about the boy, only used him to keep Lois. He never came looking for Earl. We never heard from him at all.''

''How old was Earl when he came to you, Mr. Grant?''

''Sixteen,'' he answered readily.

Up to now Norah had given little thought to Earl Dana's motivation for his crimes. She had no patience with the modern apologists who equated rape with alcoholism or drug addiction and called it an illness. That was all right as long as the addiction remained self-destructive, but once the line was crossed and violence inflicted on another human being it became a crime. By its nature rape required a victim! Norah chafed over the learned psychiatric dissertations. They agreed that rape was a form of aggression, but from there on it was all contradictory. Rape was due to high sexual drive, low sexual drive; hatred of self, hatred of society —particularly of women; strong maternal ties, maternal antagonism; fear of homosexual inclination. Take your choice. It was all the same to the victim. It didn't matter to Norah either except insofar as it might help her to get the evidence that would convict Dana.

Whether Earl Dana had already committed the first assault before moving in with Grant, whether his father had even kicked him out because of it, or whether the first assault happened later, Hamilton Grant was surely aware of the taint in the young man he considered his adopted son. As a self-contained, reticent, very private person, Grant would never have told Norah so much if he weren't hoping to enlist her sympathy. He'd come to the wrong person. Norah's pity and indignation were reserved for Earl Dana's victims. She wanted to keep it that way.

"Earl is a suspect in a rape and murder case," she told Grant bluntly.

He flinched. A low rattle started deep in his throat and emerged barely intelligible. "No . . . oh, God, no, not murder . . ." He got hold of himself too late. "I don't believe it. There's a mistake. There has to be a mistake."

It was the mention of the murder that had shocked him, not the rape. As far as Norah was concerned, that clinched it—he knew, had known for some time what Dana was doing. There were those who refused to recognize rape as a crime, who insisted that the woman had to be willing—and maybe Grant was one of them. But he couldn't extend that apology to murder!

"Does Earl have a nickname, Mr. Grant? Did he ever have a nickname . . . in school, maybe?"

Grant appeared confused. He shook his head.

There was no reason for him to deny the nickname. Norah fought a sudden rising panic. Was it possible, just barely possible, that Dolly was right after all? Was the homicide not connected to the string of rapes? Were there two perpetrators? "The army, maybe? Could he have had a nickname in the army?" she asked.

"He never talked about the army."

Norah pressed her lips together. He could have got the nickname in the army; it was still possible that Earl and Buzz were the same person. She phrased her next question carefully, so that Grant would have no way of knowing which would be the right answer and, not knowing, would opt for the truth. "When did Earl get that tattoo on his arm? Did he have it when he came to see you in early August?" She held her breath.

"Yes. He got the tattoo in June. I applied it for him."

His hesitation had been so slight that if she hadn't been looking for it, she might not have noticed. And the answer he'd come up with was not the answer she wanted. If he'd stated that Dana had had the tattoo for years, she might have had a chance of disproving it. As it was . . . "You did? With one hand?" The challenge was automatic.

"Yes, ma'am. With one hand."

"Why?"

"Because he wanted it."

"Why did he want it?"

Grant gave her a thin, bleak smile. "Why does anyone want a tattoo?"

He was fencing with her again, and she took that as an encouraging sign. "I've often wondered about that."

"I have one." With his good right hand Grant unbuttoned his shirt and revealed through the hairs of his chest an old-fashioned schooner in full sail on a wavy sea. "I was a very young salt when I got that; I considered it a mark of manhood."

"Earl is twenty-nine years old, and he's not a sailor."

"Now that I think about it, he did have a particular reason. Seems he'd met a sailor over to the Anchor Café who had a beauty. He was doing plenty of bragging over it. They had a few drinks —you know how it is—and Earl told him he could get a better one anytime he wanted. They made a bet."

"I suppose somebody over at the Anchor Café would remember that."

"I couldn't say."

"They do know Earl over there, don't they?"

"Well, he's not a regular. Earl doesn't drink all that much."

"Still, that kind of argument must have caused interest, and then the bet . . . The bartender would be likely to remember the bet."

"It wasn't that big a bet. Maybe . . . ten dollars."

"Oh. I got the impression . . . well, I'll ask anyway." Norah got up. "By the way, did Earl win?"

"I never had a close look at the tattoo," Norah commented. "It must be something really special."

Grant seemed startled. Then he shrugged. "Not as good as all that."

The Anchor Café was closed for the winter and would not reopen till the next year on Decoration Day weekend. The owner was in Florida, where he ran a similar saloon near Clearwater; his staff had gone with him. Grant had surely known that when he

155

concocted his story. Further inquiries around Jenning's Wharf simply confirmed that Grant had been known to do some tattoo work in the past, but nobody knew anything about the job on Earl Dana. Nobody had ever heard Earl called Buzz either. All Norah could find out was that he had lived with Grant until he was drafted. After he got out of the army, he came back but didn't stay long. He visited at irregular intervals, mainly holidays, sometimes staying for as long as two weeks. The fact was that nobody seemed to know very much about either Dana or Grant. For an old-timer, Grant had mighty few cronies. Of course, most of the merchants around the dock area were what he would call newcomers, and maybe he didn't care to mix with them. The few who went far enough back to remember Victor and Lois Dana didn't care to talk to a detective from New York. Though they had nothing else to do and wouldn't have till the tourists and amateur sailors started coming back in the spring, they remained characteristically close-mouthed.

After lunch Norah and Bobby decided to go back to New York. They drove to Boston, but the morning fog had intensified, and takeoffs from Logan were delayed indefinitely. They considered Amtrak, then elected to wait it out. It was after 10 P.M. when they landed at La Guardia. The train would have been quicker, but, as Hoff pointed out sourly, they had only wasted their own time.

It was raining in New York. By the time Hoff got his car out of the airport parking lot, crawled through the inevitable rainy-night traffic snarls, and delivered Norah to her front door, it was after eleven. As far as he was concerned, the trip was a failure. Norah wasn't so sure. She'd done a lot of thinking during the hours of waiting and during the flight. If Grant had lied about the bet, he must have known that the lie wouldn't stand up: he surely didn't think that just because the Anchor Café was closed the matter would be dropped. So what was he gaining by the lie? Time. Time for what? Time for Dana to get away again, to disappear.

As Hoff started to get out of the car, Norah put a hand on his arm. "Let's go pick up Dana."

"Huh? What for?"

"For questioning."

"On what grounds? We don't have any new evidence."

"All right, we'll pick him up on Eva Lynn's complaint."

"That's Rand's job. We can notify him and tell him to go ahead and get a warrant."

"There's no time for that. We'll think of something on the way, but let's go, Bobby, please. It may already be too late."

It was. Dana was gone. The landlady was still smoldering.

"I've been going up and down those stairs all afternoon to call him to the phone. I can't do it; my arthritis—it's something terrible, particularly in this weather. I don't take phone calls for the tenants; they know that. It's OK for them to use the phone in the hall, but I don't go climbing stairs to get them. It was long distance though, so I made an exception. Huh! He wasn't in the room. I told the operator to try where he works. Not half an hour later the phone rings again. Seems he hadn't shown up at the garage. This time some man gets on to talk to me—a relative, he said. He practically begged me to go up and try again. I knew he hadn't come in, but I went anyway. This time I tried the door. It was open, so I went in. And you know what? He'd cleared out—bag and baggage! That's some nerve, huh? No notice, not a word, just went. Left the rent on the bureau, still . . . he could have said something, stuck a note under my door. Some people have no consideration."

It had been Hamilton Grant calling of course. And suddenly Norah knew why Grant was so frantic. When she had casually mentioned that she'd never actually had a close look at Earl's tattoo, he'd seemed surprised. She realized now that he'd been frightened. He didn't want her to get a close look at that tattoo. She had discovered the reason for that in her big *Legal Medicine, Pathology and Toxology* in the chapter on rape, which she'd read over and over.

What made her pull at Hoff and practically drag him out the door was that Dana had skipped before Hamilton Grant's call.

16

"I just want to make sure she's OK, that's all. It's only going to take a few extra minutes to go over to Jenna Carpenter's. We have to, Bobby. Then we can put out the APB."

"And go home and get some sleep?" Hoff asked testily, but he was worried too.

"If she's there and she's OK, sure."

Hoff knew what it would mean if she wasn't there. They got back in the car, and he stepped so hard on the gas that they nearly rammed the car in front. He swore under his breath, spun the wheel, and got them out into the street. Norah sat tensely beside him without a word. They'd barely pulled up in front of Jenna's building when she jumped out and ran into the lobby.

"She's not in, miss," the doorman told her blandly.

The knot in Norah's stomach tightened. "Please ring the apartment anyway."

"It's no use, miss. She's gone. Miss Carpenter went this afternoon, and she won't be back for several days." He grinned, and the grin spread upward.

It didn't reassure Norah in the least. "Do you know where she went? Was she alone?"

Hoff came up just in time to hear the last. He groaned.

"Yes, I do, and no, she wasn't." The doorman was enjoying himself.

"Look, Buster, we haven't got time for games. Just spit it out, will you?" Hoff showed his ID. "Police officers. Both of us," he added.

"Yeah? Why didn't you say so?" The doorman was aggrieved. "And my name is not Buster, it's Bessinger. Harold Bessinger."

"Sorry, Mr. Bessinger. No offense. But we are in a hurry. OK?"

"Sure." Bessinger sniffed. Then as he looked at Norah and saw her anxiety, his shaggy brows relaxed and he smiled again. "Miss Carpenter eloped."

Norah gasped. Holy Mother of God!

Hoff relaxed. He grinned. "You sure didn't expect that, did you?" he asked Norah.

She shook her head. She stared at Bessinger. "You said you knew where she went."

"Yes, ma'am. That is . . ." The doorman was confused. The man seemed pleased; the woman was real upset. "She didn't actually tell me where she was going, but I did hear her mention to her boyfriend that he was going to love the cottage. Well, Miss

Carpenter has this place, that is, her family has this place, in Connecticut. Naturally I figure . . . she goes there weekends most of the time. . . ."

"I don't suppose you know where in Connecticut?"

"Oh, yes, ma'am. We have the address and the phone number in case of emergency, but . . . ." His jowls sagged, the heavy brows met, and he studied both Norah and Bobby from beneath them.

"This is definitely an emergency, Mr. Bessinger. I give you my word," Norah told him.

"We can't bust in on them on their wedding night!" Hoff sputtered.

"You want to call them up and tell them we're on our way?" Norah was too anxious to bother about tact.

"I don't think we have any business going at all. It's all right, Norah, believe me. There's nothing to worry about. I mean, he's married her. That obviously means he's going straight."

"The way he did with Frances Russo?"

"No. He never let himself be seen with Russo. He never used his real name. He didn't marry Frances Russo."

Norah sighed. "I'm scared for the girl."

"You don't need to be. A lot of rapists are married, and they behave normally with their wives."

"Those men became rapists after they married."

"You're an expert? You've read every case history? OK, OK. We'll call the local PD; how's that? We'll ask them to go over to the cottage and make sure everything's all right. Norah, if the girl is really in danger, that's the quickest way to get her protection."

"I suppose so."

"You know so. Look, there's nothing to worry about. Dana's past record shows that he doesn't get violent unless the woman resists. Well, Jenna Carpenter's his bride, right? She's not going to resist. According to you, it's the other way round—she's been looking to rouse him."

"But if she gets frightened?"

"Why should she get frightened? He told her about himself, you told her, and she still went ahead and eloped with him."

"I didn't tell her he's a killer."

"We haven't proved he is."

Norah explained how it could be proved.

Hoff listened carefully. "Well, sure, it sounds OK. Probably is, but . . ."

Norah gave up. "We'll call the local PD."

"Now you're being smart."

"Then I'm going down there."

"Hell, Norah, what can we do when we get there? We've got no jurisdiction. . . ."

"While we're worrying about the rights and legalities, that girl could be in mortal danger." Norah's voice rose. She was remembering her dream, seeing again the dead bodies each with Jenna's face. She couldn't tell Bobby about it, naturally—what a laugh he'd have over her "woman's intuition." "You don't have to come if you don't want to."

"I don't, huh? Great. I can just see myself explaining to the captain how come I was in the sack while you were busting in on a honeymoon couple in the middle of the night."

"I'll say I didn't tell you."

"That should take care of it—except how are you going to explain that you were driving my car? Because without my car you're not going anywhere. Not at this hour—the trains have stopped running."

"I'll sign out a car from the police garage."

"The hell you will! Come on. Let's find a phone, make the call, and get the show on the road." Hoff heaved an immense sigh over the lost night's sleep.

By the time they reached Dellwood it was 3 A.M. The rain had subsided to a fine drizzle or thick mist, depending on one's viewpoint. The lights of the deserted main street were hazy because of it, the pavements shiny. Nothing was open, not even the diner. Nothing moved. Bobby wanted to go straight on to the local station; Norah was determined to go directly to the Carpenter house. They'd picked up a map at a gas station on Route 1, and with its help they now located the Old Pond Road. They had to drive around the pond twice before spotting the dirt turnoff that climbed a small hill toward a pair of lighted second-story windows.

The rest of the white shingle house with green shutters was dark.

The car headlights made flame reflections on the glass panes as they climbed to the crest of the hill. At the crest there was a circular graveled drive leading to the front of the house. They stopped, and Bobby turned motor and lights off. The reflections disappeared; the reverberations of their approach faded more slowly till darkness and silence wrapped themselves around the car and around Norah and Bobby as they remained seated inside. Only the dim glow of those two upstairs windows continued to brood over the night. They shouldn't have been on, Norah thought.

Hoff was looking up too. "Probably they fell asleep and forgot to turn them off." He didn't realize he was whispering.

Norah eased herself out of the car. "Let's take a look around," she whispered back.

They crept across a narrow, uneven, winter-brown lawn, Hoff sweeping the way with his flashlight.

Norah moved directly to the big bay window. The sparse shrubbery was no obstruction, and the drapes were open—no reason to draw them when there was no one around to look inside. Smoldering embers in a fireplace at the narrow right end produced enough light so she could make out the general proportions of the room and see that there was no one there.

Hoff tiptoed up beside her. "Car's still in the garage. Connecticut license, so I assume it's hers or the family's. Anyhow, it means they're still here, so let's go check with the locals."

Norah started circling the house toward the rear.

Hoff followed. "Listen, it's two hours since we called. A patrol car must have checked the place out. If there was anything wrong, there'd be some indication. . . ."

Norah was peering through the glass panel in the upper portion of the kitchen door. At first as Hoff aimed his light, all they got was a reflection of their own anxious faces. Bobby slanted the beam and partially shielded it with one hand; they were at last able to see inside.

"Stand back," Hoff ordered as he prepared to force the door.

"Wait. Use this." Norah unslung her shoulder-strap bag well weighted with her police special and all her feminine paraphernalia and thrust it at him.

Shielding his eyes, Hoff swung and shattered the glass; then, reaching inside, he released the lock and flung the door open. By common accord the two detectives knelt beside Jenna Carpenter. They didn't even pause to turn on the room light but examined her by flashlight. But their speed was useless.

She was lying on the floor between the overturned kitchen table and the corner of the counter. She was wearing a white nightgown, purely white and sweetly demure except that you could see right through it without even trying. The gown was not ripped or soiled or torn. She was barefoot, her long blond hair was loose, she had no makeup on except for heavy black mascara, which was badly smudged and running in tear streaks down her cheeks. Well, she'd never cry again. She was lying on her back, but partially toward the right, right arm flung out and left arm partially across her body as though she'd reached out toward something. Her legs were normally extended, more or less together. There was no indication that she had been raped, at least not here, not on this kitchen floor. From what Norah could observe through the sheer nightgown there were no bruises.

A small puddle of blood had formed just back of her head; some of it had been soaked up by her hair, some had seeped into the cracks between the tiles, some remained and was turning viscous but not yet congealed. Hoff pointed the flashlight up to the corner of the counter. It was banded with metal, and a hank of blond hair was caught in the join. From there another stain wound down the sides of the cabinet, a minor tributary to the pool under the girl's head.

Norah got up. "I'll notify the precinct . . . uh . . . I mean the local, the county . . ." She started edging toward the main part of the house.

"Hold it. The car's still here," Hoff reminded her.

They both had the same idea, and they both looked up in the direction of the lighted room. They'd made enough noise breaking in for him to have heard, and they'd been preoccupied long enough for him to have had a chance to sneak out. Hoff pushed Norah's handbag back at her and darted out of the kitchen. She was alone in the dark with the latest of Dana's victims.

Bobby would be looking to cut Dana off outside, but suppose he hadn't had the nerve to run? Suppose he was still upstairs? Norah

162

got her gun out, slung the bag over her shoulder, and moved into the dark hallway to the living room. She put on the lights, then went upstairs.

Before entering each room, she reached in and turned on the lights till the whole house was ablaze and till there was only the master bedroom left. She held her gun firmly, turned the knob, and kicked the door open. The precaution had been wasted. The dim, cozy room was empty. It was a quietly comfortable, pastel place, very different from the garish "pad" Jenna maintained in New York. Norah noticed the mirror-topped dressing table with its array of cosmetics and perfumes in cut crystal bottles and the silver-backed brush and comb set. Long blond hairs were caught in the brush, and an open lipstick had rolled off the table to the blue carpet. Most particularly Norah noticed the bed. The spread had been removed and neatly folded on a special rack in the corner; the sheet was turned back, but the bed had not been used.

Downstairs the front door opened and was slammed shut. Steps pounded up the stairs. Hoff burst into the room.

"What the hell, Norah! You should have stayed put." Then he picked up the white bedside telephone and reported.

Sirens bleeped, lights flashed, patrol cars whined up the hill. Doors slammed as men jumped out, assaulting the night's peace. Minutes after they'd pounded inside, the charmingly rustic living room was turned into the standard homicide scene.

"Detective Hoff? I'm Al Gregory, Chief of Police." The two men shook hands. "Who's this lady?"

"Detective Mulcahaney."

Norah nodded. He was big, red-faced, aggressive, and he didn't offer his hand. So! She had more important things to think about than Gregory's prejudices.

Gregory gave her a couple of seconds to assert herself; when she said nothing, he dismissed her and addressed himself to Hoff. "As soon as we got your call from New York we sent a car out here. That was about midnight. Well, the lights were on, and Officer Roberts could hear the hi-fi. It looked OK, but in view of your warning he got out and rang the bell. Miss Carpenter came to the door. Roberts just said he'd observed the lights and wanted to make sure everything was OK. She said it was, thanked him, and that was that. He had to accept her word."

"Sure, Chief, sure."

Gregory sighed. "Well, I'd better take a look. Where is she?"

"In the kitchen." Hoff made a move.

"I know the house." Gregory waved him aside.

"It doesn't fit the pattern," Norah announced abruptly.

Gregory looked startled. Hoff stared.

"Her head wasn't bashed in; it hit the corner of the kitchen counter."

"You think somebody broke in?" the chief asked.

"There's no sign of forcible entry."

Gregory looked her over a second time. "You're suggesting she knew the person and let him in?"

"No. She would have put on a robe and slippers. She would have turned on some lights. There were no lights on except in the upstairs bedroom when we got here," Norah explained. "She wouldn't have come down in her nightgown in the dark."

"So it has to be Dana," Hoff grunted. "Maybe she did get frightened like you said she might. Maybe she was running away from him. . . ."

"Right past the front door?"

Hoff shrugged.

"There's a back door from the kitchen through to the garage. Maybe she was trying to get to her car," Gregory suggested.

"That's it!" Hoff seized on the explanation. "She ran, he chased her. In the dark she stumbled and fell, hitting her head on the corner of the counter. It was an accident, but with his reputation . . . well, Dana panicked and got out."

"Why didn't he take the car?" Norah wanted to know.

"He panicked," Hoff repeated doggedly, but he wasn't satisfied with the explanation himself. "Maybe he was afraid we'd trace him through the car."

"He could have abandoned it once he got far enough away."

"We'll search the woods." Gregory turned to give the order.

"He's had a good head start." Gregory scowled. "The house is warm, yet the blood has nearly congealed," Norah explained.

164

"He's still on foot. Unless he hitched a ride. In that case . . . hell, we'll have to put out a three-state alarm."

Norah's eyes brightened. "How far are we from the sea, Chief Gregory?"

It took only minutes to reach the harbor by car. The rain had stopped, but the clouds were still thick, hiding the moon. The few boats riding peacefully at anchor showed no lights. As well as Norah could make out, there were three or four good-size luxury cruisers, a couple of smaller, more modest craft, and the rest working boats that must belong to locals. Here, as in the woods around the cottage, there was a sense of tranquillity—but they already knew how deceptive that could be. The driver, Roberts, pulled up; his partner, Smith, got out and turned the portable spot for a slow sweep of the waterfront. There was nothing to see but black water and the white caps that indicated the storm hadn't moved far off.

"He could be out beyond the range of our light," Smith suggested. "We should alert the coast guard."

"Maybe he hasn't cast off yet," Hoff countered. "He could be hiding on one of those boats."

Norah opened the door on her side and got out. "Let's go."

"Hold it." Hoff put a hand on her shoulder. "This is as far as you go. Don't argue. You're as equal as anybody when it comes to brains, but when it comes to brawn, God made you a woman, and like it or not, there's nothing you can do about it. I'm responsible for your safety, so you stay put."

Norah started to object, but Hoff was no longer paying any

to show him what we're up to than anything else." Once more he addressed Norah. "Don't move. Keep your eyes open. If he makes a break for it, turn the light on and yell. Yell loud."

The three men moved out into the darkness, separating—one local officer at each side and Bobby in the middle. Norah stayed where she was, beside the car, one hand on the spotlight switch and straining for any sound or any shift of shadows that might indicate another presence. After a while she lost even the sense of where the three searching officers were. Though she knew they must be moving from boat to boat, she could no longer distinguish their forms from the general blackness.

At any moment she expected to hear shouts, the sound of men running, shots. Her finger quivered on the light switch, ready to cut the darkness and pin the fugitive in a shaft of brightness, but the blackness and the silence remained impenetrable.

Maybe Officer Smith was right, and Dana had already cleared the harbor and was headed out to sea. If that were so, of course the coast guard could pick him up, and surely Dana must be aware of that. On the other hand, he wouldn't be expecting them to have figured out his escape plan so promptly. Norah chewed her lips. From the first she hadn't considered Earl Dana particularly smart nor, aside from the way he stalked his victims, particularly devious either. In each crisis his instinct had been to run and hide, and he'd done it again. Only why hadn't he taken the car? Since he hadn't, he had to be here; it was the only alternative. Somewhere, on one of those boats, Earl Dana crouched in the dark waiting for a chance to cast off. Unless . . . the new possibility made Norah tense, every sense alert. Something behind her stirred; there was movement. She turned, but not in time.

An arm was flung across her neck and a hand clamped over her mouth. She was yanked backward off her feet, her air cut off so she couldn't scream. She managed a gurgle, but it was audible only to her and to her assailant. She reached backward and tried desperately to wrest the arm loose. . . .

Norah's first conscious sensation was of motion—a forward pitch and jerk as though she were riding a horse—but she was lying down. Her head ached; her stomach was queasy. Everything around her was vibrating softly. Next she became aware of a slapping sound close beside her. Water! She opened her eyes and at the same time sat up, hitting her head against a low ceiling that couldn't have been more than a couple of feet above where she was lying. The blow stunned her, and she closed her eyes again against the new throb of pain. Cautiously, remaining still, she opened her eyes again. At first all she could make out were dust motes swimming lazily in a soft gray light that slipped in through low windows on either side. Water hit the glass and ran off. Turning her head slightly, she saw that she was on one of a pair of bunks that formed a V at the forward section of the room—no, cabin. She was on a boat! Another rise and fall of the craft sent her slipping down the berth. She grasped the edge and held till the boat righted itself. Her stomach had lurched too; she swallowed and tasted bile. She was on a small boat in a very rough sea.

After a couple of minutes, when she thought she'd overcome the nausea, Norah slid along to where there was headroom and sat up. The cabin was large enough, she supposed, as such things go. Aside from the two forward bunks, there was a little dining area and a galley opposite, all plywood paneling and leather upholstery. A single step led to the door. From inside there was no way to see who was operating the boat, but it wasn't hard to guess. It had to be Dana.

Evidently they'd underestimated the time necessary for Dana to reach the harbor. It was only a couple of miles, but he'd had to walk. He must still have been looking around for a boat to use when the patrol car pulled up. Their arrival had not only interrupted but also cut off his escape, for even if he could manage to get aboard and cast off, he knew they would notify the coast guard instantly, and he would be brought back. Evidently she had also underestimated Dana, for he had instantly revised his plan. Coolly he'd waited till the men spread out to search; then, when she was alone, he'd crept up behind her and taken her hostage. And that was how he'd got away. With Norah aboard, Bobby and the others hadn't been able to stop him. The coast guard wouldn't dare to interfere either.

The drab light indicated it was already dawn. So hours had passed; they must be well on the way to — wherever Dana wanted to go. Norah peered out through the water-washed window and saw only a milky haze, sea and sky blending, the barely discernible line between them constantly shifting and slanting. Hastily she pulled back. Had that seesaw line that made her gorge rise dangerously been horizon or shore? It was near enough to shore, but whether it was Connecticut or Long Island, or whether they were already out and clearing Block Island, she had no way of knowing. All Norah did know was that it was much too far for her to try to swim for it. Cautiously she got to her feet, testing her balance against the boat's movement, which was now fairly steady, and walked the narrow space to the door and tried it. It was open. Thank God.

He hadn't tied her up or locked her in. He must feel pretty confident. Well, why not? He had every reason to be—for the moment. He'd even left her her handbag. It was at the foot of the bunk, but even as she reached for it and picked it up, she could tell by the heft that her service gun was gone. He'd taken that much of a precaution, and Norah was glad that he had. He couldn't know that she had a second gun (not standard issue) strapped in its leg holster to the inside of her left calf under her slacks. She put her hand on it for a moment, gaining assurance. The question now was when to use it.

Sooner or later, Earl Dana would have to put in. Should she wait till then? If he put in because he ran short of fuel, then that would be her best bet. There was no way of knowing how much fuel he had, and if he should put in because he'd reached his destination, then it was reasonable to assume it would be a place where he had friends and where they would help him, not her. So she had better make her move now while they were within sight of land. All she had to do was open the door, hold the gun on him, and order him to head for land. In fact, she could also notify the coast guard over the ship's radio that she had taken over, and they could come out and get her. Good. Simple.

Norah leaned over, got her gun out of the holster, and inched the door open. She faced an open, empty deck.

Of course he wouldn't be running the boat from there: he'd be up front on—the bridge? She stepped outside. The wind was strong, laden with salty wetness, and it felt good. She turned around and looked up. His back was to her, but she knew him—Earl Dana; it couldn't have been anyone else.

He was staring out to sea, apparently completely absorbed in the handling of the boat, though it seemed small enough to be readily maneuvered by one person, especially an experienced sailor, and Norah supposed he had chosen it for just that reason. Maybe it was the rough weather that concerned him? Anyhow, his preoccupation gave Norah the chance she needed to orient herself and plan the mechanics of her move precisely. What she saw was discouraging: taking over wouldn't be as simple as she had thought in the shelter of the cabin below.

To start with, access to the bridge deck above was not by a conventional staircase as Norah in her landlubber's ignorance had assumed, but by a narrow—and for her uncertain footing —precarious ladder. This she'd have to climb, clinging with just one hand as she hung out over the water, because the gun had to be in her other hand. Was there an alternative? There was no side deck, only a narrow ledge around the boat, and she wasn't about to crawl along that and try to surprise Dana from the front. Besides, the bridge was glass-enclosed at the front and sides. Its roof was the base for a spidery platform, which, except for the canvas laced to the railing, was open to the elements. The ladder to that was even steeper and more exposed. Once again Norah turned to look past the foaming wake across the vast, misty grayness. There was no one within sight she might hail.

So it would have to be up the ladder to the bridge. That decided, she considered the bridge itself. It was tiny. It wasn't that Norah feared that Dana would hear her approaching—the noise of the engine, the wind, the breaking waves would cover any sound of her movement; what she didn't like was the idea of standing so close within his reach during the long way back to shore. A sudden lurch could throw her off balance just enough. . . . She couldn't risk that. No, what she had to do was order him down, lock him in the cabin, and take over the wheel herself. Could she handle the boat in the rough sea and bring it safely in? She could because she'd have to.

It was lucky that Norah took that extra moment to check that the key to the cabin was on the right side of the door before proceeding. There was no key. Oh, God! Of course there wasn't—if there had been, he would have locked her inside.

Frantic now, she tried to think of still another way.

Handcuffs. If she could get the handcuffs on him, tether him to the railing . . . Wasting no more time, Norah went back inside the cabin for her handbag and found the pair of cuffs that were mandatory equipment. She got them ready, then quietly came out on the open deck again and carefully crawled up the ladder. One step short of the top, holding her breath against the expected click, she snapped one of the bracelets to the railing. Then she took the last step up.

"I've got you covered," she announced. "Take your hands off

the wheel and clasp them on top of your head . . . and do it slowly." She was pleased that her voice was firm and assured. "Good. Now turn around . . . easy. . . ."

Dana complied perfectly.

She gestured with the gun. "Step away from the wheel and over here to this side of the railing. Good."

He moved like a sleepwalker or an automaton, Norah thought as, keeping him covered, she reached for the open end of the handcuffs. She had not seen Earl Dana since the grand-jury hearing. Apathetic—the word jumped into her mind. That was how he looked—then and now. In the corridor outside the courtroom she'd dubbed it reserve, good coaching by his expensive lawyer. But now. . . ? There was no fear apparent in his blue eyes or cunning—not even surprise. They were simply vacant.

"Stretch out your right hand," she ordered. "The right hand only. Get it out. Now."

Again he did as he was told—meekly.

He looked innocuous and helpless. Norah reminded herself of what he was—a rapist, a man who got his kicks from brutalizing and demeaning women, from their fear and from their pain. A man who held women in contempt, Dana's contempt for her must have been bolstered by having so easily taken her hostage. He could be putting on an act, trying to get her to drop her guard. She would not underestimate him another time.

He could jump her now; at this moment, as she reached to snap the cuff on his wrist, he could with his left hand knock the gun away from her.

"You snap that cuff on. Go on; snap it on your right wrist. Do it or I'll shoot."

The boat listed only slightly, but it was enough to throw Norah forward toward Dana; yet the blow came not from him but from above. A leg swung and kicked the gun out of her hand and sent her sprawling sideways to the deck.

"Get it," Hamilton Grant snapped. He jumped down and moved to take the wheel.

The tilt of the deck sent the gun sliding almost into Dana's hands. Norah lay where she'd fallen, huddled in over the pain that had shot instantly from her wrist up through her entire arm.

170

"Sorry, Miss Mulcahaney. I didn't intend to hurt you. You brought it on yourself."

Dragging herself to a sitting position on the deck, Norah looked up from the vapid face of Earl Dana to the stern, rigid countenance of the man at the wheel.

"The lookout tower, Miss Mulcahaney. Above us," he replied to her unspoken question. "I was up there just checking that the coast guard wasn't using the fog as cover to follow us after all. When you emerged, I ducked below the canvas."

He'd watched and waited, giving her all the time she wanted to make her move! It simply hadn't occurred to her that anybody might be up on that exposed platform. In fact, she hadn't considered the possibility of a second person's being aboard. Why should she? Not that it mattered, Norah thought. Even if she'd known, she wouldn't have been able to hold the boat against the two of them. Under Grant's hand the boat was steady again, so she was able awkwardly to get to her feet. She braced herself against the wall but made no other move. The throbbing in her arm had increased, but through the pain came the realization of what Grant's presence meant. The excitement of her discovery made her forget the pain.

"How long have you been protecting and covering up for Earl, Mr. Grant?"

He turned his back on her and stared resolutely out to sea. Dana shrank farther back into the corner.

Norah continued. "Maybe you didn't realize at the beginning just how serious his problem was? Maybe you rationalized that he had a sexual urge slightly stronger than most, but that he would outgrow it?"

Grant continued to stare straight ahead.

"But when he kept on? When the attacks became more frequent. . . ?"

"It wasn't his fault," Grant broke in brusquely. "That girl . . . she teased him. She was a tramp. Everybody in town knew it."

So it had started after Earl had gone to live with Grant. So Grant had known about it from the very beginning. The girl being what she was, Norah could understand the older man's rationale, but . . . "All right, that was the first incident. How about the next one? And the one after that? Were those girls tramps too? How many were there before you admitted to yourself that it was Earl's fault and not the girls'? When did you start to worry about his being found out? You must have known that in a small town you couldn't keep the secret forever. How many times did he commit rape before you had to send him away?''

"He was all right before he went into the army. The army ruined him. What he did before that was just what any young man does . . . but afterward . . . The army ruined him. When he came back, he was . . . out of control.''

"Then why didn't you get him medical help? The army would have paid for it.''

"And have him locked up?''

"So you sent him to New York to live in a furnished room, alone. You must have known he'd only get worse living like that.'' Norah's legs felt wobbly, and she was still fighting the movement of the boat. She reached over to one of the padded seats and pulled herself wearily into it. Neither Grant nor Dana seemed to care.

"You were the one who hired Edwin Wallingford to defend Earl against Gabriella Constante's charges, weren't you?''

"Ayuh. What's wrong with that? I had every right. Earl was innocent; he was proved innocent.''

Norah didn't argue the technicalities. "How did you know that Earl needed a lawyer? I mean, he was in New York and you were in Portsmouth. How did you know he was in trouble again? He must have come to you and confided in you.'' Grant scowled. "He always came to you, didn't he? From the very beginning?''

"Who else should he turn to?''

"And so he turned to you after he killed Frances Russo. And he was really scared that time, wasn't he? Terrified. So you helped him as you had before. You had him change his appearance—cut off his hair, dye it, shave off the mustache. . . .''

"No!'' Grant whirled on her. His eyes blazed red; the ravaged terrain of his face was pitted with new craters of anguish. "What I mean is—yes, but I didn't know that. . . . I thought it was only . . .''

"Only another assault, Mr. Grant? Only another woman raped?'' Norah took a deep breath. "Yet when I told you that Earl had progressed from rape to murder, you still covered for him.

172

You called New York to warn him to get away, but he wasn't at the rooming house and he wasn't at work. How did you know he'd run off to get married, Mr. Grant? How did you know where to go looking for him?''

Grant's big chest heaved. "He'd told me about the girl, so when I couldn't reach him anywhere else, I called her."

"And she told you."

"I said I wanted to send a wedding present—money. I said probably they'd be needing it, so she gave me the address. I took the train and got there as soon as I could."

"You wanted to stop the marriage."

"Yes. But only because of what you told me happened with that Frances Russo. Only because of what you said!"

He still hadn't given up trying to shift the blame. "But you were too late."

Grant's entire body sagged. "When I got to the house, it was dark except for one room upstairs. Everything was quiet. It looked all right. I paid off the taxi and walked up to the front door and rang the bell. There was no answer. I reasoned they wouldn't be sleeping with the lights on, but I prayed to God that they were and rang again. I waited till the taxi was well away down the hill; then I went around to the back. There was a light there, in the kitchen."

Norah started to speak, then decided to save the question till he was through.

"I looked in, and the first thing I saw was Earl standing there. He was . . ." Grant indicated Dana, who was still beside the railing with the gun dangling limply in one hand like a bewildered and slightly sullen child. "I knocked, but he didn't hear. I had to pound me in." He paused. "Then I saw the girl. It wasn't his fault, Detective Mulcahaney. It was an accident."

"Why didn't you call the police?"

"They wouldn't have believed it. They would have questioned and bullied and harassed him. He's been harassed enough."

"So you decided to get him away."

"I reasoned it would be morning anyway before the body was discovered, maybe longer. After all, the cottage wasn't usually occupied at this time of year, so there'd be no reason for anybody to go looking until . . . somebody in New York began to miss the girl and wonder why she didn't return. So I turned out the kitchen light and led Earl away.''

So that was one question answered without Norah's having had to ask it. Because of the answer, the crime took on yet another aspect. "How about the owner of the boat? Wouldn't he or the caretaker at the marina have noticed it was gone?"

"That could take days too. And then, why should the two things be connected?"

And that was why he hadn't taken Jenna Carpenter's car to drive to the harbor. Bobby had been right that the fugitive feared being traced through the car.

"No, it was a good plan. If only . . . I don't understand how you happened to chance on . . ."

"You forgot to turn off the upstairs lights, Mr. Grant," Norah explained quietly. "If everything had been dark, we might not have entered the house at all."

"Oh." He looked dazed too, but only for a moment; then his uncertainty passed, and he became colder and more determined than before. "It worked out anyway, even better. Nobody's going to come near us with you aboard."

"But you'll be tracked every inch of the way. Sooner or later . . ."

Hamilton Grant's good hand tightened on the wheel. "We'll see."

He might get away with it; it wasn't impossible. "All right, assuming you do reach . . . Canada . . . or wherever . . . assuming you find a place to hide, what are you going to do with Earl?" Norah jerked her head in his direction. "How are you going to control him? How are you going to stop him from assaulting and maybe killing another woman? Every police unit will be warned; they'll all be on the lookout for him. They'll get him the next time for sure."

"The girl's death was an accident!"

"And Frances Russo's death?"

"You're the only one who says he did it. I say he didn't. Anyhow, there's not going to be any next time. I'll see to it."

"How? By chaining him up at night while you try to get a few

174

hours' sleep? How are you going to keep him hidden? His description is going to be circulated and posted everywhere. Somebody's bound to get a look at him. It won't do you any good to have him change his appearance another time. You can have him let his hair grow back out to blond, put a beard on him, get him contact lenses to cover his blue eyes, but you can't erase the tattoo.''

"So what's a tattoo? You can't jail a man for having a tattoo.''

"I'll tell you whether you can or not after I've taken a good look at it. Earl, will you show me your tattoo?''

"No!'' Grant left the wheel and placed himself between Norah and Dana.

Norah got up. "Why not, Mr. Grant? Why don't you want me to examine it? That wonderful, intricate, ornate tattoo that won Earl a ten-dollar bet? Incidentally, Earl, did you ever collect that bet? Did you show the tattoo to the sailor in the bar? Has anybody ever had a really good look at it?''

"You're not going to,'' Grant warned.

"I don't have to, do I? Frances Russo had blood in her mouth, not her own, therefore the blood of her assailant. A witness saw a man near the building immediately after the murder who appeared hunched over and hugging himself as though he were cold. But he couldn't have been cold in July, could he? I say he was clutching his arm, writhing in pain because Frances Russo bit him. I say the marks of his victim's teeth are still on Earl's left forearm. You tried to camouflage them with the tattoo, but the camouflage won't mean much under a microscope. After two months the marks are still relatively fresh, but they'll remain identifiable for a long, long time, years, maybe the rest of Earl's life. Marks of human denti-

tion are as individual as fingerprints. Did you know that, Mr. Grant? I didn't, not until recently. But for the tattoo, we probably would never have thought to look for them.''

Grant stared at Norah. "Once we were safe, Earl and me, I meant to turn you loose. Now, of course, I can't.'' He sounded almost regretful.

"I'm not the only one who's figured it out.''

"I'll gamble that you are.''

Norah felt the first chill of real fear. "They'll come after you for killing me, then. What's the difference?''

"Earl will be safe. I don't care what happens to me."

"How will he survive without you? Look at him. He's not going to be able to function on his own."

"He'll manage. Get back down and into the cabin."

"You should have found him help in the beginning."

"I said—get back down and into the cabin."

He advanced menacingly, forcing Norah to take a step toward the ladder. She glanced at Dana, who through the entire exchange had remained removed, as though unaware that he was the subject of their struggle. Somehow she had to catch his attention, make him react, make him take part. She could hardly expect that he would side with her against Grant; still, if she could get the two of them involved with each other, so that they temporarily forgot her . . .

"Frances Russo was the right girl for Earl," Norah said. "You should have let him marry her."

"Let him!" Grant exploded. "I wanted him to marry her. I urged him. Didn't I, Earl? Didn't I tell you that. . . ?"

"Why should I marry anybody?" At last Dana came out of his torpor. He shook himself like a dog coming out of the water. "I don't want to get married. I'm never going to get married."

"You married Jenna—yesterday," Norah reminded him with more pity than she would ever have thought she could have for this man.

"No, I didn't." Though he answered Norah, Dana was watching Grant. "I didn't want to and I didn't."

Evidently Grant was as surprised as she. "You didn't get married?"

"Jenna was the one who wanted to, but I explained how I felt and she understood."

"Explain it to me, Earl," Norah asked.

"Well . . . I loved her." He still watched Grant.

"If you loved her, why didn't you want to marry her?"

Dana wrenched his gaze away from the man and regarded Norah as though she were stupid. "Ham loved mama, more than life itself, he said, and he never married her."

"That was different. Your mother was already married."

The quick and facile answer served only to confuse Dana.

"You still went away with Jenna." Gently Norah brought him back to the story.

"She said it would be all right."

Norah sighed. "What happened?"

"She wanted . . . she insisted . . . When we got to the cottage, she expected me to treat her like . . . the others. But I loved her. I kept telling her that, but she still wanted me to . . ." He fell silent.

"And you couldn't."

Shying at the memory, he could only doggedly repeat, "I loved her. I loved her. I didn't *want* to treat her like the others." He sagged back, letting the railing support him. "I ran from her. I ran out of the room and down the stairs. She came after me. She was crying. I don't understand why she was crying. She threw herself against the front door and wouldn't let me out. She kept saying she wanted to help me. So I went to the back, to the kitchen door. She caught up with me. She threw her arms around my neck. She pressed herself against me. . . . I couldn't bear it! I shoved her off."

And she fell and hit her head against the counter.

Earl Dana's blue eyes lost their faraway look and fixed on the man who had been a foster father to him, pleading for justification. "You never touched mama, not once. You told me that. You said you respected her too much to put a hand on her."

Behind Norah, Hamilton Grant groaned.

She turned to look at him. It was all there in the haggard, ugly face—why Lois Dana had preferred to stay with her husband. Though he had abused her and betrayed her with other women, Victor Dana had been a normal man. Grant separated sex from love because he had to. The boy, idolizing him, had tried to live in the same standard—except that Earl Dana was not impotent. In explaining and justifying himself, Grant had turned the boy into a pervert.

At Norah's look, Hamilton Grant cringed and threw his good arm over his face as though anticipating a blow. He feared that she might put it all into words for Earl to hear. While they'd lived together, Grant had covered up for him and protected him. When it was no longer possible to keep his crimes hidden, he'd sent Dana to the city. Finally, when he was caught, Grant had hired an

177

expensive lawyer to get him off, but never once had he done anything to stop him. He claimed it was because he couldn't bear to see Lois Dana's son put away, but was it because he didn't want to give up his vicarious share in Earl's experiences? By making no attempt to stop him, Grant had actually encouraged him to continue. Grant was the real criminal.

"Give me the gun, Earl." Norah held out her hand, and docilely Earl Dana obeyed. "Now take the wheel and head for shore."

Hamilton Grant didn't protest. He shuffled over to one side.

The Constantes were going back to Puerto Rico. Pablo Constante held Norah's hand in his, and the tears flashed in his fine, dark eyes. "I can't thank you enough."

"Gabby's the one who deserves the credit, and you and Mrs. Constante too for going through with the charges. If the first woman he attacked had reported . . ." Norah sighed. She knew now what reporting a rape meant to the victim, and she couldn't blame any woman who was not able to face up to it.

"Is it going to work out with Enrique?" Patrick Mulcahaney asked.

"That is finished."

"Because of the baby?" Norah wanted to know.

"Partly, of course, but I believe it goes deeper. Gabriella questioned her own desires, her own guilt in not offering more resistance to the attack. I understand now that that is a natural reaction, but at the time . . . well, her uncertainty communicated itself to all of us and particularly to Enrique. When the grand jury accepted Dana's claim that Gabriella consented so did Gabriella herself, and so did Enrique."

"But now . . ."

"The faith between them has been destroyed." Constante forced a smile. "She will have the child and raise him. In time —who knows?—she may meet another man." Constante straightened, and the smile came more easily. "And then you will come to the wedding, Norah, you and your father."

"You can count on us. How are you getting to the airport? I could borrow a car and drive you. . . ."

"No need. Luisa Alvarez is going to drive us in her father's automobile. If it had not been in the garage the night the girls went

178

to Santa Teresa's, if they had not had to take the subway . . ." He covered his face with his hands.

Was it possible that Luisa Alvarez used the Broadway Garage? Was it possible that she was the one Dana had been stalking as his next victim? Had Dana been waiting at the subway for Luisa, and had he switched to Gabby only because Luisa's boyfried, Raul, showed up?

Patrick Mulcahaney put a hand on Constante's shoulder. "It does no good to dwell on such things, my friend."

Constante uncovered his face. "You are right."

Norah thought so too and said nothing.

"Hoff had no business going off and leaving you!" Joe Capretto growled.

Joe and Norah were in their regular booth at Vittorio's. The lights were low, the Muzak played softly a medley of Joe's favorite Neapolitan songs—and Norah was miserable. She hadn't returned Joe's call as he'd asked her father to tell her to do, and when he'd called again to invite her to dinner, she'd accepted reluctantly. She reasoned that he'd decided to break his news about Helen Scott in person. He probably felt he owed her that much. Which he did; only at this point Norah almost wished he'd told her over the phone. Anyhow, she'd already made up her mind that she wasn't going to enter into a contest over Joseph Antony Capretto. Norah Mulcahaney was a fighter, but she wasn't going to fight over any man. If Joe wanted Mrs. Scott, then he could have her—and vice versa. She just wished he'd tell her and get it over. At the same time, she wasn't going to be the one to bring up the subject. That was up to him. And he seemed in no hurry at all

In fact, Joe appeared completely at ease, ebullient even. Probably he was looking forward to tomorrow's graduation and the big family celebration afterward. Well, no matter how much he might insist, Norah now had no intention of attending. Meantime, all he talked about was the case. His high spirits didn't keep him from the usual careful review.

"Hoff had orders to stick close to you," he reiterated.

"Will you stop fussing? You sound just like Dad."

"Your father isn't always wrong, you know."

"You don't say. That's a switch."

179

"You have to admit that somehow you always manage to get yourself into trouble."

"Will you please tell me what I did wrong?"

"I didn't say you did anything wrong."

"Well, thanks very much, Lieutenant. I guess negative praise is about as much as I can expect from you. It happens that everybody else thinks I did a very good job." Norah reached for her wineglass and took a good, long swallow of the Bardolino.

"Come on, Norah. Let's not fight. You did a damn good job, and you know it."

Norah tucked in her chin. "It doesn't hurt to be told once in a while."

"You did a fine job from beginning to end, and you did it all on your own. How's that?"

"Wrong. I had all kinds of help. There was Sam Vickers at the Fourth, the women on RAI, and whatever you may think of Bobby Hoff, he's a good man. Then there was Captain Blake at . . ."

Joe grinned. "You sound like you're accepting an Academy Award."

"You helped too, Lieutenant."

"Me? I had nothing to do with it. How could I? I wasn't kept informed."

Norah decided to ignore that. "When in doubt I tried to think what you would do, and then I did it."

Joe grunted. "Don't try to shift the responsibility for your actions on me, Mulcahaney." But he was pleased. He refilled her glass. "I don't mean to be critical. It's just that . . . I care what happens to you. OK?"

"OK."

"I always will care."

She looked away. That was it; that was the opening. Now, now he would tell her. She tensed and waited. Nothing. She glanced sideways and saw that Joe had leaned back against the banquette and was sipping contentedly. Was he going to wait till they'd eaten? Was he saving it for dessert? Did he really expect her to sit there all through dinner with this hanging between them? She wouldn't be able to eat a bite! Norah's indignation grew. Despite all her good intentions not to be the one to broach the subject, it burst out of her.

"What did you want the other night?"

Joe was startled. "What other night? Oh, you mean when I called. Nothing much."

"You told my father it was important."

"Well . . ." The color rose under his dark skin. "I thought at the time it might be, but . . . maybe I was wrong. . . . I thought you might want to know that Helen Scott left town."

Norah stared at him.

"She went back to her husband."

Norah grew hot, then cold. There was a humming in her ears. She shrugged. "Why should you think I'd be interested?"

Their eyes met. Norah's glance wavered first; she smiled ruefully; then Joe smiled; then they both laughed aloud and reached for each other's hand across the table.

"She came to see me," Norah confessed. "She claimed you were still in love with her."

"Oh, boy! I figured she was up to something, but I never thought she'd have the gall to . . . You didn't buy it, did you?"

"Well . . ."

"Hell, Norah. All you had to do was ask me. Why didn't you just pick up the phone and . . ."

"She claimed you didn't know it yourself."

"Great. You might have given me credit for knowing my own mind." Joe scowled and let go her hand. "OK. Let's dispose of Mrs. Scott once and for all. I was very much in love with her once. Or thought I was, which comes to the same thing. I even considered proposing."

Mrs. Scott had given the impression that he had proposed and she'd turned him down.

"But I talked myself out of it."

"You did?"

"That's right. I . . . ah . . . felt inferior. You know—poor, Italian, underprivileged, all that."

She'd never suspected that under the suave, assured exterior Joe Capretto hid such feelings. That he confided them to her touched Norah deeply and made her feel almost protective toward him.

"All these years I've been wondering whether or not I made a mistake, what she would have said if I had asked her to marry me. Then when she wrote to say she was getting a divorce and coming

181

back to New York, I discovered several things—first, that I wasn't interested; second, and a lot more important, that I was in love with you; third, that I still didn't have enough to offer. So that was when I took the lieutenant's exam. I also realized that I'd better not keep my mouth shut too long this time, that I'd better tell you how I felt about you."

"Did you tell Helen Scott?"

"I told her I'd asked you to marry me."

"Are you sure you weren't using me to cut your ties to her?"

Joe took a deep breath, held it, then slowly let it out again. "I guess you're entitled to ask that. Yes, I'm sure."

Norah was feeling better all the time. "Are you sure you aren't now trying to avoid a mistake you made fifteen, no, sixteen years ago?"

"That was no mistake."

They were both silent for several moments. Finally Joe took Norah's hand again. "I love you, Norah. I don't know what else to say."

Her smile was radiant. "Nothing else is necessary."

Vittorio bustled up with the giant menu. He took one look and decided they weren't ready to order yet.

Author's Note

Since completion of this book, the work of the Rape Analysis and Investigation Squad has proved so valuable that it has been expanded in scope and personnel. It is now known as the Sex Crime Investigation Unit, and there are sex crime units in each of the borough commands. Because of the anticipated move to the new police headquarters building, it will not be possible to retain the much-publicized 577 R-A-P-E as the telephone number. As of this writing, a new number has not been assigned.